Waxing Moon

by

Sarah E. Stevens

Calling the Moon, Book Two

Waxing Moon

Cover Art by *Debbie Taylor*

The Wild Rose Press, Inc.
PO Box 708
Adams Basin, NY 14410-0708
Visit us at www.thewildrosepress.com

Publishing History
First Black Rose Edition, 2017
Print ISBN 978-1-5092-1586-7
Digital ISBN 978-1-5092-1587-4

Calling the Moon, Book Two
Published in the United States of America

Fire filled the hallway to Carson's room,
and I skidded to a frantic stop, unable to reach him.

Carson!

My throat felt so raw from the smoke I couldn't even scream his name. Heat pounded down the hallway, along with thick black smoke, and flames blocked his door.

The window! Maybe I could get to him from his window, from outside.

I whirled, stumbled, and ran back down the hallway. The fire seemed to chase me until my numb feet tripped on the edge of the area rug and I fell hard, sending a stab of pain into my arm where some glass stuck.

Landing, I remembered I should stay on the floor. The air was slightly clearer down there, and I crawled the last feet to the front door, lined by small paned windows shattered by heat. Glass pieces bit into my knees as I reached the door, the doorknob hot in my hand as I turned it.

I launched myself onto the front stoop, then forced myself off the ground to run around the side of the house. Flames snaked upward toward the roof; the siding below was a mass of char. How did the fire erupt so quickly?

I ran to Carson's window, now a gaping wound in the siding framed by jagged pieces of glass. The eaves above sang with rising flame and sheets of smoke poured off the lower walls. My bare feet sank into mud, deep mud, and I paused for a second, confused because the water didn't make sense.

I shook my head to clear it. Carson. I had to get to Carson.

Dedication

For Mom and Dad, with all my love.
Thank you for all the hours you read to me
and all the years you believed in me.

Chapter One

I jolted awake because of the barking—deep barks that sounded right next to me even though I slept alone in my bedroom. I sat up before I opened my eyes and even then, my brain lagged behind. For the first few seconds, I stared at the flames before understanding my house was on fire.

My house was on fire.

Carson!

The curtains at my window burned, flames shooting up toward the ceiling. I stared at them and almost forgot to move. Then panic poured through me and I jumped up. I felt disoriented: the blackness, the flames, the smoke beginning to fill the room, the roar. My heart raced in terror.

My baby was in this fire.

With a high-pitched crash, my bedroom windows exploded from the heat, and a shower of hot glass flew into the room. I reflexively turned away, arms raised to cover my face. Some of the glass hit me, hot stings against my arms and side, but I barely felt the pain. Below the thunder of the fire, I heard the smoke alarm sound a futile warning.

I didn't think to drop to my knees, to detour into the bathroom for a wet cloth, to crawl to Carson's bedroom. Instead, I ran through the house, breathed in the choking smoke, felt my hands and feet start to numb

1

from panic.

Fire filled the hallway to Carson's room, and I skidded to a frantic stop, unable to reach him.

Carson!

My throat felt so raw from the smoke I couldn't even scream his name. Heat pounded down the hallway, along with thick black smoke, and flames blocked his door.

The window! Maybe I could get to him from his window, from outside.

I whirled, stumbled, and ran back down the hallway. The fire seemed to chase me until my numb feet tripped on the edge of the area rug and I fell hard, sending a stab of pain into my arm where some glass stuck.

Landing, I remembered I should stay on the floor. The air was slightly clearer down there, and I crawled the last feet to the front door, lined by small paned windows shattered by heat. Glass pieces bit into my knees as I reached the door, the doorknob hot in my hand as I turned it.

I launched myself onto the front stoop, then forced myself off the ground to run around the side of the house. Flames snaked upward toward the roof; the siding below was a mass of char. How did the fire erupt so quickly?

I ran to Carson's window, now a gaping wound in the siding framed by jagged pieces of glass. The eaves above sang with rising flame and sheets of smoke poured off the lower walls. My bare feet sank into mud, deep mud, and I paused for a second, confused because the water didn't make sense.

I shook my head to clear it. Carson. I had to get to

Carson.

I tried to knock out the rest of the glass on the window frame, before I pulled myself up and over the window. My eyes searched for my baby in the darkness—thank all the gods! Somehow, there was no fire in his room. I landed heavily on the carpet. The floor was wet and cold shocked my skin. I didn't have sprinklers—what the hell? I sloshed through inches of water and finally reached Carson's crib.

He cried, which meant he was alive, and my heart leapt. Tears streamed down his face and his mouth opened in a howl. I grabbed him, held him fiercely and maybe a little too tight, but he grabbed me right back with arms and legs, burrowed into my body, rubbed his face into my shoulder. He was soaking wet from tears.

Or—

Something cracked overhead and I leapt back toward the window, swung my legs up and over the sill, and dropped down into the mud. I landed heavily on one side with Carson cradled against me and pain stabbed through my hip. Holding Carson to me with one arm, I crawled as far as I could—which wasn't far—then collapsed onto the ground.

I looked back at my house. Fire blazed on the roof. Carson still cried; I cried. We both gasped for air. We were black with soot, with ash, with mud. We were soaked. I was suddenly freezing. Nothing made sense.

Then a growl came out of the darkness and chills raced up my spine. I sat up and turned to see what my body already knew. A huge, black wolf. A Werewolf— it had to be. Only Weres were that big. But who was he? Why was he here? The wolf stood mere feet from me with hackles raised and mouth half-open. Red light from the fire reflected off his teeth. He crouched, muscles taut, ready to spring.

"No!" I shouted and clutched Carson to me, a surge of anger giving me strength.

Why would a Were attack us?

The wolf's ears lay flat against his head. His black lips curled around fangs and his eyes looked full of hellfire. He took slow steps in my direction and I braced myself. I needed to be patient; I'd get only one chance.

I waited until he was close, until I felt the energy of him pressing on me, making the hair on my arms prickle. Then I kicked him, channeling all my strength into the blow. I must have surprised him because my foot made contact with his chest and knocked him backward—not far, but enough for me to put my back to a tree, to brace myself for further fighting.

He growled so deep I felt it in my chest, even over the fire. I looked around for anything to use as a weapon, but there were only pine needles, pinecones, scrubby grasses, clumps of dirt. I readied my body, even though I knew I wouldn't catch him off-guard again, even as I prepared for those teeth to rip into my leg, my arm. Into Carson. I screamed at the wolf, not with words, but in fury.

My scream seemed to hang in the air. No. A siren.

The wolf hesitated. He fixed those glowing eyes on me for a long moment, then tore away into the darkness.

A fire engine pulled up, then another, sirens wailing but now barely audible over the blood pounding in my ears. Shouts. People running. Hoses with streaming jets of water. Water. The water. The wolf.

The fire. My mind tried to make a connection, but couldn't. I collapsed against the base of the tree as every bit of adrenaline fled and left me weak, shaking, nauseated.

Firefighters yelled something and I noticed my neighbors stood outside. They wore pajamas, which struck me as incredibly odd, even though it wasn't, of course, because this was the middle of the night. Carla from across the street sobbed, shoulders shaking, one hand pressed to her mouth.

Oh.

"I'm here," I tried to yell. The words didn't quite come out. "I'm here!"

I didn't think I could move again, but I had to. I hugged Carson to me and crawled a few feet, dragging one leg behind me because of the pain that jabbed through me when I tried to move it.

A firefighter ran to me, yelled, and knelt down next to me. He tried to take Carson from me and I fought him, trying to scream. He said something and I shook my head in confusion, then passed out.

****

Nurses brought Carson to lie beside me on the hospital bed with his own oxygen mask, a smaller copy of mine. I curled around him the best I could and pressed as much of my body to him as possible. He pushed against me in return. We focused on breathing together. I still couldn't process what happened.

Mothering a Werewolf challenged me, but right now I felt incredibly grateful my baby was a Were—and an extremely powerful one at that. Carson's strength would help him heal quickly from the smoke inhalation. Even now, I heard the easing in his lungs, while my own breath still bubbled tight in my chest. I was just a human with one recessive Werewolf gene—what Weres called a "dark moon wolf"—and no preternatural healing abilities.

A doctor came in and introduced herself, though the name flew out of my head as soon as she said it. She listened to my lungs, while a second doctor came in and put his stethoscope to Carson's chest. My doctor's face was deeply creased, like she perpetually frowned: not the best look for an emergency room doctor.

"We're going to give you a breathing treatment to ease your lungs." She gestured toward my oxygen mask. "We need to stabilize your oxygen levels first, then get some chest x-rays to make sure we're only dealing with smoke inhalation." The doctor scribbled on a chart and glanced over at Carson. "He will get much of the same treatment, although his lungs seem better than I expected."

"Wow, do you see my hands shaking?" I said, watching them with some interest.

The next moment, I said, "I think I'm going to throw up."

A nurse ran up with a basin, another nurse deftly picked up Carson, and I sat there for a minute. The acrid smell of the smoke on my clothes finally triggered it; my stomach heaved and lost its contents in the plastic basin. I retched spasmodically, my body trying to rid itself of the ash, the smell, all of it. It was a part of me—the smoke clung in my throat, my nose. When I stopped heaving, I saw my vomit was black.

"Gross." I said weakly, then coughed. "I'm freezing."

"Your clothes are wet," said the nurse, "Here." She

helped me out of my blue-checked nightgown and into a hospital robe, then laid some heated blankets on me. "You must have been sprayed by the fire hoses. Or did you have sprinklers?" She shot me a questioning look.

"No, I—" I shook my head and frowned. "Can I make a phone call?"

Sheila answered on the second ring, her voice thick with sleep. It took her a moment to realize it was me, then a longer moment to understand what I said.

"Jules!" she said, interrupting me as I started to repeat my whole story. "Which hospital?"

I told her. On the other end of the phone, I heard Tim ask some sharp question about what happened. Unlike Sheila, he didn't sound muzzy with sleep, but I suppose he often woke to emergency situations as an investigator for the Werewolf council. Ever since he and Sheila dated, he spent nearly all of his off-duty time in southern Oregon.

"We'll be right there," said my best friend.

As soon as I hung up the phone, the nurse took me for chest x-rays. When she brought me back to the examination room, my heart leapt painfully to see Carson again. I was relieved to see he had stopped crying—but perhaps his chest hurt too much, just like mine. Every breath ached. A nurse held him and swayed with him, but quickly handed him to me at my impatient gesture. His pajamas were gone, replaced by a child-sized gown that wrapped around him several times. His gaze darted around the room. He grabbed handfuls of my gown and whimpered as I tried to soothe him. He coughed wetly and nuzzled into me urgently.

I nursed him, as much for comfort—his and mine

both—as for nourishment and looked around the room while my brain tried to catch up with events. The clock read 2:35, although I would have sworn we'd been in the hospital for hours and hours. Not to mention the eons we spent trapped in the burning house.

A knock sounded on the door and I startled.

"Jules? Julie? Are you okay? Is Carson okay?" Sheila rushed into the room, all frantic energy and huge blue eyes. Tim followed behind more sedately, but with an equally assessing gaze. Even woken in the middle of the night with no makeup and her hair pulled into a ponytail, Sheila still managed to look good.

I nodded at them both, tears suddenly filling my eyes.

"Hey." Sheila settled onto the edge of my stretcher. I leaned into her and wiped my eyes. "You're okay, sweetie. You're going to be okay, Jules."

I tried to smile at her and Tim. "We're fine." My voice broke and I couldn't keep the flood of words in. "We could have died. We could have *died*! Sheila, my house burned down. And a wolf tried to kill us. He attacked me and Carson when we got out of the fire. Did they save anything? Did the firefighters save my house?"

"I don't know, Jules. It doesn't matter—I mean, yes, it matters, but what *really* matters—"

"A wolf? There was a Were at your house? Sheila didn't say anything about a wolf. What happened?" Tim asked. His voice slipped into work mode, trying to gather information and assess the situation.

"Wait." Sheila said. "Did you call your parents yet?"

"My parents? No. But it's practically three a.m. I

don't want to wake them up. Besides, they're on their way to Europe tomorrow on that tour, and I don't want them to worry. I can tell them when they get home in two weeks."

Sheila and Tim exchanged a glance.

"Honey, you need to call your parents," Sheila said.

I started to protest, but she handed me her phone.

"They're your *parents*. Your house burned down and you almost died. Would you want Carson to call you?"

I sighed.

My mom answered the phone and immediately flipped out, even though I started the conversation by telling her everything was okay. She didn't need to worry. I just wanted them to know the house burned down and I was in the ER, but I was perfectly fine and so was Carson. She put me on speaker and I heard my dad, his voice tight with anxiety. I explained we were really okay: our oxygen levels stabilized, our chest x-rays didn't show burns in our lungs—only smoke damage—and the doctors stitched my deeper cuts. No, I wasn't sure if the whole house was gone or if anything had been saved. No, they hadn't said when they were going to release us, and no, I didn't know where we were going to stay—actually, yes, we would stay with Sheila for a while. I added this last information at Sheila's prompting. Yes, of course I had homeowner's insurance. No, I hadn't called them yet; I'd call them first thing in the morning. Yes, the doctors were taking good care of us.

No, they shouldn't cancel their tour and drive up to southern Oregon tomorrow.

I spent quite a bit of time convincing them of this last point. They'd planned this trip to Italy and France for nearly a year and—well, Sheila said I was still in shock and not thinking clearly—but I didn't want them to miss their trip. Especially since I knew they hadn't purchased trip insurance: my dad thought it a waste of money, and he and my mom had argued about it more than once. Besides, if a Werewolf wanted to kill me, I didn't want my parents in the line of fire. My recessive Were gene must have come from one of them, but they didn't know anything about my recent entrée into the paranormal world. Finally, after promising them to call them again in a few hours, to email them every day they were gone, *and* to call the emergency tour contact if there were the slightest reason I needed them, they gave in. Actually, even after all of that, I think the deciding moment was when Sheila took the phone to reassure them she and Tim would take care of us. She could charm a baby out of his pacifier, my Sheila. She didn't have to work for a few more weeks and convinced my parents she'd take good care of me. Sheila taught at the local university, which was still on break since the fall quarter didn't start until the very end of September.

My best friend Sheila was also a Witch, an honest-to-goodness Witch descended from a proud family of Witches—well, of skipped-generation Witches, anyway, since that's how the gift usually passed on. Two months ago, I had no idea things like Witches and Werewolves existed, but I had a crash course on the supernatural after Carson changed into a wolf for the first time. He inherited the Werewolf genes from his father and—unbeknownst to me—from my family line through the recessive gene I didn't know I carried. I had no Were abilities—and never would, unless my recessive gene was activated by a bite from a Werewolf. A bite might turn me into a Were, but also might kill me. At about even odds, I couldn't risk it. Even if I wanted to.

We all quieted as a nurse bustled in, glanced at the oxygen meters still hooked up to my finger and Carson's toe, and asked me how I felt. She said the doctor would be in shortly to talk about follow-up care before we were released.

When she left again, Tim said, "Tell me everything. What happened, Julie?"

I told them the whole story. Sheila sat next to me on the bed and she squeezed my arm at appropriate moments. Tim moved to stand behind her, his hands on her shoulders, and nodded as if etching all the details into long-term memory.

"Carson called the moon at such a young age," Tim said with a slight frown on his face, after I finished. He studied my baby, conked out asleep in my arms after nursing.

"What?" I said.

Tim glanced at the door and lowered his voice. "He must have called the moon and raised water as an instinctual defense against the fire." He gestured to the spots of mud that lingered on my legs even after my feet had been cleaned in order to dress my cuts.

Raising water from the ground was a Were power, similar to the way the moon influences tides. I used to think Werewolves—if they existed at all—would just be humans that turned into wolves, but I learned they had the power to perform what I thought of as moon-magic. Since Weres drew their strength from the moon, they could influence things like water, shadow, creativity, and madness. Now I understood: the mud, the water, the wet pajamas. Except Carson was only a baby.

Carson's lungs already sounded better. I cleared my own throat, which provoked a coughing fit. By the time I finished, tears flowed down my face. Just from coughing, though. I really was fine. I frowned at Sheila's expression.

"Is that...unusual?" I asked, after catching my breath.

"Unusual? For a six-month-old full moon Were—who manifested at four months—to call the moon and raise water?" Tim shrugged. "How would we know? Carson's so strong we can't use normal standards to judge him."

"When did you first call the moon? How long after you manifested?" Sheila asked Tim.

"I didn't call the moon until my pack Full taught me how. I was twelve. I changed to a wolf for the first time when I was eleven, slightly earlier than average. To teach us how to call the moon, our pack Full demonstrated for me and the other young Weres, and we began by learning to shift darkness and hide. Not raising water. In fact, on a night like tonight, with the moon little more than half-full, I'd be taxed to make more than a mud puddle. Next week, I could draw up a decent trickle."

Tim paused for emphasis. "But I'm not a full moon Were, just a waxing moon. And I'm certainly not...whatever Carson is."

We all pondered his last statement for a minute. I rubbed my forehead, right between my eyes where stress always hit me. Hard enough to believe Carson changed into a wolf at the full moon, even though I'd seen it myself twice. He shouldn't be able to access any of his other Were powers at this age.

"Did you recognize the other Were?" Tim asked.

"No. But I haven't met that many. Like I said, he was really big and black." I thought for a minute. The only black Were I knew was Ian McGregor, the younger brother of Carson's father Mac. But this wolf hadn't been Ian; I was positive. Besides, Ian wouldn't want to hurt me or Carson—he loved his nephew. He visited during the last full moon and the two of them romped all over the backyard.

"Are you sure it was a 'he?' " asked Sheila.

"Yes." I answered, then frowned. "I think so, anyway. It seemed…like a 'he.' Male."

"Thank goodness the fire engines scared him off," said Sheila.

Tim's usually mellow eyes narrowed. "I think I should go by your house and check things out. I can tell you how bad the damage is and also look for…any other signs."

"Signs of what?" I asked.

Tim just shrugged.

Chapter Two

The doctors released us about five a.m., by which time I felt absolutely exhausted, yet somehow wired. They'd pumped me full of drugs to clear my breathing—perhaps explaining the jitteriness—prescribed my very own inhaler, and started me on a course of steroids to combat the inflammation in my lungs. Carson slept in my arms, though he kept startling and making small mewling noises. When that happened, I hugged him tighter and soothed him with whispers. Taking care of him somehow helped me: every time I thought about the flames chasing me, the smoke-filled air, my house collapsing, I fussed over Carson instead of falling to pieces.

The police department provided us with a car seat, after relaying the dire news my car burned to bare metal after part of my roof unexpectedly collapsed outward into the driveway. I thanked them for the seat and tried not to let the phrase "bare metal" echo in my head.

When we pulled up to Sheila's house, Tim sat on the front step in wolf form. He rose and stretched his forelegs, then shook his head vigorously and loped to meet our car. I must have looked away for a minute, because when Tim—as a human—opened my door, I barely stifled a shriek. His eyebrows jumped in response.

"Are you okay?" he asked.

"Of course. You just surprised me."

"Not that. How are you feeling? What did the doctors say?" Tim looked across me and addressed his second question to Sheila.

"I'm fine. They said we'd be fine," I said, preempting any other response. "We're both on steroids and inhalers. Well, Carson has a nebulizer, but he probably won't need it for long with the Were healing. He's practically better already. We're just tired."

Or I should be tired. I was tired, but...I reflexively glanced back to where Carson slept in his seat. He was fine, of course, safe and sound.

I jumped when Sheila spoke. Dammit, what were they trying to do to me?

Sheila's forehead creased with that line she hated between her eyebrows. "I said, let's go inside and get you comfortable."

"Right." I said. "Comfortable."

My hands shook as I unbuckled Carson's straps. Damned medicine. I felt my heart race, too. Sheila preceded us into the house, while Tim held the door and brought up the rear. He closed it very softly behind us, but tension snaked up my back. My gaze darted around the room cataloguing exits—front door, three windows, back door down that hallway through the kitchen—before I realized what I was doing. I leaned down into Carson's head and inhaled, only to choke on the harsh smell of smoke and ash. I cleared my throat violently and swallowed hard.

Sheila came back into the room, and I still stood in the entryway like an idiot.

"I put down the futon in the office for you. I'll get the sheets now."

"Thanks." I made my feet move in that direction. Tim hovered behind me.

We both waited while Sheila made the bed, Tim silently handing her pillows and a blanket. Carson slept against my shoulder, his mouth open, his chest rising and falling only slightly shallower and faster than usual.

"I don't have a pacifier," I said. "I don't have a pacifier for Carson."

"Do you think he needs one? He's sound asleep right now," said Sheila.

"He loves his pacifier. And I don't have one!"

"Jules, it's okay. It's going to be okay. *You're* okay. Do you want Tim to go buy a pacifier somewhere?"

"I know. I know—I'm fine. But Carson—I can't believe I don't have a pacifier!"

Sheila crossed the room to me, but I backed away from her, shaking my head wildly to fend her off. Then she reached me and put her arms around me, talking to me softly, saying something I couldn't even hear because the sound of my sudden sobs drowned her out.

****

I pulled myself together. Sometime, in the course of my crying, Sheila had taken Carson and snuggled him into a nest on the futon bed. He slept soundly. I looked at him for the space of several breaths and rubbed my eyes, then realized my glasses were probably a melted lump somewhere and sighed. Good thing I didn't really need them too much, not even to drive legally.

"I'm sorry."

Sheila frowned at me. "Sorry for what? For being human?"

16

"What, so if I was a Were I wouldn't fall apart?"

For once, Sheila seemed at a loss for words. She just stared at me.

"You know that's not what she meant," Tim said. "You and Carson both nearly died in that fire. Your house burned to the ground, Julie. Anyone would be upset."

I almost ignored his platitudes until his words sank in. I swiveled toward him.

"Did it? Did my house really burn to the ground?"

He nodded, slowly, and spoke with care. "Yes. The fire was too advanced when the firefighters arrived. The roof collapsed. They were still hosing down the building while I was there, so it's impossible to know yet if any of your things might have survived."

Sheila said something, but I didn't listen. Tim's face wore a sympathetic look, but his eyes were shuttered.

"Tell me the rest."

Tim looked at Sheila.

"Dammit, Tim, what else? What aren't you telling me?" I forced myself to lower my voice, because I didn't want to wake Carson.

"Jules." Sheila put her hand on my shoulder. "*If* Tim has more news, maybe it can wait until you've had a little sleep. And a shower?"

God. A shower. Suddenly, the reek of smoke still clinging to my hair overwhelmed me. I pushed the curls behind my ears defiantly and firmly decided the shower and sleep could wait.

"I need to know." I set my jaw and matched Tim's stare. "Tell me what you found."

"Okay." Tim sat across the room from Sheila and

me. When he glanced at her briefly, the tension in his body told me he wanted to cross the room and touch her, to center himself. Out of deference to me or for some other motivation, he remained in his chair, though he leaned forward. He took a deep breath, and told me.

"Your house was burned down by Salamanders."

The words didn't match his tone.

"What...salamanders?" I echoed.

"No, not salamanders—Salamanders."

This time, I heard the capital letter, but remained bewildered.

"What the hell are you talking about? Salamanders? Like, lizards?"

Tim's face registered surprise. "Sheila?"

"I know what they are." Sheila's voice shook.

"Great. So glad you're both part of the *in crowd*. Since *my* house burned down and *my* life nearly ended, do you think one of you could please enlighten me?"

"Dammit, Jules." My sarcasm seemed to revive my best friend. "Could you drop the attitude for a while? Yes, shock and trauma and all of that, but you're being a total jerk. Tim's just trying to help."

I meant to yell back, but the frustration on her face stopped me. I tried to give her a grin, instead. It probably looked like a grimace, but I gave my best shot.

"God, Sheila. Attitude is the only thing keeping me going right now."

"I know, Jules. But you're safe here—" She stopped. "Tim, are we safe here?"

"We should be. I'll know if they're around."

"Hey, still waiting to hear who 'they' are."

Tim said, "Salamanders are paranormal creatures, like Werewolves. They draw their strength from the sun and can call on its powers—fire, heat, light—similar to the way Weres draw on the moon to raise water, shift darkness, and such. Judging by the scents at the scene, at least three Salamanders called fire at your house. Not an accident, Julie. Arson. Someone—a group of someones—wanted you and Carson dead."

"Why?" Sheila asked.

Me, I couldn't even form the word. Dammit, I should have taken a shower and gone to bed and dealt with all of this later. Sheila had been right. As usual.

"I don't know," said Tim. "Yet."

"I know Salamanders are…antithetical to Weres, but I thought you mostly co-existed peacefully."

"We do."

"Well, apparently not!" said Sheila.

"So these people turn into giant lizards? Instead of wolves?" I asked, not understanding why Sheila stifled a small laugh at my question.

Tim said, "No, they don't change form. Sometimes when calling the sun, Salamanders have a different cast to their eyes or their complexion—minor changes—but they remain fully human in shape."

"Then why are they called Salamanders? If they're not lizards?"

Tim frowned, then finally crossed the room to stand beside Sheila's chair. When he rested his hands on her shoulders, tension visibly drained from his body. Sheila unconsciously leaned back against him and his thumbs traced circles on her white t-shirt. They were physically opposite in so many ways, with Sheila's striking looks and Tim's extra-in-a-crowd-scene appearance; Sheila's long blonde hair and smooth tan, Tim's closely shorn black curls and dark brown skin.

Yet there was an undeniable sense of rightness between them. I'd even stopped teasing Sheila about Tim being just another in her long line of throwaway men.

I realized my hands still shook and I clasped them together to hide the tremors. As Tim spoke, I forced everything else out of my mind to focus.

"You'd have to ask a Salamander for a full version of their history, but as I understand it, they believe they're descended from a powerful sun-being, a lizard creature from the sun that came to Earth and mated with a human long ago."

Sheila looked up at Tim. "Really? I always thought they were called Salamanders because people used to think salamanders—the real ones—lived in fire."

"Why would people think salamanders lived in fire? Aren't they amphibians?" I asked.

"Because salamanders lived in rotten logs and crawled out when the logs were thrown into a fireplace."

"Well, both explanations sound equally bizarre to me," I said.

"I don't care how they got their name," said Sheila. "Why are they trying to kill Julie and Carson?"

The million-dollar question. The one I'd been avoiding by focusing on the peripherals. I didn't even know they existed. What could they possibly have against me?

We both looked at Tim.

He ran his fingers over his hair. "I'm going to check in with the council. They might know something helpful and they need to be informed about the attack. I'll report the rogue Were, too."

I nodded. Tim wasn't in southern Oregon in his

official capacity as a council investigator, but it made sense to consult them when any Were was attacked—especially when another Werewolf was the attacker, in addition to these Salamanders.

"What about the wolf?" I asked. "Did you find out anything more?"

"Definitely a male Were. He circled your house. I even found a paw print outside your window. I don't know his identity, didn't recognize his scent."

A strange Were and at least three Salamanders tried to kill me and my six-month-old baby.

"I need to talk to Eliza," I said. "I guess it's too late to call her?"

Eliza Minuet was a full moon Were who'd been best friends with Carson's father Mac since childhood. After Mac's death, she transferred her love and devotion to me and Carson. If Carson was in danger, she needed to know because she'd do whatever it took to keep him safe. No matter what.

Sheila handed me the phone. "You know it's never too late to call Eliza, Jules."

Eliza picked up right after the first ring. "Hello?" Her voice sounded sharp with alarm.

"Hey."

"Julie? What's wrong?"

A wave of emotion swept over me and I fought back tears, swallowing hard before I could speak again. "Yeah, it's me. We're okay. Salamanders burned down my house and tried to kill us. There was a Were, too. He attacked me, but he ran away because the fire engines got there."

"Mother moon," she said. "Are you okay? Really?"

"Yes," I said, then undercut my adamant statement

with a fit of wheezing coughs.

"Where are you? Is Tim there?"

"I'm at Sheila's house, and yes, Tim is right here."

"Did he recognize the Were's scent?"

"No. He was big and black and strong. With sharp teeth." I remembered how they'd glinted red in the firelight, pictured them tearing into Carson's small body, and took a deep breath. It hadn't happened. We were okay.

"Julie, listen to me. I'll be there as soon as I can. Until I'm there, I don't want you out of Tim's sight. Do you promise?"

"Yes. I promise." A small part of the tension thrumming through my body released.

"Okay. Good. Can I talk to Tim for a minute?"

I passed the phone over and the two Weres immediately traded information, discussing strategies for keeping me and Carson safe. I looked at Tim for a minute, his brow creased in concentration, then stood up.

"Can I get that shower now, Sheila?" I tried to smile.

Sheila sprang out of her chair and ushered me to the bathroom. She found towels, offered me a choice of several shampoos and body washes, and otherwise fussed over me until I gently pushed her out of the bathroom and started the shower.

I stayed in the shower until the hot water ran out. After washing my hair three times, I was pretty sure it didn't smell like smoke. I'd used handfuls of different shampoos—rosemary mint, pink lemonade, and "Butterfly Nectar"—so I wasn't sure what my hair *actually* smelled like, but it smelled sweet.

I tried to focus on the little things: clean hair, fresh water, thick towels. I was alive. I wanted to appreciate the faint glow of the sky through the bathroom window. Dawn should have comforted me. Instead, I wondered if Salamanders gained power in the daytime. If the rising sun somehow called them from hiding. If they'd find us. How quickly they'd find us. What they'd do when they found us. Why they wanted to kill me, when I didn't even know they existed.

I shook my head, furious with myself, then stopped to cough. When I could take a breath again, I scrubbed the fog off the bathroom mirror with the intention of doing something to make sure my curly hair didn't dry into a frizzy mass. Instead, I stood there, transfixed by my reflection. I didn't even look like myself. I looked—

I grabbed the towel and scrubbed my head vigorously, turning my back to my mirror so I didn't see my face, reflecting pale and bloodless. The black circles under my hazel eyes. Towel hanging limply from one hand, my other hand rose slowly. My fingers traced over my right cheekbone, probing the blue-black bruise centered on the small cut I'd seen. It stung, now. In fact, the pleasure of my shower suddenly disappeared behind a litany of pains, both major and minor, making themselves heard.

Goddammit.

Once dry, I stopped short with the realization I had nothing to wear. Literally nothing. Not even underwear. I sank to the bathmat, hugged my knees, and pulled the towel tight around myself.

Sheila knocked on the bathroom door, calling softly. I jolted awake, lifted my head off my arms and

Sarah E. Stevens

blinked as the room came back into focus.

I cleared my throat several times before my voice emerged.

"I'm okay. I—I fell asleep, I guess."

Sheila's voice sounded gentle. "I brought you some pajamas. Here. And a toothbrush." She cracked the door and held a t-shirt, stretchy cotton pants with paisleys, and an aqua toothbrush still in its packaging. I reached for them and clenched my teeth against the protests of stiff muscles. There was a pair of clean underwear on the pile: zebra stripes and red lace. I wasn't a hundred percent sure if this was an effort to cheer me up after my brush with death or just Sheila's normal style. Probably the latter, I decided, thinking about my own underwear with some chagrin. Burned to a crisp or lying in an ashy, sodden mess.

I took a while to get dressed, as I fought with various parts of my body that didn't want to move. Decently attired, if not making much of a fashion statement, I finally emerged from the cocooning bathroom. Sudden panic coursed through me—was Carson okay—and I hurried to the office to make sure. Tim sat on the edge of the bed next to Carson, who slept more or less peacefully, sprawled on his back. His tiny chest rose and fell quickly just a hair quicker than normal. Tim stared out the window in a way that would have looked like daydreaming had it been anyone else.

"Is Carson okay?"

"A bit restless, but sleeping."

"Thanks for staying right by him."

"I'm not about to leave either one of you alone right now," Tim said and gave me a nod both serious and caring.

Sheila appeared in the doorway with two mugs curling steam. "Jules?" Her voice quiet, nearly a murmur. "I brought you some chamomile tea. I thought it might be soothing for your throat."

"And my nerves, right?" I tried to smile at her as she handed one mug to me and the other to Tim.

"Irish Breakfast for you, my wild wolf."

"Just what I like," said Tim.

The tone behind his words brought a blush to my never-discomfited best friend and left me caught between rolling my eyes and throwing hot tea at the two of them. I settled for taking a sip, tasting plenty of honey. The heat and sweetness eased some of the tight bitterness in my throat and chest.

We sat in silence. I watched Carson, Tim watched the window, and Sheila alternated watching the three of us. When I finished my tea, Sheila took my mug and suggested I try to get some rest. I nodded, too tired to even formulate words.

"Tim will stay on watch. Call if you need anything. Anything at all," she said.

I curled up beside Carson on the futon and tumbled into sleep almost before the two of them left the room.

Chapter Three

Carson woke me with a sudden cry. His little eyes sprang wide open in alarm and he reached for me with both hands. His wispy baby hair was damp with sweat from whatever he'd been dreaming.

"Shh, sweetie, it's okay." My voice sounded strangely tight and congested to my own ears, but served to calm him slightly.

I sat him up on the bed and looked around the room for his nebulizer. Once I found it, I looked down at my son and realized he seemed to breathe just fine. He wasn't coughing at all. Me? I felt like an elephant sat on my chest and I heard my lungs whistling in a thoroughly annoying—and somewhat alarming—way. I set down the nebulizer and picked up my inhalers, after which I took some deeper breaths without exploding into coughs. I ached all over. While I tried to stretch out some of the pain, I heard a knock on the door.

"Come in," I said, then repeated myself loud enough to carry.

Sheila poked her head in the door. She held her phone, hand cupped over it.

"It's Eliza. Are you up to talk?"

I nodded and took the phone.

"Julie, hi. I'll be there tonight, okay? I'm in Cody, Wyoming waiting for a flight to Salt Lake City, then to Medford. I'll rent a car at the airport and be down to

Sheila's place in Ashland before bedtime. Are you feeling okay? How's Carson?"

I took a second to catch up. Cody must be the closet airport to Greybull, the small town in northern Wyoming that Eliza's pack called home. "We're okay. Sheila's taking good care of me and Tim's here… Are you sure you don't mind coming?"

"Julie, don't be ridiculous. I booked the flights last night, right after we got off the phone. Of *course* I'm coming. That's what friends do. You almost died— there are Salamanders and a Were involved and who knows what they'll try next. I can help."

I pushed aside my initial inclination to protest more, to feel guilty she'd drop everything to come when I needed her, and allowed myself to just be grateful. I said, "Thanks, Eliza. I know Carson will be safe with you here."

"No problem. You'd do the same for me. Besides, I can even justify it as pack business, kind of. The Full's quite worried."

"Did Lily ask you to come?" I said.

"Well, let's just say the pack's happy to take advantage of our friendship. The Full's charged me with protecting you until the council can figure out what's going on. We're Carson's pack, too, you know. You're pack by proxy, if nothing else."

Eliza was one of the strongest Weres in the Greybull pack, a full moon Were herself, second only to Lily Rose who led the pack as *the* Full and also mayor of Greybull. And a stripper in her spare time— not really, but I liked to imagine that, because of her over-the-top name and glamorous looks. Lily Rose was the antithesis of what I expected of a Werewolf and she threw me quite off guard the first time I met her. I thought the pack leader would be much bigger, stronger, and well, male-er. Since Carson's father Mac was a member of the Greybull pack before his murder, the Greybull pack firmly claimed Carson as one of their own. Eliza and Lily Rose continually urged me to move to Wyoming and bring Carson into the pack, but I didn't want to live in Greybull. Or anywhere else in Wyoming. No way.

"Lily says the whole council is very concerned for your safety," Eliza continued.

My eyebrows raised. I was fairly certain "your safety" really meant the well-being of Carson the uber-powerful Were baby, at least as far as the council was concerned. I somehow doubted they worried about the safety of Julie Hall, human. Of course, they also had a vested interest in learning more about the rogue Were who attacked me. They couldn't allow stray Werewolves to make trouble for the packs.

"Okay. Um. Thanks for coming," I said, wishing for better words. What could I say to a friend who dropped everything and flew to my side in a time of need?

"I'll see you soon, Julie, okay? Put Sheila back on the phone for directions. You should save your voice—you sound awful."

When Sheila ended the phone call, she stood there, arms akimbo, and assessed me with a long look.

"Oh, before I forget." She strode out of the room and came back with a package of pacifiers, one blue and one orange. "This is the right kind, isn't it?"

"Yes. Thank you." I blinked furiously to hide my tears.

Carefully, I focused my attention on Carson as he finished nursing then fussed with the little footed sleeper the hospital had given us and changed his diaper.

Sheila let me perform those tasks in silence. When I was composed again, I looked up at her and asked, "What's next?"

"Well." Her mouth curved in a smile. "I think we'd better get you some clothes. Unless you'd like to run around in my extra pajamas all day."

So less than twelve hours after nearly dying in my burning house, I flip-flopped across the Rogue Valley Mall to shop for the basics: bras, underwear (thankfully not with zebra stripes), jeans, t-shirts, a sweatshirt, new sandals for me, onesies, stretchy pants, and new pajamas for Carson. And some extra pacifiers, just in case. Plus, I bought a pretzel with hot cheese because I never went to the mall without getting a pretzel and I didn't think it was time to break tradition. At Sheila's prompting, I also picked up a new cell phone. I wouldn't have thought about it, but she was right: that was absolutely essential. We stopped in town for a new baby sling to carry Carson, this one a beautiful woven print of blue and purple, so I thought we covered all our immediate needs. Since I escaped the fire without my purse, wallet, credit cards, debit card, or anything else, Sheila paid for everything. I'd made a quick call to my homeowner's insurance who promised me living expenses and longer-term reimbursement for my property and belongings. After setting the rather onerous process in motion, I resolved to put money on the back burner and focus on more important things.

Like finding out who tried to kill me and Carson.

And why.

I held Carson while I finished my pretzel—without dropping any cheese or salt on his head, quite an accomplishment—and listened to Tim and Sheila make small talk in such an obvious attempt to soothe me that I actually got annoyed. At a lull in their forced conversation, I spoke.

"I want to see my house."

Sheila frowned. "Are you sure? It might upset you."

"I'm sure it will upset me. But I need to see for myself."

An understatement. I felt an almost physical pull to go back, to see the house, to revisit our near deaths.

Tim nodded, as if he expected as much. "Let's go then," he said.

The drive from the mall to my house in Jacksonville took twenty minutes. Twenty minutes during which tension strangled my back and neck, and turned already stiff muscles into torture. Twenty minutes to wonder if the Salamanders would be there, drawn back to the crime scene—as I was—ready to attack again. Twenty minutes to pretend my labored breathing meant I needed my inhaler. Twenty minutes of clenched fists before I realized what I was doing. Those twenty minutes seemed much, much longer. Yet not long enough to prepare myself.

I smelled the fire first, before the house even came into view. I retched then turned it into a cough. Sheila turned around in the front seat to look at me. I gazed back, face like stone, and dared her to say something. She gave me a nod before facing forward again.

Tim parked down the street from my house and I

got out of the car. A small fire truck still sat in front of the house and yellow caution tape blocked my driveway. Two firefighters leaned against their truck, chatting with each other while they watched the wreckage of my house. My gaze followed theirs before I was quite ready.

My car, my poor old car, sat in the middle of the blackened driveway. At least, I assumed it was my car. A mass of metal and melted upholstery, though the rear windshield somehow still looked whole without even a crack. A landslide of char from my roof and siding covered the crushed hood. Water still dripped from the wreckage of the house, spreading a greasy, black puddle down my driveway and into the street.

"Holy crap." I realized my own voice broke the silence and further noticed Tim and Sheila frozen in tableau. Tim stood at full alert, looking as much like a wolf with cocked ears and rankled fur as possible to look in human form. His eyes scanned the scene and I felt sure he absorbed every scent in the area. Sheila, on the other hand, looked only at me. Her back to the house, as if it didn't even matter, she stood with her whole body canted in my direction. Her blue eyes looked enormous, gaze locked on my face, and I wondered what she saw. Me, I felt encased in marble, as if the faintest movement would crack me.

We stood like that long enough one of the firefighters noticed us, pushed off from the truck, and started in our direction.

"*Jules*, do you want me to get Carson?" The emphasis in Sheila's voice made me think she spoke before.

It took another minute before I understood her

question.

"Yes, please." I said.

With Sheila holding Carson, I walked toward the black hole of my house.

When I passed the firefighter, he said something to me. I brushed past him with a meaningless gesture and felt thankful Sheila hurried to take care of any necessary explanations.

Holy crap. I mouthed the words this time. My house.

Several walls still stood. The rest was a litter of roof and burned things, blackened items I could almost recognize. Here and there, scraps of paper and cloth floated like jetsam on the wet ashes. Everything destroyed. Utterly.

I had nothing to say. Didn't know what to do.

I turned to Sheila, standing next to me, and held out my hands for Carson. I hugged him, buried my nose in his hair, which, thankfully, after a bath this morning no longer smelled like the fire, though everything around us did.

Carson squirmed in my desperate embrace, trying to look around in his six-month-old-I'm-my-own-baby-and-don't-forget-it way.

"Can I walk around?" I asked.

One of the firefighters hovered behind us. "You can look," he said, "but don't go inside and stay back from the walls, because they're not stable."

Sheila and Tim followed me as I traced the perimeter of my house. My former house. Kitchen. Living room. My bedroom. I stopped there and poked around on the ground, full of footprints, mud, and charred bits. I looked up at Tim and he mutely used his toe to point to a half-covered mark on the ground. When I looked closer, I saw part of a print. I stretched my hand out. Half a paw print that would have been the size of my outstretched fingers. Huge.

"Did you follow the tracks last night?" I asked.

"As far as I could." Tim's voice sounded grim. "He took to the road and confused things—quite clever."

"In a car?"

"Not clear. The Salamanders definitely parked down the road a bit. The Were may have met up with them."

"Are they…around? Any of them?"

"No."

I almost asked if he was sure, but stopped myself. He wouldn't say it if he weren't sure.

God, I had a headache.

Carson fussed a bit and I jiggled him on my hip while we walked the rest of the way around the wreckage. After a minute, I said, "I guess there's not much else to do here."

We silently drifted back into the car. Sheila continued to watch me with worried eyes. I was just glad she didn't say anything.

I stared back at the house as we drove away.

"Now what?" Sheila asked Tim.

"Now we wait for Eliza. I'm not leaving you two alone without another Were to protect you. As soon as she's here, I'll widen my investigation around Julie's house and we'll find them."

Whoever they might be.

Chapter Four

When Eliza arrived right after dinner, she strode over to me, grabbed both of my shoulders, and searched my face for a long minute before pulling me close for a hug.

"Julie." My name took on an unfamiliar weight as she let go of me and looked again, cataloging my visible injuries—bruises here, some cuts there. She hugged me tight one more time, nodded slightly, and turned to Tim.

When she spoke to him, the entire atmosphere changed. The air became thick with static charge.

"Tell me everything you know." Eliza had no authority over Tim, but I wouldn't guess that from her tone. After his report, the council officially assigned Tim to investigate the attempted murder and find the Were involved. So technically, he outranked Eliza. However, as the stronger Werewolf—full moon to his waxing moon—as my close friend, and a representative of Carson's nominal pack, Eliza held the high ground on both power and moral imperative. She didn't hesitate to let it show.

"As I've notified the council," Tim said and continued after a pause so short I wondered if I imagined it, "Salamanders set the fire at Julie's house. At least three, maybe four. They called a strong fire and firefighters fought hard to contain the blaze. The fire completely destroyed the house. Julie and Carson were lucky to escape—the Salamanders clearly meant to kill them. Julie woke up because the rogue Were barked for some reason, maybe to alert the Salamanders to approaching witnesses, maybe in jubilation, or a natural reaction against the flames. She rescued Carson, who called the moon and drew water to protect himself. After escaping the house and rescuing Carson, Julie managed to fend off the Were until firefighters arrived at the scene and he fled. The Were is a mature male, black fur, according to Julie, and quite large, confirmed by the size of his prints."

"Where did the Salamanders go?" asked Eliza.

"Don't know. They left in a car parked down the street. I found the Were's scent all over the neighborhood—he may have watched the house for quite a while. Weeks."

News to me. I frowned at Tim.

"When the Were ran, he crossed the road several times and I lost his scent. He might have gotten into the car with the Salamanders."

Eliza continued debriefing Tim then turned to me with pointed questions. I told the story from the beginning, then halted at several points—including a full description of the water in Carson's room—before she was satisfied she'd caught up with all the known information. Which didn't seem like much, frankly.

By this time, it was nearly nine o'clock at night. Carson had been asleep for a full two hours, probably a response to the prior sleepless night, and I felt like propping my eyelids open with toothpicks. However, when Eliza said she wanted to go to the house right then, in lieu of waiting for the next day when the scent trail would be colder, I sat up straight and said I wanted to go, too.

Sheila frowned. "If you go, I'm coming. Gotta keep you out of trouble, Jules."

"Actually, I'd rather you stay here with Tim and watch Carson. I don't think he'll wake up, but if he does, you could give him a bit of rice cereal." I stopped short. "Oh shit," I said.

"What?" asked Sheila.

"I was supposed to work today. I didn't even call them," I said. A month ago, I returned to my job at the Jacksonville branch library. Carson spent his time at a daycare center near our house.

Eliza looked dubious. "I'm sure they'll understand. Can you take a few weeks of vacation until we sort out all this?"

"No. I used up all my vacation for maternity leave." I rubbed my forehead, focusing on my right temple where it felt like someone was stabbing me with a long, thin needle.

"Leave without pay, then," said Sheila in a decided voice. "You can't go back to work—at least this week." I opened my mouth to protest, but she continued. "Jules, don't be an idiot. Think about it; do you want to leave Carson at daycare? Do you want the library burned down around you? We have to figure out who's responsible for this and you can't do that while sitting behind the research desk."

"You mean, I can't just Google 'murdering Salamanders' and 'rogue Weres' and find the answer that way?" I essayed the weak joke and received an approving smile from my best friend.

"Just leave it to me, Jules," Sheila drawled and

gave me a wink. "I'll call them in the morning and arrange some time off."

Unsure whether to feel patronized or relieved Sheila would take care of it, I opted for the latter. "Okay." Decided, I turned to Eliza. "Well, what are we waiting for? Let's go."

The first few minutes of our drive were quiet, as I engaged in some deep breaths to ease my tension. Eliza watched me out of the corner of her eye while she drove the rental car up Highway 99 toward Jacksonville. It was one of those beautiful evenings at the end of the summer, with the air crisping into autumn. Darkness flooded the valley floor with the waxing moon occasionally sending light through the cloud cover and onto the slopes of the Cascades.

"I'm glad you're okay, Julie." Eliza let out a slow breath.

"Yeah, me too."

"I should have been here. If I'd been here, I could have protected you."

I shrugged. "Well, you've got a pack and a life back in Greybull. You can't move to southern Oregon."

"I know. But we can't protect you while you're here all alone."

I frowned at her pointed tone.

Eliza hit the brakes slightly when she saw the drive-through coffee kiosk approaching. "Do you want a coffee or something?"

I smiled in spite of everything. "No, it's too late."

"What? There's a time and a place when Julie Hall doesn't want a coffee?" Eliza grinned at me. "How about a chai? A decaf latte?"

"Very funny." The decaf latte actually sounded

kind of tempting, but I made a face at her anyway.

"Mother moon, Julie. How do we get ourselves into these scrapes? You really could have been killed last night." She shook her head. "Goddamn firebugs. Why are they after you? And a Were allied with them?"

Passing headlights illustrated the frown on Eliza's face as she continued. "It's nearly impossible to outwit a called fire. You were lucky, really lucky. Thank the moon Carson called water. He really is strong. What a Were he's going to grow up to be…"

After a moment and another sidelong glance, Eliza said, "You know, you don't need to worry about your job here. The Full's promised you pack support and a position in Greybull. You could just quit your job at the library."

"Eliza."

"Your house is gone and there's no reason for you to rebuild here in Jacksonville. Take the insurance money and buy something in Greybull. The pack really does need someone to help with our archive—"

"I keep telling you. You can't call a room full of musty boxes an archive." I tried to distract Eliza's mini-rant, but she continued as if I hadn't spoken.

"Exactly. You could sort through things, organize them. The records might even have information that would help us understand Carson, why he's so strong, how he's likely to develop, how to help him. No one's been through that stuff for decades. If you moved, you wouldn't have to worry about being alone with no protection. The pack would provide you with a salary, with housing, with training for Carson—"

"Just stop it! Eliza, I'm not moving to Greybull!" Greybull: population eighteen hundred and some, home of a pack of Werewolves, all of whom would dote on Carson the uber-strong Werewolf and secretly pity me for being merely a dark moon wolf. At the same time, they'd caution me against wanting to be a Were, continually rubbing my face in the fact that I'd risk my life if I were bitten, if I tried to become a Were in truth. My whole life would revolve around the pack, as I dug into their history and their records. Carson would grow, gain even more abilities, and become central to the pack. Maybe even pack leader, someday, *the* Full. Heck, leader of the national council. There weren't any other Werewolves as strong as Carson. And me? I'd be stuck socializing with Weres who pitied me or other humans in town from whom I'd have to keep this enormous secret.

No way in hell would I move to Greybull. Carson and I would manage on our own. His uncle Ian would help, as would the rest of the MacGregor family, although Carson's grandparents weren't strong Weres. Tim—surely Tim could teach Carson what he needed to know. And Eliza, too, if she stopped harping on the need for me to move closer to her pack.

"We've been over this time and again, Eliza." I tried for a light tone. "I'm not the Wyoming type, okay? And I'm not part of your pack. You and Lily—" I consciously neglected to use her pack title, "can't force me to move to Greybull."

I faced straight ahead. "I'll be fine right here. I'll rebuild my house. This is my home."

I would never, ever move to Greybull. Unless—but I stopped that thought before it fully formed. I couldn't risk some Were biting me to turn me from a dark moon to a true Were. I couldn't risk death.

Eliza lifted her hands off the steering wheel in mock surrender. "Consider the subject dropped." She didn't need to add "for now." I heard it anyway.

I decided to switch gears. "What are you hoping to find at the house?"

One shoulder shrugged. "I'd like to get a handle on the scents, that's all. So I know them."

"Do, uh, Salamanders smell different than humans?"

"Firebugs *stink*. Like strong sunlight or a struck match."

I glanced at her in surprise. "I'm not sure sunlight has a smell, but I like the smell of matches." Or I did. Before. "So. I take it you're not a Salamander fan, then?"

"No self-respecting Were is. They..." One hand traced a circle in the air as Eliza sought the words. "They feel compelled to flaunt their supposed superiority. Linked to the *sun*, not the *moon*. The moon only reflects the sun's light; the sun is the real source." Her voice mocked the sentiment. "They're never...subtle. When firebugs are in the room, it's like they need all the attention, all the light, all the focus on them. They suck the very oxygen from the air."

She shrugged again. "I can't describe it."

I wisely chose to stay silent, instead of pointing out Eliza herself had a tendency to commandeer a situation, to bring roiling energy into a room and raise the hairs on the back of my neck, to occupy more space than even her admittedly tall figure necessitated. Not in a bad way—or, at least, not always—but I'd seen Eliza use her very presence to cow others. Tim, on the other hand, downplayed his strength, faded into the crowd, unless he needed to make a show of power.

"Have you known a lot of Salamanders?"

"I've run into them from time to time. Steered clear of them as much as possible, for obvious reasons." Scorn filled her voice.

"All right," I said. "Weres don't like Salamanders, check. But Tim said you usually get along okay? Live and let live and all of that? I mean, they don't go around the countryside trying to burn down Were houses, right?"

"Right. Probably because they know they'd lose in any honest fight." Eliza glanced at me as if daring me to contradict her claim. I just nodded. "Although some of those firebugs…you never know what they're going to burn."

"Are there lots of Salamanders?"

"Define 'lots.' "

I huffed an exasperated breath, and Eliza flashed a grin before answering my question. "Probably about the same as Weres. Maybe eight thousand in the US. They don't have a tendency to congregate the way we do, though."

"So no packs? Or, whatever a group of lizards would be called?"

Eliza considered for a moment. "A school of Salamanders? A slime of Salamanders?"

"I like it. A slime of Salamanders."

"Okay, then. No, they don't have slimes."

I snorted.

Eliza dropped her playful tone and her expression tightened. "We're close. I want to focus."

I'd been so diverted by our conversation I hadn't realized we were mere blocks from my house. I clenched my fists and hoped Eliza couldn't hear the sudden jump in my heartbeat with her damned Were senses.

Eliza cracked the window and slowed the car. We drove the last few minutes in silence, Eliza scenting the air, me trying to ignore the wisps of char in the breeze. We parked the car almost exactly where Tim had stopped earlier in the day. There weren't any firefighters at the scene now, though the yellow tape still hung forlornly across my driveway. The fire must be solidly doused, then, no fear about smoldering ashes. This time of year, southern Oregon was like a tinderbox—full of dry grasses and evergreen needles— so I know the firefighters must have been concerned.

I forced myself to look away from the burned shell even as it called to me. I wanted to run to the house, to feel the charred wood and broken bits under my hands, to roll in it, to taste it, to somehow understand. I could have stayed there forever, just staring. I heard the roar of the fire, glass shattering, my own voice screaming. I jumped and my hands flew to my throat when I saw flames in the road—then I realized the red glow was from taillights, just the lights of a car passing. I blinked furiously and finally pried my clenched jaw open to ask—in what I desperately hoped was a normal voice— if Eliza picked up any scents.

She stood next to me, one hand extended, face locked in an expression I couldn't read. Her eyes were black and fierce.

She spoke in a murmur and I felt my throat loosen slightly.

"Yes. This way." She gestured toward the side of the house, near my bedroom.

I tripped, following her, and cursed my lack of night vision. As we walked, I sensed energy rising, spilling off Eliza, and felt my skin tighten in response. I tucked my hair behind my ears, annoyed at the prickles, and shifted my shoulders to relax still-aching muscles. Eliza stopped and I nearly walked into her.

"What is it?" I whispered.

She froze for a long minute, breathing shallowly, then spat out, "Stay here." She sprang forward in two graceful steps and knelt down where Tim had shown me the paw print.

Eliza turned, her face pale against the dark of the night. I took half a step backward—an involuntary reaction to the wildness in her eyes—then gasped as she pulled on shadow, tugging the nearby darkness into a thick shroud, and leapt out in wolf form. Her hackles raised, lips drawn away to reveal sharp teeth white in the moonlight, mouth half-open as she sniffed the ground once, twice, again, again. She raised her head, tension apparent in the muscles of her shoulders and haunches under the buff fur, ears drawn painfully alert.

Without another look at me, she was gone. She sprang so quickly I jumped again then tensed in sudden alarm at the sharp crack of a branch breaking under her foot. The crack of fire, of wood buckling under flame. No. I fought the fear and surfaced. The wolf raced into the scrubby trees behind my house.

Eliza left and I was alone. I crossed my arms in front of me, cursing the traitorous trembles, the anxiety snaking up my spine.

I *was* alone. There were no Salamanders here. Eliza wouldn't have left me if there were anything to fear. She just ran after his scent and she'd be back in no time at all. Just like Tim, she'd lose the rogue Were on the road and be right back for me.

I walked back and forth in front of the ruins of my house. One of my neighbors had a light on and I debated the merits of knocking on her door, but I wasn't sure I could handle her sympathy and the inevitable discussion about the fire. Or her questions about why I hung out here on the street. Eliza would return in just a minute, anyway—though it seemed like she'd been gone for a long time. I crossed to the car and leaned against its side. I took out my phone, thought about calling Sheila, but didn't.

"Where's the baby?"

I stifled a scream. My heart raced as I searched the shadows and found the figure under the cedar tree. He took three steps toward me and repeated, "Where is the baby?"

"Who are you?" My voice didn't shake and I stood up straight.

He held out a hand and fire blossomed in his palm. "Does that answer your question?" He moved his mouth in a wicked smile that never reached his eyes. "Now answer mine. Where is the mutant Were baby?"

The man—the Salamander—looked my age, late twenties, with long brown hair tied at the nape of his neck. His glasses reflected the flames still burning in his hand.

"None of your goddamned business." I spat the words as my fury mounted. "You burned down my house!"

The flames on the man's palms shot up. "Shame you didn't stay to really enjoy the flames last night. For the last time, where's your son?"

"Shall I call 911?" I said, holding up my cell phone. "The police would be quite interested if I died in a fireball the night after someone burned down my house. You want to draw that sort of attention, Salamander?" I spoke loudly, half-hoping one of my neighbors would hear us.

The Salamander's eyes narrowed. "You think the police would be able to identify your remains after I'm done with them?"

I fought the shudder that raced up my spine, swiped open my phone, and punched the three numbers, pausing before I hit send.

"This isn't over," the man said.

With a rushing whoosh, the cedar tree caught fire, sending orange flames into the air as branches popped and crackled, dry tinder in this heat. I jumped away, slammed my back into the car, and by the time I could focus on anything except breathing, the Salamander was gone.

Flames surged up the tree and limned its branches, and I knew one of my neighbors must be calling in the fire right now—and I didn't want to hang around for the slew of questions that would follow. Better that no one realized I'd been here tonight, that the investigators decided a mystery arsonist targeted the neighborhood, not me personally. Or my baby. I slipped into Eliza's rental car and started the engine with fumbling fingers, using the keys she'd left in the ignition, hoping all the while no one would make note of me. The lights turned on automatically and I let them, since acting furtive seemed like a bad idea. I wouldn't go far; Eliza could follow the scent and find me.

I drove a couple of blocks and pulled over on a

busier street. I locked the doors. Twice. And left the car idling, just in case.

Where the fuck was Eliza?

I called Sheila. "Hey. Eliza's run into the woods. A Salamander appeared out of nowhere and demanded I tell him where my 'mutant Were baby' is and set fire to a tree before he fled."

"What?" Sheila said.

After a muffled sound, Tim was on the phone. "Where did Eliza go?"

"No clue. She changed and raced off without a word."

"How long has she been gone?"

I shook my head and looked at the dashboard clock. "Fifteen minutes? Twenty?"

Tim cursed. "What happened with the Salamander?"

"He wants Carson. I don't know why. I threatened to call 911, he said he could burn me to death and leave no identifiable remains, then he set the cedar tree on fire and ran off." I took a long breath.

"Okay. If Eliza doesn't come back in five minutes, come back here. If you see any more Salamanders, leave right away, go somewhere very public, and call us back."

"Right. Is...is Carson okay?"

"He's just fine, don't worry."

"Okay."

I sat in the car and listened to fire engines scream to my block. Again.

Three minutes later, Eliza ghosted around the corner and padded over to the car. Her dark wolf eyes appeared enormous. She wreathed herself in shadow and stepped forth, tapped on the car door until I unlocked it, and snapped at me, "What the hell happened? Are you okay?"

"What the hell happened to *you*? Where did you go? How dare you just run off like that without telling me anything."

"Julie, I smelled a Salamander back there, near your house and there's a tree on fire. *Are you okay?*"

"With no thanks to you, I'm absolutely fine."

"What happened?"

I almost demanded she explain herself first, but decided she needed to know about Salamander. He might lurk around even now. I quenched my anger and told her everything.

"Is he still around?" I asked. At her look, I clarified, "The Salamander. Do you still smell him?"

"No."

"Then again, I guess you didn't smell him earlier, or else you wouldn't have run off like that."

Eliza didn't say anything. She didn't even apologize. Instead, I sensed…something. My own shoulders tensed further in reaction to the strained way she held herself, as if curled inward around something painful.

I spoke first when it became clear she didn't intend to enlighten me.

"Did you?" I cleared my throat, thankful for a steadier voice—I wasn't sure if it had been shaking in anger or fear. Both, perhaps. "Did you figure out where he went? The Were?"

"What?" Eliza wrenched her attention from the darkness long enough to hear what I said. "No. Tim's right. The track and scent are muddied in the road."

"Is he a strong Were? Can you tell?"

"Yes." The sound was clipped.

"What about the Salamanders?"

"What?"

I wanted to smack her. "Earth to Eliza. What did you learn about the Salamanders?"

"Nothing."

"Nothing?" My voice rose several octaves, and at last, Eliza looked at me.

"Nothing new. You learned more than I did. Tim's right, I traced three primary scents, maybe an older one. I'll recognize them next time." She spoke with exaggerated precision, as if talking to a three year old, and I flinched at the sudden hurt caused by her tone.

Eliza didn't seem to feel snubbed, but sat like stone as I drove us back to Sheila's house, taking a very roundabout route and looking behind us after every turn.

Chapter Five

The next morning dawned too early, considering I got to sleep around midnight. Carson woke up around three a.m. and then fought sleep for an hour before catnapping until six, when I gave up and brought him into the kitchen. I was trying to figure out how to work Sheila's super-duper fancy coffeemaker when she walked in.

"How the hell do you manage to look so chipper?" I grumbled.

Sheila winked at me and deftly took over with the coffee beans. "Practice, young apprentice."

"And what the hell is that?"

"Why that, dear Jules, is called a highchair. Used for babies and toddlers."

"Gee, thanks. What is this so-called highchair doing in your kitchen?"

"Well, right now, it's serving as a chair—a *high* chair—for yonder baby, what's his name, young Carson, I believe."

I threw the kitchen towel at her and she laughed. "I went out last night and bought it, Jules. So you don't have to perch Carson on your lap all the time. As his favorite auntie, I wanted to make sure he wasn't scalded by black coffee and his morning-grumpy mama."

"We're not moving in here, you know."

"Hmm. Actually, you are, you know. Moving in

here." Sheila held up a hand. "At least for a while. Your place is obviously wrecked and I'm not sending you to some hotel. You'll stay here until we figure out what's going on and what you're going to do next."

I sank down in a kitchen chair.

"I need coffee," I moaned. "I can't argue with you without coffee."

"Ah-ha! I'll remember that." Sheila snagged me a mug and let the coffee brew directly into it, then delivered the mug with a flourish.

"You're not supposed to do that, you know. Let the coffee drip into the cup. All the caffeine comes out first or something." I peered into the dark brew. "Then again, never mind."

I took a quick sip, scalding my mouth slightly in that oh-so-pleasurable-first-coffee-of-the-morning way. Carson pounded on the highchair tray with a spoon and shrieked. Happily, I think.

Sheila fixed herself a cup of Earl Grey tea and allowed me to imbibe my drug of choice for a while without further comment.

"Are you sure you have room for us here? Me and Carson, plus Eliza—your townhouse is getting crowded quickly," I said.

"I think we'll be fine. You and Carson can have the office for as long as you want and Eliza will be comfortable curled up in wolf form. Besides, if we need extra space, we could always use Don's house."

"Don from your department?"

"He and his wife are away until the fifteenth, and I'm watering their plants. I really do think we'll all be fine here, though," Sheila said. She frowned then continued. "So what's up with Eliza? She hardly said a word after you two got back last night, even in the face of Tim's questions. And his disapproval. I've never seen anyone stonewall him like that."

I refilled my mug. "I don't know. After she went haring off after the scents at my house, she became very…withdrawn. Just stressed, I guess. Maybe she's upset at herself for leaving me with a Salamander lurking about."

"Well, I'm upset about it. Makes sense she would be," said Sheila.

"Yeah, me too. I still don't understand why she didn't scent him. He couldn't have been far away. She really hates Salamanders." I frowned and thought for a minute. "Hate might not be the right word. They disgust her. I think she's upset any Were would ally with them. That's probably worse than our rogue trying to kill me, in her book."

Sheila gave a wry laugh. "She's going to love Tim's news, then."

"What's Tim's news?" Eliza spoke from the doorway and both Sheila and I swiveled in her direction. I plastered a pleasant look on my face and mentally rewound the conversation before shrugging it off.

"Well, good morning, sunshine. Aren't we a bunch of early risers?" Sheila drawled and crossed the kitchen to hand Eliza a coffee cup.

"What's Tim's news, Sheila?" I asked.

"Hmm. He'll be down soon, I'm sure. I wouldn't want to spoil the surprise. Don't worry, it's nothing bad." She refused to say any more, answering further questions with lifted eyebrows and an amused shake of the head.

****

Tim didn't waste time. As he crossed to get his own fill of morning caffeine—thus answering the question about why non-coffee-drinking Sheila owned a fancy coffeemaker, top class beans, and a grinder I couldn't operate—he tossed the news over his shoulder at the table.

"There's a new addition to our team arriving this afternoon with the council's blessing. The Salamanders are sending one of their own to help investigate." Tim turned around with his coffee. His eyes focused unerringly on Eliza.

I paused with spoon in midair, resuming the task of feeding Carson when he banged his little fists on the tray in protest over the rice cereal hovering just out of reach. Two spoonfuls later, Eliza still stared at Tim with narrowed eyes.

"Well, sounds reasonable to me," I volunteered. "Takes a Salamander to catch a Salamander."

"More than that," said Tim. "The gesture's meant to show this group is rogue. Their actions aren't sanctioned by the leadership."

Eliza's mouth was set in a thin line. "I don't like it."

"I don't care if you like it." Tim took out a box of cereal from the cabinet and filled his bowl. "You can't handle it? Then feel free to go back to Greybull right now. I know your pack full wants you here to help protect Julie and Carson, but the council can dispatch other Weres if needed."

"I'm not leaving."

"Good, then. We're all in agreement. I don't want any tension on my team."

I sucked in a quick breath at his choice of pronoun and Eliza straightened in her chair. She didn't challenge his statement, though, only nodded once.

"So." I glanced between the two of them before deciding it was safe to continue. "I thought the Salamanders weren't organized into packs, or uh, slimes or anything? But they have some sort of central authority to send people around?"

"Slimes?" repeated Sheila.

"You know, a pod of dolphins, a murder of crows, a slime of Salamanders?"

Sheila's laughter cut through the remaining tension and even Eliza grinned. Tim's deep chuckle caused Sheila to lean into his side, one arm around his waist. His arm circled her shoulders and pulled her tight.

"I've heard of a lounge of lizards, but a slime of Salamanders? That's good," Sheila said.

"Is it really a lounge of lizards?" I asked.

"I think so."

"So what *is* a group of Salamanders called?"

Tim shrugged. "Just a group of Salamanders, I guess. You can ask our Salamander, later."

"*Our* Salamander? Goddamn firebugs." Eliza muttered at a careful pitch, loud enough to hear, but soft enough Tim could choose to ignore it.

But he didn't.

"None of that, Eliza," he said, sharply. "No 'firebug' talk."

Eliza pushed away from the table and rose to her full height, making it quite apparent she topped Tim by about an inch. The hair rose on the back of my neck and I held my breath as the air in the room seemed to crackle.

Abruptly, she wheeled on one foot like a ballet dancer and left, slamming the back door behind her.

I flinched at the sound and held myself rigid as tears sprang into my eyes for no reason. No reason at all. Just a loud noise. *Ridiculous* that I wanted to jump up and flee. There was nothing to run from.

Tim exhaled, slowly. "She'll calm down, once she's adjusted to the idea. She seems a little on edge." He frowned.

Sheila nodded and pulled away from Tim long enough to hand him the milk from the fridge. She then crossed to me and rested one hand on my shoulder.

"You're going to be okay, too, Jules."

I cleared my throat. "Of course. I'm fine, Sheila."

I busied myself with feeding Carson the rest of his cereal and then washed him off, since he ended up with as much cereal on his clothes and face and arms and hair as in his belly. Bibs were useless with my boy.

"So," Sheila said, brightly. "Want to go to the shooting range, Jules?"

****

I'd always been fairly anti-gun. But then again, I was also anti-letting people kill me or my son. After I discovered some things going bump in the night were actually real, I'd decided I better learn how to shoot a gun. I had one lucky shot in Las Vegas—a shot that saved Tim's life—and I still had nightmares about the man I killed. But after a lot of soul searching, I came down on the side of better him than me or mine.

Upon our return to southern Oregon, Sheila brought me to the shooting range once or twice a week and taught me the rudiments of gun handling. Sheila was a crack shot. She had three older brothers, one of whom was a cop, and she grew up in a hunting family in Idaho—a background that didn't match her diva personality, but there it was.

Sheila and I spent a chunk of the morning shooting at targets. Soon, I started to relax and actually felt like it helped my stress level. Sheila outshot me, as she always did.

"I hope Eliza's back," I said, as we got back into the car to go home.

"She probably ran off some steam and is home making up to Tim," said Sheila.

"Oooh, making up to Tim?" I wiggled my eyebrows suggestively.

Sheila snorted. "As if."

"Just kidding."

"Well, obviously." Sheila gave me a funny look and I shrugged.

****

Eliza and Tim did seem to have ironed out things in our absence. They were in the living room: Tim on the sofa reading a book and Eliza stretched on the floor playing with Carson. Carson looked overdue for a nap, so I carried him upstairs, nursed him, and tucked him in. When I reemerged, the gang had assembled in the kitchen and Sheila was cutting coffeecake.

"Coffeecake?" I asked.

Eliza shrugged in the middle of pulling her hair back in a ponytail. "I made coffeecake. When I got back from my run."

"You…" I covered my confusion by taking a piece. "Thanks, looks good."

Sheila—bless her soul—had made another pot of coffee, so we all helped ourselves to elevenses.

"I think we should go back to the site as soon as possible, fan out in a pattern and search for any further signs of our enemies," said Tim.

Eliza nodded. "Agreed."

"I'll stay here and look through my spell books for something to combat fire. I wouldn't be much help with the tracking," said Sheila. Her granny Emma had left her forty-odd volumes of journals from the Martin family Witches. In the last months, I'd helped her get through the first five journals, organizing the spells into an electronic database searchable by category and ingredient. The amount of material we'd gotten through was paltry at best and we kept getting sidetracked with family stories, gossip, witchy politics, and odd bits of information. Sheila practiced her witchcraft a lot more after our adventure in Las Vegas and had a number of handy spells at the ready, but protection from flames hadn't been high on our priority list.

"Carson won't wake up for another hour or two, so..." I trailed off. I didn't want him staying here without at least one Were to guard him, but I knew the search would go quicker with both Eliza and Tim there.

A knock on the front door interrupted our planning session. Tim raised his head and drew in a deep breath through his nose.

"Our Salamander's here. Earlier than expected."

Eliza's face wrinkled in distaste.

We all followed Sheila into the living room, Eliza bringing up the rear.

"Welcome," said Sheila, as she pulled open the door. "I'm Sheila Martin, hostess and resident Witch."

"Tim Rogers, council investigator and head of this team." I watched as Tim drew the mantle of authority across his mild face.

The Salamander stepped through the door. He was lanky with spiky strawberry-blond hair and an enormous smile.

"Hi, I'm Julie Hall. Uh, the one who almost got killed."

"I'm Newt." He held out his freckled hand to each of us in turn, eyebrows raised as if waiting for it.

"Newt the…" I stopped myself, barely.

His blue eyes crinkled up. "Yep, Newt the Salamander."

I stifled a giggle. Even Eliza, who stood stiffly at my side, quirked her mouth to one side before tightening her lips once more.

"Nice to meet you, Newt," I managed.

"Oh, come on. Go ahead, you're going to lose it sooner or later. My sister's name is Sally."

At that, I dissolved into a snort, then gave up the fight and laughed wholeheartedly. Newt joined me, his freckles catching sunlight through the window, and his blue eyes shining. Sheila leaned against the door as she closed it, giggling under her breath.

After a few moments, I wiped my eyes and said, "Really? Your sister's name is Sally?"

He nodded. "My parents' strange sense of humor."

"Yeah, I guess so. I know a family with kids named Harbor, Piers, and Ocean—their parents are really into sailing—but…well. Sally and Newt. I think I'd like to meet your parents."

"They were pretty funny."

I noted the past tense and wasn't sure what to say next.

Newt didn't miss a beat, but broke into another

sunny smile and walked toward Eliza. "Sorry, I didn't catch your name?" He held out his hand.

"Eliza Minuet." I wasn't sure if I imagined the hesitation before they shook. "Full moon Were from Julie and Carson's pack. Here to protect them from…their enemies." Eliza's smile looked fierce and bared too many teeth, more like a threat.

"Not our pack," I interjected without thought. When everyone turned to me, I flushed, but continued. "That is, we're not officially part of Eliza's pack. I'm a dark moon, not a Were. And Carson isn't part of a pack right now."

Was that a growl? I glanced at Eliza. I'd imagined it. I think.

"You need pack to protect you." Eliza enunciated every syllable, her gaze locked on Newt as if to clarify why she thought we might need protection.

"Regroup, folks. Focus," said Tim.

"Okay." Newt glanced around the room, his cheerfulness not squelched by any apparent tensions. "Where's the strong baby wolf and what's the status here?"

We settled awkwardly around Sheila's living room, silently negotiating placement. Sheila and Tim claimed the sage green couch, while Newt sat on the matching armchair and stretched out his long legs. After a moment, I perched on the rocking chair. Eliza sank cross-legged on the floor beside me. She somehow exuded the air of indolent lounging while simultaneously acting like a guard dog. I took the opportunity to study Newt. He didn't look at all amphibian, but neither had the Salamander last night—that one had looked as much like a hipster as anything else. Neither of them looked anything like fire, which was good, because I'd been worried even our Salamander ally would trigger something in me. If I had seen him in a coffee shop, I would have given him a big smile and remembered nothing more than the cheerful sparkle in his eyes, like sunlight off water. And his freckles. Those would be hard to forget.

"We were just discussing how to divide responsibilities for the next few hours. Sheila will stay here to work on some spells and Carson is napping." Tim glanced between Newt and Eliza. "I think Newt and I should go to the site of the fire and widen our search net, while Eliza stays here to watch—"

"I'm going. That is." Eliza paused and brushed her hands on her jeans, getting rid of imaginary dirt. "Tim, I would like to go to the site, if you don't mind staying here with Sheila, Carson, and Julie."

"You want to go with Newt?"

Eliza nodded decisively. "Yes."

"I'd like to go, too," I said. "Carson will be okay for a couple of hours with both of you watching him. You don't mind, do you Sheila?"

"Of course not. I dote on him," she assured me with a wink.

Tim walked over to the front window and stood there for several minutes, looking out.

"All right." He turned and addressed both Eliza and Newt. "Newt, see if you can recognize any of the Salamander scents. Then you and Eliza scout the area in a series of concentric circles. I want to know if any of the Salamanders or the Were have come back to the site, or if you locate any sign of their base of operations.

"Julie, you can go along. But I want you to stay with one of them at all times and I *don't* want you to feed this obsession with your burned down house. Okay?"

"Of course," I said, choosing the easiest response.

"Eliza?"

"Yes?" she said, shoulders visibly stiff.

"Newt's in charge. You listen to him, you report to him, you inform him before you take any action." He leaned on the word "before," just in case anyone in the room missed his meaning.

Eliza opened her mouth to argue, but Tim stared her down. Finally, she just nodded.

"Hey, Tim?" Newt interjected in an easy tone.

Everyone except Eliza turned to him.

"Just for the record, I might not be able to recognize Salamanders by scent at this point, especially with other strong odors around. My sense of smell is many times better than a human's, but doesn't approach a wolf's."

"Right. Of course." Tim mock-smacked himself in the forehead and gave his most genial smile. "So…"

"If I'm close enough to another Salamander, I'll smell it or sense it in other ways, either through its body heat—nearly two degrees higher than human average—or because of the way Salamanders disrupt the earth's magnetic field. We're very sensitive to magnetism, actually." Newt broke out in another grin. "That also means we never get lost, so you can consider me your guide Salamander."

I smiled back, his grin and manner infectious.

Chapter Six

The drive to Jacksonville consisted of silence on the part of Eliza, punctuated by small talk between me and Newt. I learned he was originally from Colorado, he loved to ski—which other Salamanders found quite odd, since it went against the whole heat- and sun-loving thing—and his sister Sally lived in Florida. He was twenty-five, two years younger than me. This was the second time he'd been sent to help investigate Salamander wrong-doing.

"Sent by?" When Newt cocked his head, I rephrased. "Do Salamanders have some sort of central authority, like the Werewolf pack council?"

"Kind of. We're not nearly as...hierarchical as Werewolves. But we do have an elected governing body."

"You'd have to. With all the rogue firebu—Salamanders causing problems. Burning houses down. Killing people." Eliza contributed to the conversation for the first time.

Newt was silent for a moment.

"You know," he said, slowly. "Not many Salamanders are arsonists. A lot of us are firefighters, devoted to saving lives by unobtrusively controlling fire, guiding wildfires away from buildings."

I saw Eliza's gaze flick to the rearview mirror and then away, quickly, as a trace of flush crept across her face. She shifted her shoulders and studiously focused on driving.

"So. Um. Not sure how to ask this and pardon me if I'm rude, but are you a strong Salamander?" I twisted around to look at Newt in the backseat.

"Yep. But strength for us is more about practice and technique than innate ability. Not like dog—I mean, Werewolves." Newt winked at me over his mock slip of the tongue. Eliza pretended to ignore it.

Worried any further conversational gambits on my part might lead to more tension and wondering about Tim's wisdom in sending these two to work together, I sank into silence and watched out the window as we drove past pear orchards and houses. As we came into the small town of Jacksonville—old-fashioned storefronts, meticulous flower boxes, everything poised to cater to the tourist and music festival crowd—I quelled my mounting tension with deep breaths. I breathed easier this time and my reactions were more under control as we turned off the main street, snaked around several blocks, and pulled up in front of what used to be my place.

"Wow," said Newt, as he hopped out to investigate the wreckage of the house. He unerringly trotted over to my former bedroom window. I followed him, and after a beat, so did Eliza.

"They started it here." He pointed. "And...hmmm."

We trailed in his wake as he walked around the house and showed us several spots where the Salamanders initiated the fire: under my window, under Carson's window, near the front door, on the roof. Newt explained Salamanders could control the fire's behavior, how hot it burned, where and how quickly it spread. The degree of control differed with the skill of the Salamander. According to Newt, most Salamanders manifested the ability to call fire around puberty, just as most Weres began to change form and call on the moon at that time. The strongest Salamanders devoted lots of time to practicing their skills, calling various types of fires, working with heat energies, pushing themselves to call flames without a direct physical link to their targets. Apparently, some 'Manders needed to touch fire in order to control it, while some could direct the flames at varying distances.

"Well, these Salamanders definitely meant to kill you," Newt concluded, rocking back on his heels and surveying the site. Hands in his pockets, his cheerful tone contrasted with the stark reality of his words.

Eliza stood with her back to us, studying the surrounding area. Hopefully, she paid more attention than last night, just in case there were other 'Manders around.

"Can you tell anything about the other Salamanders?" I asked Newt.

He shook his head. "Nope. Can't smell them over all the fire trace. Not even where the one burned that tree down yesterday. I *can* tell you they weren't highly skilled. Otherwise, you never would have made it out of this." His gesture took in the charred ruins. "Though any 'Mander can be dangerous, of course. Just like a Were."

Abruptly, Eliza let out a sound more suited to a wolf throat—part shout, part bark, with a deep growling note that made my heart accelerate. The next moment, she flickered into wolf form and raced away, body low to the ground, ears pressed against her head, hackles raised. She took a leaping bound across my yard, then jerked to a stop and smoothly morphed back into her human self.

"I smell the Were nearby," she said, through gritted teeth. "I'd like to go after him."

"Go. Don't follow him too far; don't endanger yourself," Newt said. I glanced at him, surprised at how completely he assumed authority in that instant.

Eliza growled assent and dropped back into the wolf. The muscles in her haunches bunched as she leapt out of sight around the corner of my neighbor's house.

Middle of a sunny day on a residential street. I looked around carefully, hardly believing Eliza changed out in the open where anyone might spot her, even if she did pull darkness while she did it. A giant buff-colored wolf racing through my neighbors' yards was not exactly a low-key event in Jacksonville, Oregon. There didn't seem to be anyone around, though, so I guessed it was okay.

Newt continued to stare after Eliza.

"She really doesn't like me."

"I know." We exchanged a rueful smile. "Can you sense the Were?"

Newt's face lost focus. "No," he said after a minute. "I can't sense anything right now, no Were, no 'Manders."

"I guess we just wait for her to come back, then."

Newt nodded and we walked around the building again, stopping to examine this or that bit of char.

"Um." I poked my toe into a pile of ash. Once sodden, the debris was nearly dry in the semi-arid climate. "Can you tell if the building is structurally sound? The walls and that part of the roof that's left?"

"Not really. No more than you can."

"Oh." I'd been hoping for a different response, but plowed forward gamely. "Well, I'm going to look around and see if there's anything…" I looked at my house. The thing formerly known as my house.

Although I could have easily crawled over the living room wall in its current state, I nonetheless picked my way through pieces of fallen roof to enter through the front door. Charred wood left black streaks on my new jeans as I brushed past, taking each step carefully. There really wasn't much worth saving. Everything not burned was broken, blackened with soot, or warped with water. I stared in rue at my bookshelves. My treasured books lay waterlogged and puffy, those not buried under pieces of the roof. The kitchen was the worst: shards of plates and glasses, the oven door hanging open and askew. The fridge was utterly intact, but I didn't dare open it lest the smell of food mingle with that of the cold ashes and increase my stress-induced nausea. I poked among the general wreckage with one sneakered toe.

I gasped and sank down to the ground, cradling the treasure in my arms.

"Julie?" Newt's voice preceded him by a nano-second as he slid to a halt by my side.

"I'm okay."

"Did you cut yourself?"

"No. I found something." I held it out for his inspection.

Newt's voice sounded dubious. "Is that a chicken?"

"Yes. My grandmother collected them. Chickens. She left them to me, all of them. Thirty-two of them.

Not real chickens—ceramic and stuff, like this." I took a second to regroup. "This was one of her favorites."

I looked down at the blown glass chicken, blue and purple swirling through the translucent body, brilliant red on the beak and comb.

"Oh."

"I know." I rubbed the back of my hand across my eyes. "Stupid, huh? Getting all excited about a glass chicken that probably cost all of ten dollars when she got it."

"Hey. No, not stupid." Newt squeezed my shoulder. His hand was warm to the touch and sunlight caught his freckles, momentarily making them glitter like gold. I blinked.

"Let's look around. Maybe there are some more undamaged chickens."

I clutched the glass chicken tightly as we poked about in the wreckage, finding nothing else except a few isolated plates and cups that escaped the carnage. Even my cookware had warped or appeared stained with black residue. Cheap stuff to begin with, it didn't merit saving. No more unbroken chickens. Looking at the shards of the few we found hit me as hard as if they'd been real animals, now mutilated.

Newt and I made our way outside again. I placed my salvaged chicken gently in the car and leaned against its side, pushing my hair behind my ears. Newt looked this way and that, with a rather grim look on his usually sunny face, and I suddenly realized, "Eliza's been gone for a while."

Newt nodded. "I know. Too long."

"Should we…go after her?" I asked, but answered my own question before he could respond. "We probably couldn't find her. Shit."

"Let's walk around and see if we notice anything else."

Newt in the lead, we trooped about my yard and the surrounding houses, especially near the black and skeletal cedar tree. Nothing but eerie silence. None of my neighbors were home to run out with greetings or condolences, no cars drove on the street. I wasn't sure whether or not Newt gathered additional information about the Salamanders while we walked around, but I let myself believe we did something useful so I didn't feel like we just killed time.

Newt noticed Eliza's return first, and pointed in the direction of the Sequoia in my neighbor's yard. Sure enough, Eliza trotted from the shadows in the next minute, then did an about face, stepped back under the tree, and emerged in human form.

"You found him! You reek of him. Even I can smell it."

I swung to Newt, then back to Eliza in time to catch a surprised lift of her eyebrows, which as quickly relaxed and shuttered her expression.

"You found the Were? Did you fight? Are you okay?" I asked.

Eliza said, "Yes, I found him. We tussled, but no one was hurt."

"What?" I asked.

"I scented the Were and took off after him. He led me through the woods back there—" Eliza gestured. "I chased him for a while, and caught up to him."

"No. Wait. You fought, but no one was hurt? That's the part I don't understand. I've seen you fight."

She met my gaze levelly. "He's a full moon Were,

very strong. Like me. I didn't want to kill him, since his death would answer none of our questions. He focused on getting away, rather than hurting me."

"Did you recognize him?" Newt asked.

"No. No, of course not. No. If I had further information for you, *firebug*, then I would share it."

Her voice made the hair on my neck rise, and I shook my head to dispel the effect of her Were power.

Newt laughed; an abrupt chortle that rose out of him and sailed airily in the quiet day. "All right then, dog. Heel. We're going back to report to Tim."

And just like that, without the slightest indication of concern, Newt turned his back on Eliza and started walking to the car. I stood frozen for a minute, watching Eliza. When I was sure she wouldn't leap on our Salamander, I followed. After a moment, Eliza stalked after us, got in the car, and drove back to Sheila's house without uttering a single word to either of us.

Three times I started to ask her more about the Were she encountered. Three times a glare from Eliza stopped me before I'd gotten out a question.

Some team we made.

Newt seemed unmarked by the tension. He sat in the backseat, whistled something I didn't recognize, and interrupted himself to ask me questions about things we passed. Newt thrilled to learn that Medford—the biggest town in southern Oregon, equidistant from where I lived in Jacksonville and Sheila's house in Ashland—was the home of Harry & David's, the renowned fruit and fine foods company. I gamely promised to take him to their store to buy some Moose Munch as soon as we had time. Which might be never, if we were attacked again. Or maybe this afternoon, since I, personally, ran out of leads to follow. Unless Eliza and Tim went back to the house, picked up the other Were's tracks, and figured something out.

I opened my mouth, shut it as Eliza's expression quelled me once more then defiantly spoke anyway.

"Do we need to worry about the Were tracking our car to Sheila's house?" I asked.

"No."

"No because it's too hard to track a moving vehicle? Or no for a different reason?" I prodded again.

Eliza let out a huffing breath. "Yes."

"Yes what?"

"*Yes*, it's too hard to track a moving vehicle. Besides, I don't think he'll follow us."

"Why not?" Newt's completely reasonable question caused an extreme reaction from Eliza. She nearly snarled at him before relaxing her mouth. Her jaw appeared clenched with tension.

After a minute of us staring at her, Eliza said, reluctantly, "I'm not convinced the Were is working with the Salamanders." She raised a hand to cut off my sudden questions. "I didn't smell Salamanders on him, okay? I don't know what it means either."

"So we have two different enemies? Hunting us?" I pinched the bridge of my nose, hard. "God, I have a headache."

"Was this other Were stronger than you?" Newt asked, matter-of-factly, as if the question wouldn't provoke Eliza.

"No. And neither are you, *Salamander*."

Newt laughed again. "All right then, *Were*. Maybe we'll just have to find out one of these days."

"Hey. Remind me to take that day off, okay?" I said, happy to see Eliza roll her eyes in response before she dropped into silence again.

****

When we arrived at Sheila's house, I bounded in the door first, impatient to see Carson even though I knew he was well taken care of—and protected—with Sheila and Tim. My boy bounced on Sheila's knees as she played "The Grand Old Duke of York" with him. As soon as he saw me, he reached out his arms frantically toward me and I swooped him up.

"Hey sweetie, did you have a good nap?" I crooned to him and continued to speak in a lilting tone while I sat down. Carson made it perfectly clear what he'd missed about me by pulling on my shirt as I situated him to nurse. Preoccupied with getting him settled, I failed to notice the tension in the room until everyone fell silent.

"Eliza." Tim's voice held a hint of anger. "Full report and *now*."

Eliza stood straight for a moment and used her height to pointedly look down on Tim then dropped to sit on the couch, poised in mock-relaxation.

"I scented the Were in the woods behind Julie's neighbor's house. I changed form and gave pursuit, chased him for a few miles. He knew the terrain and tried to lose me in a small river."

"Might have been the Applegate river," I interjected.

Eliza nodded. "I caught up with him past the river on a wooded hillside. I tried to restrain him, or alternately, disable him. Didn't fight for the kill. He's strong. Ended up flinging me into a tree trunk and stunned me for a minute. When I gave pursuit, he took to the river again. I walked both banks for a half mile or so with no success. I was worried he'd somehow double back to Julie and the fir—the Salamander, so I returned and found them safe. The Were seemed more interested in escaping than fighting me."

"Describe him."

"Dark fur, nearly black. Large. Just like you said. A full moon of mid-strength, I'd estimate."

"Age?"

"Hard to say in wolf form. Mature adult."

Tim strode around the room for a minute, his hands locked behind his back.

"And? Tell them about him maybe not being in league with the Salamanders," I prompted with some disregard for grammar.

Eliza spoke slowly. "I scented no Salamander on him. But…we have every reason to suspect he's a threat to Julie and Carson."

"Wait a minute," Sheila said. "If he wasn't with the Salamanders, why was he at the fire?"

"You know," I said, as an idea coalesced. "Maybe he woke me up on purpose with those barks. Maybe he helped. Another few minutes and I might not have woken up at all."

"*No*," Eliza said. "If he was helping, why attack after you escaped the fire? Why did he run away from me? Why did he fight me? We *must* treat him as an enemy. He may or may not be allied with the Salamanders, but he's still an enemy."

We all pondered her declaration for a minute.

"I just don't understand it. Why would anyone want to harm us? Not to mention two disparate groups—rogue Salamanders *and* a Were?" I stroked Carson's chubby hand, his fingers curled on my shirt. His eyes closed, his cheeks flushed pink. I saw a blue vein through the translucent skin at the inside corner of his eye and his wisps of hair were sweetly sweaty.

Newt looked at Eliza. His tone casual, he repeated his earlier question. "Did you recognize the other Were?"

"*No*." Eliza stood up and walked three paces toward the kitchen. "If I'm done being interrogated, can we have lunch?"

Tim didn't look as if he agreed the so-called interrogation had ended, but nonetheless didn't object as he followed Eliza into the kitchen. Newt jauntily joined them.

Pausing behind them, Sheila lowered her voice and asked me, "What's up with Eliza?"

I shook my head. "Worried, I guess. I'm sure she's upset the other Were escaped her."

"I'm surprised he was skilled enough. Our girl's quite a hunter and I would bet on her in a fight."

"I guess he might have outweighed her? And he knew the area?"

"I suppose."

Tim called from the kitchen to ask where the mustard was, so Sheila promised to bring me a sandwich and disappeared after them. I stared into space, alone with my thoughts and feeling less sanguine than my words indicated.

****

"I guess that's why the Duran Duran song is 'Hungry Like a Wolf,' huh?" I said, eyeing the remnants of a couple pounds of lunchmeat, most of a loaf of bread, and two bags of chips.

Sheila yawned and settled one arm on Tim's shoulders after the stretch. "I think it's 'Hungry Like *the* Wolf.' " I threw a chip at her, which she caught neatly one-handed. "At this rate, I'm going to start charging the pack council for room and board," she teased Tim.

"I'm going back to find that Were. Without Julie. I can't be distracted by worrying about anyone." Eliza pushed back her chair and stood. "I'll search along the river; he can't hide his tracks completely."

"You and I will both go," said Tim. Eliza pursed her lips, but nodded assent. Tim continued, "Newt, you'll stay here and keep watch?"

"Sure."

With those quick plans made, Eliza and Tim drove off, Sheila went back to her spell books, and Carson and I laid down for a nap. When we climbed the stairs, Newt leafed through some magazines and prowled the living room, so I assumed he'd keep himself busy somehow.

Carson and I woke up an hour and a half later. I took advantage of the relative quiet to snuggle with my little boy and let my mind wander. As soon as it wandered in the direction of things like fire, enemies, and Eliza's odd behavior, I yanked the leash firmly and forced myself to think about Carson's cuteness, the perfect weather in southern Oregon during early September, and the surprise bonus of shopping for all new clothes *and* furniture. Which surely was an upside of this whole thing, right?

Thinking about those logistics reminded me I needed to stop by the insurance office and fill out a whole bunch of papers to start the reimbursement process. I also needed to face rebuilding the house, but didn't want to even think about that now—not until we were out of danger, at least. But I'd need money soon, so Carson and I went downstairs to suggest an exciting outing to the insurance office.

"Okay," said Sheila. "Maybe afterward we can stop by the garden center and the food co-op, so I can pick up some ingredients." She gestured to a couple of pages full of neatly handwritten notes.

"Is it near Harry & David's?" asked Newt.

"Nope, sorry." At Sheila's quizzical look, I added, "Our Salamander has a penchant for Moose Munch and just realized he's near the source."

"Well, who doesn't like Moose Munch?" Sheila smiled and we kept the conversation light as we piled into her candy-apple red convertible, Newt folding himself into the backseat.

We continued the façade of a normal outing through my visit to the insurance office, where they gave me a preliminary check for five thousand dollars, updated me on the progress of my claim, provided me with what seemed like ten million forms, and told me about the living stipend I'd receive until my house was rebuilt. The whole insurance response impressed me. Time consuming and form-laden, yes, but it really seemed like I would receive full value for everything I owned and they'd rebuild my house any way I chose, up to market value of the old structure. Carson showed his best-behaved baby self as he chortled in his car seat and practiced hanging onto his toys.

As Sheila drove down Oak Street toward the food co-op, Newt said, "Okay. 'Manders are following us."

Sheila reflexively stepped on the brake in alarm.

Newt twisted around in his seat to look out the back. "I thought I sensed them behind us earlier, when we were on the main road. Now I'm sure. They're definitely following us. Don't stop, Sheila."

"But what do I do?" Sheila asked. Both her hands tightened on the wheel and she kept darting glances at the rearview mirror.

"Just drive. I'm trying to spot them." Even now, Newt's voice hadn't lost its cheerful timber, making it seem like this was more of a game than a life-and-death matter.

Sheila drove around semi-aimlessly for several blocks, as both Newt and I craned our heads this way and that trying to find the Salamanders. I kept rubbing sweaty hands on my jeans.

Sheila gasped. "Newt! The car's overheating!"

"Shoot. Okay. Hold on." His freckled brow tightened in concentration as he did...something.

I wasn't sure where to look and ended up somehow dividing my attention between the temperature gauge, checking on Carson, watching Newt's intent face, and scanning the cars nearby. The car's temperature fluctuated wildly.

"Newt?" I forced the words out of my tight throat. "Is the car going to catch on fire?"

"No." Sweat started to bead on Newt's forehead. "I'm pulling out the heat and sinking it into the ground. We're going to be fine. I just—I can't find them while I'm focusing on the heat."

In fact, his eyes half-closed in concentration, so I started searching nearby vehicles in earnest. I shifted my feet in vague discomfort without identifying the source. After a moment, I spotted them.

"There! Wait." We turned a corner and I twisted around wildly then pointed as the other car turned, too, nearly a block behind us. "That car! The woman in the passenger seat looks just like Newt."

"What?" asked Sheila.

I waved my hand impatiently. "No, no, I mean, focusing like him, all intense. And they followed us for at least the last three turns. It's them!"

I watched their car in the side mirror, then cursed violently as I saw heat mirage shimmering near the gas cap on the side of our car. I rolled down the window and stuck my head out to get a better look. The cherry red paint started to blister and swell. "The gas tank. Newt! They're trying to make it explode."

Newt clenched his jaw, sweat pouring down his face. I felt heat radiating off him, even though he sat in the backseat. The air around him shifted like distortions above hot pavement.

Sheila sped up and ran a stop sign, careened around a corner—coming extremely close to a parked car—and made a series of quick turns to try to hide our car in traffic. I watched out the back window, hoping we'd lost them, but the silver sedan screeched around the last corner we'd taken.

"Shit."

"It's okay. I needed the break. Stay as far away as you can—they're less effective at a distance," said Newt.

Damn. I moved my feet again before realizing why.

"Newt, the floor's getting hot."

"Gas line," said Sheila.

The sedan traveled right behind us again, despite Sheila's efforts. I glanced at the temperature gauge, in the red zone. The paint on the side of the car wasn't any worse—but I saw heat once again radiating from the area.

"Do something!" I yelled.

"I am doing something. I. Am. Stopping them. From burning. The car," Newt said, through gritted teeth. "Two. Against. One."

"Sheila."

"I'm *driving* the damn car, Jules."

"Fuck." What was the use of having a Salamander and a Witch on my side if they couldn't attack the enemies?

"Evasive maneuvers, Sheila!"

"It's not a space ship," Sheila yelled, but nonetheless sped up and headed toward a more congested area. I could tell she wanted to pass through a bunch of stoplights and escape the other car, which was a good idea. Hopefully, the Salamanders weren't eager to attract attention and wouldn't run red lights. Unfortunately, the timing was slightly off. At the second red light, we stopped with the 'Manders right behind us.

"Sheila! Put the roof down!"

She shot me a wild-eyed glance, but hesitated only a split second before pushing the button for the convertible top to retract. I turned all the way around in the seat, and got a good look at three people in the other car. They looked at me, too.

"Julie," Newt only said the one word, but I heard the strain in his voice. The gauge on our dashboard kept jumping madly up and down and the engine whined in protest. The floor was so hot I couldn't keep my feet down. The third Salamander must have thrown his strength into the fight when the car stopped.

"Hold on." I tried to time it perfectly. I unbuckled my seat belt. As the roof tucked itself in and just as the light turned yellow for the traffic going the other direction, I grabbed Sheila's steering wheel lock from the floor of the car, gave a mental prayer, and hurled it at the windshield of the car behind us. The lock hit the windshield with a loud bang and cracks spiderwebbed the glass. Car horns honked around us.

"Go! Go! Go!" I screamed as the light turned green. I knelt backward on the seat and Sheila accelerated, pushing me flat and breaking every traffic law in the middle of downtown touristy Ashland.

Several near misses and a couple of crazy turns later, Sheila stopped the car high on the side of the mountain above Ashland, where houses were big and rich people territorial of their view. She pulled around with the car facing in the direction we'd come, so we could ambush the enemies if they happened to follow us despite the broken windshield and late start.

As soon as the car stopped, Newt jumped out and hurried to a nearby landscaping rock the size of a coffee table. He pressed both hands on it and I watched the dirt covering the side blanch to pale brown, then crack and start to flake off. When he stood and came back over to us, the air near the rock shimmered with heat-illusion.

"Sinking the heat," he explained. "Redirecting it without touch is a lot harder. I can hold a lot of it, but back there when all three of them poured power into the car, it was a bit intense." He smiled.

Intense. Yeah, that was one word for it.

We sat there for a few minutes, watching the slope of the road carefully, and relaxed stage by stage. Sheila tried to call Tim's cell phone, but it went straight to voice mail which probably indicated he was still in wolf form and his phone was…well, somewhere in magical limbo. Wherever Werewolves' clothes and things went when they changed.

"I can't sense them," said Newt. "Which means they can't sense me."

I nodded, thankful for the reassurance.

Somewhere in the middle of all the ruckus, Carson managed to fall asleep.

" 'Evasive maneuvers?' " Sheila lifted an eyebrow at me.

"Red alert?" I suggested and we both started to laugh hysterically.

After we calmed down, Newt said, "I don't get it."

That set me off again and a minute passed before I could say, "You know, the TV show? Spaceships and aliens and holes in the time-space continuum."

"Oh. I never watch that kind of thing."

"You don't?" Sheila sounded horrified, but like she tried to cover it.

"Nope."

"Wow," I said. "Why not?"

"I don't know. I like things more realistic."

His answer prompted a renewed fit of laughter and I raised my hands, gesturing weakly and wiping tears off my face. I couldn't look at Newt, lest his puzzled expression prompt further hysterics. Instead, I closed my eyes, took some breaths and said, "You, a Salamander, thinking space travel is unrealistic."

"But," Newt's voice held a smile, "Salamanders

are real. Space ships and those ridged-forehead guys aren't real."

Well. True enough, I guess, and a sobering thought. I was still getting used to this so-called reality complete with Werewolves, Salamanders, and Witches.

"By the way," Newt said. "Good job getting us away from them, Julie. I wouldn't have thought of that."

"Yeah, the lowly human comes in handy sometimes."

Newt looked surprised. "I didn't mean—"

"We know," said Sheila. "Jules, you okay?"

"Yes, of course! Of course."

"Quick thinking, Jules. Even though a dozen people probably ended up with a description of my car and the police'll knock on my door any day now."

"Shit. I didn't even think of that, Sheila."

She shook her head. "No big deal. *If* the Salamanders press charges, we'll deal with it then. Better a ticket—or whatever—than our car becoming a fireball in the middle of downtown Ashland."

I swallowed and rubbed my arms against the vivid image spawned by her words.

"Hey." Sheila's voice was softer now. "We're okay. No fireball. No fire at all."

I nodded and leaned back to adjust Carson's car seat straps as an excuse not to meet anyone's eyes.

"How did they find us?" I asked. "Do you think they have Sheila's house staked out?"

Newt shook his head. "If they were hanging around her place, I would have felt it. The Weres would have smelled them, too."

"Maybe they just got lucky?" said Sheila.

"Happened to drive past us and sensed us? Like we sensed them?"

"I got a good look at them. The Salamanders. Did you two?" I asked.

"Cursorily, through the mirror," said Sheila.

"I saw them, but was pretty focused on the heat energies. Not letting the engine overheat. The gas tank explode. You know, minor stuff." Newt grinned and I rolled my eyes at him.

"Okay. Well, the one I saw last night wasn't with them, so there must be at least four, all together. Um, three of them were in the car, two men and one woman. The man driving had bleach-blond shaggy hair, the messy-on-purpose kind. Like a surfer. Late twenties or early thirties. He wore sunglasses. Didn't look huge, probably average height, but it's hard to tell in a car. We'll call him Surfer. Next to him in the passenger's seat was…let's call her Kitty, because she had these crazy cat-eye sunglasses." I held my fingers up to demonstrate.

"I'd peg her for late thirties, but I could be wrong." I thought for a minute, questioning myself. "Her skin looked kind of leathery. Like she'd tanned too much in high school and now started to wrinkle more than she should, you know? She had long brown hair with highlights—the kind that almost look like stripes. Vivid red lipstick."

"Mutton dressed as lamb, huh?"

"What?" I stared at Sheila for a minute, before understanding. "Oh, yeah. Exactly. Okay. Surfer, Kitty, and…hmmm. Mr. Average."

"Mr. Average?" Newt laughed.

"Well. He was nondescript, one of those faces

you'd pass over in a crowd, ya know? Like, a good cover for his secret identity as a rogue Salamander?"

"Jesus, Jules. Can you give a better description than that?"

"Neat dark hair with a side part. Smooth-shaven, middle-aged." I shrugged. "That's about all I got—he was in the backseat."

"Surfer, Kitty, and Mr. Average."

"And Hipster Guy," I said. "That's what I've been calling the one I saw last night—the one with the ponytail and the glasses. He wore sandals."

"Sandals make him a hipster?" asked Sheila.

"No, it was his whole vibe. You'd understand if you saw him."

Newt raised one eyebrow at me and nodded. "I'll call the master and go over descriptions with him."

"Master?" I asked.

"The head Salamander."

"You call him master?"

"As in master of skills, not a slave owner or something. It's a traditional title. Like in martial arts."

"Folks," said Sheila. "Let's cut the chitchat and figure out if it's safe to go get spell ingredients, if we should go back to my house, or if we need to find somewhere else to hide. What do you think?"

Chapter Seven

With Newt as our lookout, his eyes half-closed as he focused on sensing body heat or electromagnetic forces or whatever he said Salamanders used to find each other, we managed to get to a grocery store—not the co-op we'd been heading for earlier, but a place in the opposite direction—and the grange, which sold farm and garden supplies. Sheila picked up a whole bunch of seemingly random items, but I knew they all had a spell-related purpose. We then took a circuitous route toward Sheila's townhouse on Mountain Ave, canvassing the area in a complex grid-like pattern to make sure there weren't any 'Manders lurking. Newt didn't find any, so we decided as long as they weren't nearby—and since Newt would detect them if they came within striking range—we could safely return. Maybe they had been lucky to find us—their good luck, our bad. Maybe their smashed windshield decapitated them all. A girl could hope.

The car radio showed six thirty when we pulled into the driveway, and Tim and Eliza still weren't back. I told myself not to worry. They might spend quite a bit of time tracking the other Were, since he seemed good at covering his scent. They were both strong, competent Werewolves and no news was good news. Usually.

We didn't discuss their lateness, but I saw Sheila's growing anxiety about Tim. She glanced up and down the street several times, and checked her cell phone in a way meant to be casual. Nonetheless, she forced a bright smile and announced she was going to order food, because none of us had the presence of mind to buy anything for dinner while we were at the grocery store. She disappeared into the kitchen to find the phone number for a local pizza place.

Carson woke up somewhere between the grocery store and the grange, so he practiced sitting up for a while until his stomach and back muscles were so tired he folded over like a taco. I put him on his stomach and he rolled this way and that, looking around the room for fun things to put into his mouth. Like pieces of leaves, a paper clip, and part of a potato chip, all of which I had to forcibly remove.

The pizza and doughknots—divine little bits of pizza dough coated in butter, garlic, and parmesan cheese—arrived before the rest of our team, a fact we did not discuss via tacit agreement. Instead, I, for one, focused on stuffing myself with pizza: sourdough crust, tons of vegetables, sesame seeds...couldn't get this kind of pizza in Greybull, I was sure. I chalked it up mentally as another reason to use the next time Eliza brought up the joys of Wyoming and why Carson needed to live with the pack.

"What is it, Jules?" asked Sheila, and I realized with a start I'd been staring off into space with a piece of pizza half-raised to my mouth.

"Nothing," I said and quickly took a bite. I had been thinking about how horrid I would feel as a dark moon wolf in pack territory. How extraneous I'd be. Even more so than now, even though *of course* I'd been thinking all day if I were a real Were, I'd be out there helping Tim and Eliza. What would it be like to be a Werewolf? I glanced surreptitiously at Newt, who always knew he had abilities unmatched by humans, who grew up in a family of Salamanders, who probably took his powers for granted. And Sheila, only twelve when her granny shared knowledge of her gifts.

Ah well. At least I'd been the one to end our Salamander pursuit, albeit through an inelegant method. Mere human that I was.

Newt turned his head and opened his mouth as if to speak. The front door opened with a bang and we all jumped, me almost choking as I swallowed a bit of crust. Sheila leapt to her feet and ran to throw her arms around Tim, who preceded Eliza into the house.

Newt shrugged and completed his sentence. "They're back."

Tim's nostrils flared and the mild mask dropped off his face. "What happened? You were attacked?"

I rose, dusting off my hands on my jeans. "We're okay. We met up with the Salamanders while driving."

"Newt?" Tim's voice sounded just short of a barked command.

Newt straightened in his chair. "Three 'Manders followed us in a silver sedan. They tried to cause our car to overheat and burn—it's easy to fling heat from a distance, but harder to start a fire without throwing the flames physically from your hand, not very subtle in the middle of town. Anyway, I kept the car safe, absorbed the heat and sank what I couldn't hold into the ground, while Sheila engaged in 'evasive maneuvers.' Julie saved us by throwing Sheila's wheel lock at their windshield at a stoplight. We drove a grid around the townhouse, but didn't find them. Not sure if they know where we are or if they happened upon us by coincidence while driving."

Eliza stood stock-still as she absorbed the news. "No one hurt?"

I told her we were all fine, but my assurances didn't seem to affect the tension I saw pulling tight around her body.

"What about the rogue Were? Did you find him? Are you guys okay? You were gone a long time." I questioned Tim and Eliza, neither of whom seemed injured. Tim gave me a smile around Sheila's head, still pressed into him.

Eliza said, "We're fine," without meeting my eyes. Instead, she bee-lined for the pizza and helped herself to a piece with pepperoni and mushrooms. Bolting half of it in the space of a few seconds, she poured a glass of water and drained that. Only after sating herself slightly did she sit down, choosing a chair around the kitchen table with her back to the wall. She helped herself to more pizza.

Tim squeezed Sheila one last time then gently set her aside, though he kept one hand in his.

"Pizza?" he said as if it were a question, though I'm not sure why, since we all knew his super Were senses could have told us every detail of what was on the table.

I gave Carson a few more rice puffs to practice mouthing as he sat at the high chair and helped myself to another doughknot in anticipation of the Were team's report.

"So what's your news? Did you find the Were?" I asked again.

Tim shook his head, mouth full of pizza then

swallowed. "No. I went downstream for several miles, checked both banks, but found no trace of the rogue Were. Not sure if he is particularly good at covering his tracks or if he'd gone another direction." He glanced at Eliza, busying with eating, and continued. "Eliza took the upstream direction, but says she didn't find him either."

Surely, I imagined that faint emphasis.

Newt pursed his lips thoughtfully and glanced around the table.

"Well," he said brightly, after a moment. "What's on the agenda for this evening, then? I'll take first watch."

"No, I'll do it." Eliza pushed back from the table. "I can't relax right now and my sense of smell is better."

I didn't know if Eliza actually decided to accept Newt or if she was just too stressed to bother, but her last comment didn't even sound like a pointed insult to our Salamander.

Without waiting for anyone's acknowledgement, Eliza cracked open the back door, wreathed herself in shadows, and slunk out the door in her buff-colored fur.

"I hope the neighbors don't see her," I said, noting darkness hadn't quite fallen yet. Tim quirked an eyebrow at me and I remembered Eliza could call on the moon for concealment. Super Were abilities again. I huffed a small breath.

I left a half-eaten piece of pizza on my plate, suddenly not as hungry. Carson rubbed his eyes even with his late nap; we'd had a rough few days. Grateful to have something to do and some reason to escape the group, I stood and announced, "I'm going to put Carson to bed."

"Julie." Tim's voice commanded my instant attention, even though I wanted nothing more than to flee all of this for a short while and pretend things were somewhat normal while I tended to my baby. He waited for me to look at him before continuing. "Do you trust Eliza?"

"What? Yes. Yes, of course." I looked at Sheila for agreement. After a moment, Sheila nodded, but then spoke, words tripping over her tongue.

"She *has* been acting awfully strange. Withdrawn. Angry. Tense."

"Oh yeah? Well, I feel withdrawn, angry, and tense," I said. Sheila made a shushing motion with her hands and I dropped my voice, conscious Eliza might be right outside. "Do you trust me?"

Tim sighed and I thought he was going to drop the subject. Instead, he leaned forward. The intensity of his presence made the hairs on my arms and neck raise, but I stubbornly ignored the prickles. "Eliza's the strongest full moon in her pack, right?"

"Right. And?"

"Except for Carson."

I opened my mouth to point out Carson wasn't exactly part of her pack, then realized the implications of his observation. "You think Eliza's jealous of Carson? Threatened by Carson?"

"I don't know what to think," Tim said. "Just pointing out possibilities."

"So what, you think Eliza *wants* Carson to be killed?" My voice rose again, but I didn't care. "She saved his life two months ago in Las Vegas. If she'd wanted him dead, he'd be dead. We'd all be dead. She saved *your* life, Tim."

Tim spread his hands. "I don't have any answers, Julie. Just asking questions."

"Mac was her best friend—practically her brother and Carson is *his* baby and part of her pack." I shook my head as Sheila started to say something. "I know I keep saying Carson and I aren't exactly pack, but that's just the point. I say it because Eliza truly believes we are—in her mind, we're part of her pack and that's half the reason she wants to protect us. You know how she is. Loyal. Completely and utterly. She would never..." I didn't even know how to finish the sentence.

"I agree with you, Julie," said Newt, startling me as I'd nearly forgotten his presence. "Eliza's loyal to a fault, both to you and to her pack, and I don't think she'd ever betray you or Carson. Certainly not by allying herself with a group of goddamned firebugs." I reflexively returned Newt's smile.

"But..." The note of humor dropped from his voice. "*Eliza is lying.*"

Tim sighed and dropped his head into his hands. "I know."

"How do you know?" I asked.

"Scent."

"You can tell she's lying by scent?" Jesus Christ, I didn't know if that made me want to be a Were even more or run away screaming from all my paranormal friends. I frantically searched my mind for anything I might have lied about in the past, but stopped myself with an internal shrug.

"Best lie detectors ever." Tim tapped his nose and barred his teeth in a smile.

"I don't need to have a Were's sense of smell. I can

just tell. She's lying about something." Newt looked back and forth between Sheila and me. "You two know her. Can't you tell she's lying?"

Surrendering, I sank back into my chair and wondered aloud, "But lying about what? And why?"

We all sat there for a minute, thinking about Eliza's recent behavior.

I said. "When she got here, she seemed really tense and worried, but that seemed normal. I mean, normal given the circumstances. Then, when she heard we were going to work with a Salamander—no offense, Newt— she was angry. After we were at the site and smelled them and saw what they'd done, it got worse. I think she realized how close it was. That Carson and I really almost died." I cleared my throat. "When she scented the Were, she just took off. She was furious, I think. Really upset."

Sheila said, "Should we just ask her?" When Tim and I looked at her, she elaborated. "Let's just tell her we know she's lying. Tim, she must know you, at least, can tell for sure. Threaten to send her back to Greybull if she won't come clean."

When I made a surprised noise, Sheila said, "Well, Tim *is* the leader of this investigation. If he says she goes, she goes. Right?"

"Right." Tim's voice was flat, as if he didn't like to imagine that scene any more than I.

"My brain hurts," I said.

"Not to mention your lungs, hey Jules? You sound kind of wheezy."

"Gee, thanks." I left the table and picked up Carson. Sheila was right; I needed my inhalers. "Carson needs to sleep. Let me know if you paranormal superbeings figure things out while the human puts Carson to bed."

Chapter Eight

I must have been more tired than I thought, because I accidentally fell asleep with Carson and didn't wake up until two a.m. when he started crying. I rolled over and nursed him, then managed to get out of my clothes and into pajamas before falling back into bed. I flirted with the idea of getting up to brush my teeth, but couldn't find the motivation. Carson roused briefly a few more times in the night and I dealt with him in a half-awake trance. At five a.m. I looked at the clock and thought, "Please, just sleep until six, please pretty please." Imagine my surprise when I opened my eyes next and the clock read eight thirty. Carson stretched out next to me, pacifier next to his cheek, his tummy rising with the sweet and even deep breaths of sleep. An altogether peaceful picture. I stretched for a while, listened to the throaty rasps of a scrub jay outside the window, and finally sat up.

Carson opened his eyes and smiled at me, then reached up into his own little stretch. After nursing him, changing his diaper, and dressing him in his newly-bought-and-freshly-washed-thanks-to-Sheila clothes, I pulled on my jeans and a clean t-shirt, and headed downstairs.

The living room was quiet, but I found Sheila in the kitchen, sipping a mug of tea and reading some abstruse academic article about feminist rhetorical strategies. That was Sheila: the world in chaos with rogue paranormal beings running around trying to kill us, but if she had a few free minutes, she'd find something to read.

"Hey, sunshine, you slept in." Sheila smiled at me, made a funny face at Carson, and got me a cup of coffee without asking. That's why she's my best friend.

"I know. Can you believe it?"

Sheila moved on to making Carson rice cereal and asked permission before mashing him a bit of banana. I devoted myself to coffee before anything else.

"Where is everyone?"

"Newt's on the front steps with a phone call to his master. Tim's sleeping, after taking most of the night on watch. Eliza went for a run."

"Is she still...acting strange?"

"Mostly quiet. The same, I guess."

As if summoned by her words, Eliza opened the back door and stepped into the kitchen. She wore running shorts and a blue t-shirt, with her fawn-brown hair pulled back into a ponytail. She gave a short smile as a hello and pulled up the neck of her shirt to mop sweat off her face. Breathing deeply—though not seeming winded—she tilted her head from side to side, rolled her shoulders, and dropped gracefully into a kitchen chair, only to bound up again and get a glass of water. Settling down for the second time, she drained the glass and finally said, "Morning."

"Good morning. Did you have a nice run?" I asked, even though I personally thought the words "nice" and "run" should never be used together. Ever.

"Yes. Beautiful around here."

Sheila nodded. "In southern Orgeon, we can't

complain about the scenery or the climate, that's for sure. In fact, when I was interviewing for the job at the university and heard about the low salaries, people kept telling me, 'But the scenery's worth twenty thousand dollars a year.' " Her voice aptly mimicked the naïve enthusiasm of established faculty who didn't need to worry about mortgage payments or student loans.

I snorted, Eliza grinned at me in return, and for a moment, things seemed almost normal.

The rapport broke as a phone rang in the living room.

"That's my cell," said Eliza, a note of puzzlement in her voice. I watched as she crossed into the other room to pick up her phone from the coffee table. She glanced at it and her mouth set into an expressionless line as she registered the caller. After a moment's hesitation, she answered the call with a jab of the finger.

"Yes?"

I looked at Sheila, surprised. If Eliza answered me with that tone, I thought I might hang up. Sheila made an I-don't-know expression. We both dropped any pretense of not listening.

"Uh-huh. I'm busy, you know." Eliza turned her back to the kitchen. "We discussed that. I don't have anything more to say." After another moment. "This is pointless, okay? Please don't call again. Just move on. I wish you well." She disconnected and looked at her phone for a second, before she placed it down and walked back to the kitchen.

"Who was that?" I asked, even though I could tell by her scowl she didn't want to talk about it.

Eliza moved to the cabinet to get a bowl for cereal.

I watched her sleek ponytail twitch with her abrupt movements. "Just someone I dated for a while who has a hard time understanding 'no.' "

"Ah-ha." I hoped some light-natured teasing might get us back to our moment of ease. "Who's the unlucky guy?"

Eliza set down the cereal box with a thump and Sheila raised one hand as if that were supposed to mean something to me.

"The unlucky *girl*," Eliza said, "is a friend of a friend from a pack in southern Wyoming near Rock Springs. It turns out she's not my type."

"Oh," I said, then stopped, utterly blank about what to say next.

"Excuse me, I'm taking my cereal out on the porch."

As the kitchen door closed behind her, I turned on Sheila.

"What the hell? Did you know Eliza was a lesbian?"

"Yes, of course. How did you not know?"

"What, I'm supposed to be able to tell? To just know without her mentioning it?"

"No." Sheila's eyes flashed. "I'm just surprised you never even thought to ask about her love life before. It's not something she hides, Jules. She's private, but she talks when her friends *ask* her normal questions."

"Shit." I rubbed my forehead. Without prompting, Sheila got up and poured me more coffee. "Shit. I can't believe she and I never talked about any of that—about relationships at all. I just assumed...shit. And now she probably thinks I'm some kind of obnoxious heterosexual, with my heterosexist assumptions, or that I have some kind of *problem* with the fact she's gay, or…I was just surprised."

"Shit," I said, again. "I am the worst friend ever. Sheila, I am a horrible, horrible friend! I never even asked Eliza if she was dating anybody! I am a lousy, rotten, self-preoccupied friend and Eliza is probably mad at me and has now realized I'm an awful friend."

"Jules. Shut up." Sheila reached across the table and cuffed me on the arm. "*Now* you're being a selfish, preoccupied friend. Sitting here worried about whether or not you're a good friend when Eliza is out there." She pointed at the door. "Go. Go talk to her and clear it up. I'll stay with Carson."

"Shit," I said once more to just myself this time. "You're right."

I downed half my coffee for fortitude, ignoring the slight burn in my mouth. After reflecting, I also prepared a mug for Eliza—with cream and sugar the way she liked, although I cringed a bit—and hoisted the mug as a peace offering.

She sat on a folding camp chair at the end of the back patio. I held out the mug to her and she took it, blowing on the coffee and sipping before setting it on the ground.

"I'm an idiot," I said, pulling another chair up. "I can't believe I never asked about your love life. I don't care, you know. I mean, it doesn't bother me that you're a lesbian."

Eliza quirked her mouth. "Some of your best friends are lesbians?"

"Shut up." I rolled my eyes. "Cut the straight girl a break. Seriously, I don't care if you date men, women, both or, or ani—" My hyperbole stumbled into silence as I remembered I spoke to a Were.

Eliza laughed out loud and I relaxed.

"It's not a big deal, Julie. I just…" She shook her head. "Everything's pretty tense right now and I know you didn't mean anything by assuming it was a guy. We're still friends."

"Yes," I said, jumping on the word. "Definitely still friends. Now we can be friends who discuss our love lives—not that I have one."

"Not that mine needs to be discussed."

"Okay, well, that too. But we can talk about it later, if it gets interesting. If you meet someone special, okay?"

"Okay."

We finished our coffee in mostly companionable silence. When we headed back into the house, Eliza first and holding the door for me, a thought caused me to falter and nearly trip. She didn't… Frantically, I cast my mind back through events. Her protective attitude toward me. The way she liked me to scratch her ears when in wolf form. Her anger at my enemies. The easy camaraderie and trust between us. The strain and tension I sensed in her now. Tim sensed she was lying…would she, if she covered up emotion, lying by omission, would that seem the same? Could she…?

I squelched the thoughts. Not possible. I was just being self-centered again, I told myself quite firmly.

Chapter Nine

The feeling of quasi-normalcy Eliza and I established didn't last long. Carson rolled around on the floor with Sheila at his side, while Eliza and I sat on the couch. We tentatively filled the room with idle chat when Newt finished his conversation outside and came in the front door.

He looked around the room, then pulled the rocking chair forward to face the couch.

"So," he said, "no one else will call you on it, Eliza, but you're lying about something and I want to know what."

Eliza sprang to her feet and I echoed her, my hand flying to her arm as if to physically restrain her. Newt not only remained sitting, but leaned back in the chair, rocked it slightly with his toes, and looked up at Eliza. The light in the room seemed to brighten as he smiled broadly.

"Hey," he said. "Just want to know the truth."

Eliza's spine could have been made of steel—or steel wire, drawn so tight she might snap.

"The truth?" A note of growl crept into the words. "The truth is your friends, *firebug*, nearly killed Julie and Carson."

"Eliza. Who are you fooling? What are you hiding?"

"Don't tempt me. I'm stronger than you."

I stepped back as the hairs on my arms rose. My skin felt tight from the energy spilling in the room. I looked wildly at Sheila, who looked just as wildly at me.

Suddenly, Newt laughed and stood up.

"All right," he said. "This was going to happen sooner or later, so might as well be now. You think you're stronger? Let's see."

Eliza made an inchoate noise of assent, but Newt held up a hand to finish his thought. "If I win, Were, you answer my questions."

Sheila snatched Carson from the floor and moved toward me to hand him over. Both of us stopped with our backs against the front door. Newt and Eliza faced each other in the small open space of the living room carpet. Newt extended his arms slightly, palms up and hands cupped. The light around him intensified until he seemed to glow, strawberry-blond hair incandescent, freckles gleaming like bronze. Eliza stood ready to spring, still in human form, yet her body expressed everything of the wolf. She seemed oblivious to her surroundings, to anything except the Salamander.

Newt's face changed when he realized their fight was likely to wreak havoc on Sheila's house and his best weapon would leave this place a smoky ruin. A slight frown line creased his forehead. He raised one hand in the direction of the windows and more light streamed in—literally streamed into the room in rays, until he was nearly invisible in the brightness. I held Carson's head to me, afraid it would hurt his eyes. He started to fuss, not crying exactly, more annoyed at being held still, even though surely he could sense the roiling energy filling the room.

To combat the blinding light, Eliza pulled on shadow, coaxed it from under the chairs, the closet door, until wisps of darkness hung around her like a moth-eaten shawl.

She leapt at Newt, and the two of them disappeared in a chaotic whirlwind of light and shadow, a furious knot of wrestling bodies. I half-expected lightning and thunder to fill the room. Carson writhed in my arms, more and more restless; abruptly, my arms were full of prickles and shocks and coiled...something. The next moment, I grasped fur and tried to hang onto Carson as his wolf muscles scrabbled for traction. He twisted in my arms, growled in frustration, and nipped my shirt, his teeth grazing my collarbone.

Carson dove out of my arms and hit the floor, tail wagging but ears flat against his head. He yipped and jumped into the fray, even as I lunged to catch him.

I had a brief moment to think, incongruously, Carson must love that he already knew how to run when in wolf-form. I took a half step toward the indistinct struggle and paused, helpless.

"Eliza! Newt!"

Tim's voice roared their names like a command and the roiling mass seemed to freeze.

"Stop *NOW*!"

As the light seeped back into the atmosphere and Eliza's form—still human—also became visible through the dissipating darkness, Tim continued. "Look what you've done to Carson. Look at Julie, *team*."

I flinched at the anger behind his words and only then—as he directed attention to me—realized the extent of my own reaction to the fight. My panic might be residual from my recent trauma, fear for Carson's safety, or just an overspill of the extreme emotion in the room. Regardless of the reason, my heart raced and I could hardly breathe with my body wracked from shuddering. Eliza and Newt, still on the floor, both turned to look at me and Sheila put one hand on my arm. I spun away from her. My side vision caught Carson as a wolf pup frolicking on the floor, looking oblivious to the larger picture and distinctly pleased with himself.

Sheila took off running, which seemed really strange. Eliza leapt up and crossed the room in two steps, grabbed me by both shoulders, and forcibly turned me to face her.

"Did he bite you? Julie, *did he bite you?*"

I didn't understand at first, then shook my head as tears streamed down my face. I tried to tell her Carson bit my shirt, but suddenly remembered the sense of teeth grazing my skin. I sucked in a breath and ended up coughing until I gagged. I yanked down the collar of my shirt and looked to make sure, but no, he hadn't bitten me. Not broken the skin, anyway. I shook my head again and dropped down to the floor. I focused on breathing, in and out, and not coughing or choking. Sheila appeared again by my side, and held out my inhalers.

Ah. Smart girl. I took them gratefully, timed the coughs and inhaled as deeply as possible, sucking the medicine into my poor lungs and holding my breath as long as I could before exploding again in coughs. Once, twice. Switch to steroid inhaler, once, twice. Sheila rubbed my back and said something vaguely soothing that I barely heard. The sound of her voice calmed me, though, and I sat and stared at the mottled brown fibers of the carpet. I knew I could trust her and Tim to take care of everything. After a few minutes, my chest loosened, though my throat still felt strangely knotted.

"I'm sorry," Eliza said. I looked up at her as she knelt before me, hands on her knees, body craned forward. Her brown eyes were so deep they seemed to have a gravitational pull. "Are you okay?"

I nodded, not trusting myself to speak yet.

"I'm sorry, too," said Newt, addressing his remark to both Tim and me. "I was the instigator. My fault."

I shook my head then cleared my throat to explain. "Wasn't just you. Eliza, I trust you."

Eliza dropped her gaze then her eyes flicked back to mine.

"I trust you, but you've been acting…odd. Angry. Stressed. Secretive. Everyone says you're lying about something. Tim can tell, you know that." I stopped to cough again, holding up my hand so no one would interrupt before I could continue. "I don't believe you mean me harm—I *can't* believe that, after everything we've been through together. I trust you. But I want to know what's going on."

Eliza's face twisted in something that looked like anguish. She dropped back and brought her knees up, face down, hugging herself with her arms. When she spoke again, her voice was hoarse.

"I can't, Julie. I just can't. Just," she swallowed audibly, "give me time. Give me the rest of today." She looked at me again. "Trust me a little bit longer. Let me figure something out. I promise—I swear to you—I swear on mother moon may she never hear my call—I mean you no harm. Not you or anybody. I just…let me be sure, first. I have a responsibility."

Sure of what? I wanted to ask. What responsibility? To whom? Instead, silence covered the room, as everyone ceded right of response to me.

Finally, I said, "I trust you, Eliza."

She broke into a smile and her body relaxed. She grabbed my hand. "Thank you for giving me more time. Just today. Thank you for understanding and trusting me."

Sheila let out a slow breath I thought might have been echoed by Tim.

Newt laughed, a sound both jarring and somehow suited to the emotional release in the room. He stretched and said, "For the record, Eliza, I trust you, too." He and Eliza looked at each other for a moment. Eliza dropped her gaze first, perhaps embarrassed by her overt hostility toward our Salamander, and Newt continued, "I just want the full story. Something's missing."

Tim called us all to order. "Tonight, then. At dinner tonight, if not before, we have a war counsel. Everyone fully present and we share all information."

Eliza nodded.

"Well then," Sheila drawled, "if we're all okay now, can someone convince Carson to become human again before he rips up my carpet?"

I laughed then groaned. My baby: a gray wolf alternately chasing his tail and scrabbling furiously at the carpet edge between the living room and the kitchen tile. I'd seen him in wolf form before during the last two full moons, but this was the first time he changed out of cycle. The spillover energy in the room must have prompted his shift.

"What I am going to do with him?" I said out loud.

"Move to Greybull?" Eliza said then grinned as I opened my mouth to retort angrily. "Kidding, Julie. Or, well, not exactly kidding, but kind of."

I swatted at her, mostly glad things seemed back to normal. Yes, Eliza still hid something, but at least we were no longer hiding the fact she hid something. If that made any sense. I shifted uncomfortably, remembering my earlier unformed thoughts and the warm look in her eyes, then consciously dismissed my crazy ideas. Her secret must be something else.

"Okay." Eliza uncrossed her legs and pulled darkness smoothly, emerging as her sleek, buff-colored self, each strand of fur touched with a hint black at the tip, and padded over to Carson.

Carson yipped excitedly and pounced on her, sinking his teeth into the fur at the base of her neck.

Eliza's mouth opened in a loll and she collapsed on her side to wrestle with the cub for a while.

My heart ached, somehow, watching them play together, enjoying something I could never share. Never. I reined in my thoughts, firmly. Carson rolled over and showed his belly, then scrabbled at Eliza with his little claws as she mock-shook him.

After several minutes of playing, she dropped down, gave a low rumbling growl, and poked him hard with her nose. They both shifted and Eliza sat up, loosed her hair, and sleekly pulled it back into her characteristic ponytail. Carson pushed up on his hands, weight on his tummy, and kicked his little feet against the floor. He grinned at me, as if to say, "Did you see that, Mama?"

"Yes, yes, you're very clever," I said, hoping it didn't sound like a grumble. I picked him up and relished his baby weight nestled against me.

I looked around at the team.

"Today," I said, "we find the Salamanders."

Chapter Ten

After some discussion, we divided into two teams for the rest of the day. Tim asked Sheila and Newt to drive the area in a crisscross pattern with the hopes they'd find the 'Manders. Tim and Eliza planned to search the wooded areas around Jacksonville in the hopes of finding our rogue Were. I approved of Tim's decision to separate Eliza and Newt, although their spat and the ensuing discussion seemed to have greatly lessened the tension. In fact, I caught Eliza's level gaze on Newt more than once and I wondered if she reassessed our Salamander. Initially, Tim asked me to accompany Sheila and Newt, but my stomach churned at the idea of another fire attack on the car—at the thought of the gas tank exploding—and so I asked if I could go with him and Eliza to the woods, instead. Somehow, the Were seemed less threatening.

Tim considered. "I'm not sure, Julie. Eliza and I need to be in wolf form to follow any tracks and scents we find. We're likely to end up off road in the middle of the woods."

Shit. I couldn't stay home alone with Carson, and I really didn't think I could handle driving around, waiting for someone to catch us on fire. But the alternative...

"Use us as bait," I said.

"What?" Tim and Sheila said at the same time.

Eliza frowned.

"The Were can sense us, right? Smell us? If he's close enough? If he's after Carson and we're in the middle of the woods—seemingly alone—do you think he'll be able to resist?"

"I don't like it," said Eliza.

"Wait a minute, let's think it through." Tim tapped his chin.

"I think it's brilliant," Newt said, and gave me a huge smile of approval. "Julie's right, you know. Drop her off in the middle of the woods, near where you lost the Were's scent in the river. Slink away as far as possible without compromising her safety, wreathe yourselves in darkness, and wait."

"The Were can still scent us, darkness or no," said Eliza.

Tim nodded agreement with Eliza, but said, "However, it might still work if the Were felt he could get to them before we could. Or if he thought he could take us. Or..."

"We could 'or' all day, folks. The worst thing that can happen is he scents the Weres and doesn't show up." Sheila flipped her long hair behind her shoulders, where it shone in the sunlight.

I wasn't sure I agreed with her assessment of the worst thing—I could think of about ten million things that would be worse than the Were not showing up—but I didn't quibble. Instead, I said, "I think it's worth a try."

Tim stared off in space for a moment then made the decision. I'd go into the woods, as bait. Me and Carson.

Before we left, Sheila passed out protective

amulets she'd crafted the night before. The last set of amulets she'd made for our team, back in Las Vegas, had been spelled safety pins, complete with bright plastic animal heads. Those had worked by increasing our luck, a fairly subtle spell. Today, she passed out intricately woven string bracelets, one for each of us. They looked almost like the friendship bracelets kids made for each other.

"Wow, so you made these last night?" I studied mine, woven from threads of brown, green, and purple.

"Yup. Some pulled guard duty." She winked at Tim, Eliza, and Newt. "Some labored long into the morning hours," she preened a bit, "and some slept."

I knew she was teasing and didn't mean to chide me for being a useless human, so I bit my tongue on an angry retort and nodded stiffly at her. "Thank you very much."

"Oh shit, Jules." Sheila looked at me in exasperation.

"I mean it! Thank you. I appreciate you using your witchcraft to help us all."

Sheila sighed.

"Sheila, how do these work?" Newt peered at the bundle in Sheila's hand.

Sheila handed him one of bronze, azure, and pink string. "It's three workings in one. A strength charm, a deflection of malevolent magic, and a do-not-notice-me."

"Um." Everyone turned to look at me. "Won't the do-not-notice-me spell interfere a bit with our 'Notice Me! I'm Alone in the Woods!' plan?"

Sheila opened her mouth then closed it again.

"Put it on as soon as you see the enemy Were?"

Newt suggested.

"Sure. 'Hey, Were, hold on one second, let me tie this bracelet. Okay, got it. Now try to attack me.' "

"On the other hand," said Tim, "do-not-notice-me might make this ruse actually feasible, if it fools the Were into thinking you're alone by blunting his sense of Eliza and me."

"True." Sheila seemed relieved her work wasn't totally useless.

"Well, I guess I'll carry ours and put them on if we can." I pocketed the two bracelets, mine and Carson's, interlaced with azure, forest green, and butter yellow. "It's not active if it's not on, right?"

"Right," said Sheila. "Needs to be on your skin."

Eliza studied hers carefully. "What determines the colors you used?" Hers, I noticed, was two shades of brown, a cinnamon and an ash, intertwined with sage green and pale blue.

Sheila flushed slightly, then gave a broad grin and drawled, "Witch secrets, my dear friends. Just colors attuned to you."

I glanced at Tim's wrist, where he'd already fastened his: deep red, dark purple shaded nearly to black, two types of vibrant pink, and a gold thread weaving them together. Sheila's own bracelet was gray, white, and burnt orange. I wondered if she hadn't gotten them mixed up, but wisely voiced nothing.

"All right." Newt gave us all a wicked grin. "Game on, peeps."

****

Newt and Sheila left right away with the admonition to call me the minute they encountered any Salamanders—my cell phone wouldn't be in limbo-

109

land, one side benefit of me accompanying the Weres. We had a somewhat argumentative discussion about whether or not the bracelets would work once the Weres changed form; I'd asked if they'd be lost in limbo, or somehow present albeit not in physical form. Sheila and Eliza decided the bracelets would accompany the Weres as wolves, even if the bracelets weren't exactly tangible, thus should work as planned. During this discussion, I nursed Carson again, changed his diaper, and felt confident he'd collapse into a morning nap while we drove.

Of course, Carson chose to prove me wrong and spent the twenty-five-minute drive between Ashland and Jacksonville screaming, even though I sat right next to him and tried to provide comfort. He was bright red and sweaty when we arrived in Jacksonville, while I was a nervous wreck of anxiety and frustration. I *hated* when he threw a fit in the car and I could do nothing to help him. As soon as I whisked him out of his car seat, he stopped crying and began to hiccup. Five seconds after I put him in the baby sling, he was asleep against my chest.

"Well, at least he's sleeping now," said Eliza, looking at him dubiously, as if wondering how such a sweet baby could make such a godawful noise.

We parked alongside the road out of town, close to where the Applegate River ran. The three of us picked our way through the woods and down the riverbank.

"This area is full of his scent," said Tim. "Some old, some new."

"How old?" I asked.

"Weeks."

"He's been lurking around my house for *weeks*?"

Tim shrugged. "Guess so."

"Um. How new? The newest scent."

"New. He's been all over this area within the last day, which bodes well for him finding you."

"Great. I think."

Eliza called for us to join her over near a thick growth of manzanita trees. She gestured down river.

"How about Tim and I wait here? If I call a bit of darkness, this should be a good place to hide. And," she tapped her wrist, "the don't-notice-me should help."

I turned in a circle, surveying the area. "Where should I go?"

"Somewhere out in the open, so we'll see right away if anything approaches," said Tim, studying our surroundings. "How about over there?"

He pointed to where the woods were clearer, tall pine trees and less underbrush, up on a hill about half a football field from the river.

"Okay. And I just sit and…wait." I tried not to sound dubious. This was *my* plan, after all.

Eliza frowned. "He'll think it's a trap. Now that we're actually here and looking at the area, why *would* Julie and Carson just sit around on a hillside? It'll be completely obvious they're trying to lure him out."

"Shit." Eliza was right and I had a stupid plan. This would never… "Wait a minute. So we make it obvious. Even more obvious, I mean. How about I go over there and start yelling? Demand he come out and face me? He might think I'm crazy—crazy-angry—but maybe he'll be curious enough to actually come close?"

Eliza rubbed her forehead. "Tim?"

Tim nodded decisively. "It's the best plan we have, so let's give it a try. If this doesn't work, Eliza and I will come back later this afternoon and hunt him down. Without you and Carson, Julie."

"Okay. Agreed. It's worth a shot. Off I go, then." I walked a few steps before turning back. "Will you wait in wolf or human form?"

"Wolf," they answered in unison.

With Carson snoozing in the sling, I walked over to the slight ridge we chose. I circled the area, winding through pine trees, blackberry bushes, and the occasional deciduous tree, until I found a spot where I could see in all directions and nothing could sneak up too close. Hopefully. The woods were silent. This early in autumn, most of the grasses and weeds were brittle yellow, bleached by the sun and lack of rainfall. The trees stood tall and dark green, littering the ground with old pine needles and cones. My steps crackled, but I reminded myself noise was okay. This was not subterfuge, after all, but rather the opposite. From my spot on the ridge, I had a clear view around me: woods, small clearings, riverbank slanting down to water. Brewer's blackbirds, sparrows, and the occasional scrub jay flickered in the trees, the only movements I detected.

I cleared my throat and chased away self-consciousness. Facing the river, I called out, "Yoo-hoo! Hey, Werewolf!" The sound quickly swallowed by the woods, I forced myself to continue. "Get your ass out here, Were. I'm waiting for you. Hey, wolf!"

My anger started to rise with my voice. "Werewolf, get the hell out here and show yourself. What's the matter, not brave enough to face me in daylight? You want to skulk around at nighttime and threaten me? Threaten me and my baby? Well, grow some balls,

Were and meet me face to face. What's the matter, are you afraid?"

I continued in this vein for quite some time, then had to stop and use my inhalers, trying to hold tight to my chutzpah while doing so. My throat hurt and I wondered if the Were was even close enough to hear me. I fought not to look toward Tim and Eliza's hiding spot. Instead, I did the baby two-step and circled my staked-out territory, patting Carson on the back while he slept in ignorance, and shouted for the Were. Exasperated and out of taunts, I started to sing "Who's Afraid of the Big, Bad Wolf" over and over, when, without a sound to announce him, the Were appeared. A large black wolf, his shoulder as high as my waist, eyes deep and unreadable, standing next to a Douglas fir about fifty feet from me.

Inadvertently, I stepped back, then lifted my chin and stood my ground. He remained motionless. And huge. Even bigger than I remembered.

"What's the matter, Were," I snapped, as much from fear as anger. "Scared of a human? Don't have the guts to come closer and finish what you started? Isn't this what you wanted?"

He paced slowly toward me, one foot then another. His gaze fixed on me, and as he passed through a patch of sun, I saw his eyes were dark amber lightened to honey by the rays. Honey. Strangely inappropriate thought.

Chills ran up my spine and I tried to say something else, to taunt him further—why, because I was an idiot—but couldn't make the words form. My tongue stuck in my suddenly-dry mouth. I managed to loosen one of the arms clutching Carson and dug into my pocket frantically, grabbing for the bracelets, mine and Carson's, as if I could somehow tie them on in the few moments while he came nearer and nearer. His ears stood alert, head slightly lowered, body taut.

I backed into a tree and stopped short with the bark pressing into me. The Were paced about twenty feet from me and I found myself wondering how much time I'd have, after he sprang. One heartbeat? Two? Enough time to duck behind the tree? I tried to keep my focus on the wolf, even as I used my peripheral vision to look for a stick, a big stick. I could hit him with a stick. Why didn't I have a gun? With silver bullets? Or any bullets? How was I so unprepared?

Where were Tim and Eliza? Why were they waiting?

As I articulated the thought, what looked like a wind-tossed pattern of shadows sprang into the space between me and the black Were. Suddenly, I saw Tim: a gray wolf, nearly as big as the black, in true fighting stance with his head down, teeth barred, hackles high. He growled at the black wolf, a low fierce noise I felt in my chest, and he rushed to close the distance. For a moment, the black Were seemed caught between flight and fury. He made an aborted leap to the side, then crouched and lunged to meet Tim's attack. They crashed together, snarling, and I jumped, feeling the tree bark catch in my shirt.

With the Were's attention focused elsewhere, I tied Carson's bracelet, then mine with shaking fingers, wishing I'd had the presence of mind earlier to fix some sort of slip knot. That done, I grabbed a stout branch I spotted earlier and brandished it. As if a branch would help. Carson stirred restlessly and I bounced up and down, hoping he wouldn't wake up, hoping he wouldn't change form and join this fight. No. Not this time. I held the baby sling against me with my left arm as firmly as possible, while I clutched the stick in my right.

Tim and the other wolf separated again and circled each other slowly on stiff legs. Low rumbles filled the air and then, in the blink of an eye, one of them leapt and they wrestled, a knot of fur and fury, tearing at each other with teeth and hind legs. I took half a step forward to help then stopped. Someone yipped in pain and someone barked in response. The sound shuddered through me, the snarls like aftershocks. I couldn't tell what happened: they were a fused mass of gray and black fur in violent motion.

When they next broke apart, Tim favored his front left leg, shifting his weight slightly in a way I thought might be a feint. The black wolf crouched low to the ground in anger, teeth barred and sharply white in the speckled sunlight. He charged Tim with a powerful thrust of his hindquarters, knocked the gray wolf off his feet and the two of them renewed their struggle.

"Come on, Tim, come on," I said under my breath. "Come on."

And suddenly, the two wolves were still. Tim lay frozen on his back. The black wolf had his teeth around Tim's throat and a low growl reverberated through the silence. Tim didn't move, very carefully didn't move except for the rise of his furred chest as he drew in gulps of air.

Shit!

Pine needles cushioned my steps. One, two, three.

The wolves' attention remained fixed on each

other.

I raised my hand, held my breath, and threw the branch as hard as I could.

The stick hit the black wolf in the back, just as I hoped. He jumped and released his hold on Tim's throat, then swung toward me. This close—only ten feet or so—he looked even larger, like a nightmarish hellhound, amber eyes startling in their intensity over his sharp teeth.

Tim twisted and found his feet, his fur rising in anger. Every hair on my own body stood on end in response to the Were energy spilling from the two wolves.

Carson's eyes popped open wide. He strained to turn toward the other Weres.

"No!" I yelled. "No!"

A bark rang out. A sharp, commanding bark out of nowhere. No, from Eliza who appeared out of the midst of don't-notice-me or called darkness, I didn't know which. She stood three big steps to my right, with her ears and eyes pointed at the black wolf, stretched to her full height like a casting in bronze. Her tail hung behind her.

Both of the other Weres stopped in their tracks. Tim tilted his head and cocked one ear, but kept his focus carefully on his opponent. The black wolf froze, jolted out of the fight. He stepped forward, not in the direction of Tim, who he almost seemed to forget, but toward Eliza. Then he took two steps backward. His fur twitched, almost as if reacting to a fly. He lifted a foot then put it back down.

In that moment, Tim jumped, using the full force of his body weight to crash into the black wolf and bear him to the ground. Carson shrieked—a sound more eager than afraid—and struggled against me.

"No!" I grabbed him. "Dammit, Carson! Do not change!" I held his head with both of my hands, locked his gaze to mine, and hoped he understood me.

Eliza barked again and grabbed my attention. Again, she sounded, nearly a howl, and the Weres paused in their fight. This time, she took advantage of the moment and raced into the fray.

She crashed into the two other Weres, then came up crouched over Tim.

Over *Tim*.

Eliza barred her teeth inches from Tim's face. One of her feet pressed on his neck. Tim looked as shocked as a wolf could look. As shocked as I felt.

After a moment, Eliza backed off and Tim rolled over, but stayed close to the ground. The black wolf stood scant feet away from the two of them. Eliza swung her head in his direction, then made a whuffing noise. The black Were stepped backward, letting out a half-whine I couldn't interpret. Eliza approached him, nose first, but the other Were backed away from her, then turned tail and raced away down the slope. He slalomed around trees, crashed across the wide, slow river, and emerged on the opposite bank. The black wolf stood there and looked at us for a minute, then ran.

"What the *hell?*"

I looked at the two wolves, who just as intently studied each other.

"*What the hell?*" I strode over to the two of them. "Change back *right now* and tell me what the hell happened!"

Carson batted at my face. I didn't know if he was

playing or annoyed at my yelling, but at least he didn't turn into a wolf. I jiggled him and stared at my two friends.

A shimmer of darkness licked the area, faded, and left Tim kneeling on the ground with his hands on his legs. He stared at Eliza. After clearing his throat, he spoke in a voice that sent chills up my spine because of—not despite—its mildness.

"Eliza. Explain."

The buff wolf stood there a moment longer, then resolved through shadow into Eliza. She straightened her shoulders and pushed her ponytail behind her, where it hung as precise as usual. She looked at Tim first, then me.

When she spoke, she addressed her fellow Were first. "Sorry about that, Tim."

Tim's eyebrows rose.

She continued. "I wasn't going to hurt you."

"No, you weren't." Funny, how the words of agreement instead sounded like a threat.

"Eliza?" Desperation tinged my voice and I winced.

Eliza closed her eyes for a moment, then sank cross-legged to the ground. After a shared glance, Tim and I followed suit. I let Carson out of the sling and sat him on a mat of pine needles, where he proceeded to bounce up excitedly for a moment, before slowly folding into a taco. I propped him up against my leg.

"That's Tony."

"The Were?" Tim asked.

"Who's Tony?" I said, at the same time.

"Tony Blythe. Dave's older brother."

"Dave Blythe? You mean, that Dave?" None of it

made sense to me. The pack council had put Dave to death after we discovered his involvement with the mafia and the murder of Werewolves.

"Yes, *that* Dave."

"And that was Tony? His brother? The one who went wolf? Five years ago, after their parents died?" I asked.

"Yes." Eliza looked at me intently. "I thought it was. When I first scented him, I thought it was him—but it had been so long—no one even knew if he was still alive—and..."

"So he's pack. That Were was part of your pack," Tim said. His voice warmed slightly.

"Yes."

I nodded, putting it all together. "Conflict of loyalty. Pack versus friends."

"Yes. No. *You* have my loyalty, Julie. You and Carson. And you are my pack. And," she gestured widely, "I'm part of this team, all of us together. But...I just had to be sure." Her voice dropped so the last sentence was barely audible. To my human ears, anyway.

"Tony must know his younger brother was executed by the council. And he wants revenge. Because we're the ones who caught Dave and turned him over. Because it was my fault," I said, slowly.

"But you weren't at fault," said Eliza. "Or, at least, not any more than me or Tim or Sheila or...the council, really. They decided to put him to death."

"Yeah, but Tony's not going after the council, is he?" I said. I rubbed my face, weary beyond belief. "It was my fault." I raised a hand to stop Eliza from interrupting. "Okay, *our* fault. We should have seen it coming. We should have been able to stop Dave—to make him understand..."

"Dave made his choices and no one else can take responsibility for them," said Tim.

"But he was a pup. Just a pup! Only seventeen. Blame our pack, if anyone. We failed him." Eliza's voice shook with raw anguish and she blinked, hard. I reached over to grab her hand.

"Yes, he was a pup, but his actions caused the deaths of two Weres, the suffering of more, and the perverted deaths of many humans." Tim counted off the crimes on his fingers.

"Um, Julie." Eliza nodded at Carson.

"Oh, shit," I said, and scooped pine needles out of my baby's mouth. "Here," I said, popping in his pacifier instead, so he could continue to play with the needles without choking to death.

"Anyway," Eliza shook her head, "I guess it doesn't matter now. Tony's decided to take revenge on Julie—or perhaps all of us."

"I don't...I still don't understand, though. If he's been prowling around here for weeks, he had plenty of opportunities," I made a wide gesture with my hands, "to kill me. Plus, just now, he ran away."

"Outnumbered," said Tim.

"I don't understand it either, Julie," admitted Eliza. "That's why I hoped I was wrong. Hoped for another explanation."

"I know. I understand," I said and hoped she sensed my full apology for all her recent behavior.

She smiled in return—a real smile—and I knew she felt forgiven.

Chapter Eleven

Minds whirling, we headed back to the car. I sank into my thoughts while Tim called the pack council, and Eliza called Lily Rose, pack Full. Tim finished first and started driving.

"Lily was *not* happy," Eliza said, after ending the call.

"Sounds like an understatement from the part of the conversation I heard," I said.

"First Dave, now Tony—she thinks we're airing pack dirty laundry to the whole council. Proving we can't police our own at the same time."

"Is she…going to get in trouble?"

"Trouble from the council? No. But it's possible some young hotshot Were might think she's weak and try to move into Greybull, take over the pack."

"Does that happen often?"

"Not too often. Unless a pack gets a reputation for weakness."

I turned that over in my mind for a minute. "How strong is Lily, anyway? Stronger than you, I guess, or else you'd be Full?"

"If I wanted to try for it," Eliza said and flashed a grin. "Frankly, I'm not sure if she's stronger or not. We've never dueled—not for real, anyway. I'm not interested in being Full right now, though. Maybe later."

I wondered what she thought about in the space before she continued.

"Anyway, Lily's quite strong. Most full moon Weres would have a hard time taking her."

"Julie?" Tim broke into our conversation. "Could you call Sheila and update her?"

"Oh, sure." I punched speed dial.

"Hey. Where are you guys?"

"Hi. We're driving around Lithia Park," said Sheila, referring to the large pie-shaped public park in downtown Ashland. "Newt thought he sensed something up this way. What about you?"

"We're on our way back. We found the Were—or he found us." I updated her quickly. She sucked in a long breath when I told her the Were was Tony Blythe.

"Wow."

I heard Newt's voice in the background.

"Where? Okay." Sheila wasn't talking to me. Newt spoke again, not loud enough for me to understand.

"Jules?" Sheila's urgent tone made me clutch the phone. "Newt found them. We're up at the top of Lithia Park, near the swimming area. He doesn't think they'll sense him because of the bracelets. We're going to try to ambush them."

I bit back my first words and settled for saying, "Okay. Be careful. We'll be there in"—I checked out the window—"fifteen minutes."

"Okay. Tell—never mind. See you soon." The phone cut off.

Eliza turned around completely in her seat and Tim's gaze darted to me in the rearview mirror. He'd started speeding and I hoped the don't-notice-me extended to traffic cops who liked to pull people over on Highway 99.

"Um, they found the Salamanders and they're going to ambush them."

Tim nodded, jaw tight. "We heard."

Right. Super Were senses again.

"Plan?" Eliza said.

The two Weres discussed strategy. Eliza was particularly skilled at calling the moon to cause madness in others, but she needed to be in close range. The combination of called darkness and Sheila's bracelet might allow her to get near enough, though none of us knew exactly how the 'Manders electromagnetic senses operated. Eliza also thought she could call a substantial amount of water, since we were only four days from a full moon. Calling water would be easier so close to Lithia Creek and the reservoir. Tim said he could take the Salamanders in a physical fight, especially in wolf form.

I started to say something then thought better of it.

Tim's eyes met mine in the mirror and he said, stiffly, "What you saw earlier wasn't a fair picture of my fighting ability."

Eliza kept a studiously straight face. She said, "True. If Tony's been wolf for five years, neither one of us could take him in a fight—regardless of Sheila's charms—and you certainly weren't expecting me to attack you."

I detected a note of smugness in her voice and spoke to puncture it. "Yes. Since we're all on the same team, no reason to think you'd attack Tim."

Eliza winced. "Sorry. Again."

"We can have a rematch sometime, if you'd like."

I rubbed the prickles off the back of my neck.

"All right. Stop the Were posturing, both of you. Focus on the Salamanders."

"Right." Tim switched gears. "Julie, when we get there, I want you and Carson to stay in the car and out of the fight. In fact, maybe you should drive into town and wait for one of us to call you, give the all clear to come back."

"What?"

I looked at Eliza for support, found none, and lashed out angrily. "No way. No way will I leave you all in danger—danger *because of me*—while I flee downtown and grab a latte."

Eliza grinned. "No one said anything about a latte, Julie."

"Stop it. You know what I mean. I'm not running away from this. It's *my* fight."

"*Our* fight," said Tim. "And we can't fight effectively while worried about you and Carson."

Shit.

"So..." I scrambled for a solution. "Let's drop Carson off with...Dana. Eliza, let's run by my friend Dana's house and ask if she can watch Carson—I can call her now—and then he'll be safe and I can come and help."

"How exactly are you going to help?" Tim's matter-of-fact question felt like a punch in the gut.

"I...we can stop by Sheila's, too, and I can get a gun. Or maybe she has an extra one with her. I'm sure she brought a gun." Dammit, why hadn't *I* brought a gun?

Tim said, "You suggest we detour to your friend Dana's house, then across town to Sheila's house to get a gun, then back into town and up to the park, the place where our friends may even now be involved in mortal combat?"

I collapsed back in my seat, utterly defeated. If only I was a real Were. One stupid recessive gene. What good could I do?

"Fine. You're right. I'll drop you off, but I won't drive away. I'll wait in the car. If they come near the car, if we're in danger, *then* I promise we'll leave right away."

They both knew me well enough to hear the resolve in my voice.

Tim and Eliza continued to plan as we sped toward Ashland. I looked at Carson, full of power though only a baby and dug my fingernails into my palms, wishing I could do anything useful to help.

****

We didn't have to search for our team. We just followed the smoke.

As we drove up the road through the park and reached the top near the beach area, a small plume of smoke appeared against the blue sky, tracing a path upward. I wondered how long before the fire trucks appeared—September was prime wildfire season in southern Oregon and everyone watched the horizon.

Tim pulled into the gravel lot and stopped the car. With a glance at the several other cars to make sure we had no audience, he tossed me the car keys with an admonition to stay put, nodded at Eliza, and changed form. Shadow chased over his body and left the gray wolf behind. Eliza followed suit and the two of them disappeared into the woods.

I checked on Carson, who seemed just fine, and scrambled into the front seat just in case we needed to make a getaway.

Then I waited.

I found myself staring into the woods and jumping at noises, no matter how innocuous. Even the sounds of children splashing at the pebbly beach were imbued with menace. I crossed my fingers—literally crossed my fingers, even though it felt stupid; it was something I could *do*—and hoped the fight wouldn't expand to include any bystanders. I craned my head this way and that, hoping to see something more than the faint smoke spiraling into the air above the trees, which hadn't seemed to attract anyone else's attention yet.

Three minutes passed.

A woman emerged into the parking area from the beach, grabbed a tube of sunscreen from her car, and headed back toward the water. She noticed me sitting there and gave a cheery wave in that small-town way. I waved back and smiled over gritted teeth. The car grew hot, even though we parked in the shade, and I swiveled around to check on Carson again. He'd fallen asleep and I sent up silent thanks. The last thing I needed was a screaming baby. He seemed kind of sweaty, but I decided against starting the car to run the air conditioning and just made sure all the windows were open.

Five more minutes passed. I told myself to stop looking at the clock.

A branch cracked and I jumped. And looked.

Him.

The black Were stood right at the edge of the woods, nearly on the gravel, mere feet from my car. His flanks heaved with his panting and I somehow had time to marvel how he found us—he somehow kept pace with us—he'd followed us here. Or maybe he knew to meet the Salamanders here. Maybe they planned some sort of ambush. At the same time all those thoughts ran through my head, I tried to start the car. My hands shook and the keys clanged together. Which key? Where was the right key? Shit! I fumbled the key ring and dropped it on the floor with a clatter. I couldn't take my gaze off the black wolf, his amber eyes trained on me in turn. What was he waiting for? I risked a glance down, saw the keys near my right foot, and kicked them back toward me. I stretched my hand down, keeping my attention on the wolf so I'd see him when he sprang, when he—

The wolf's entire body jerked suddenly and his head swung to the left. He glanced back at me with those unreadable eyes, and he sprang into the woods, silent and invisible as a shadow.

He'd attracted my attention on purpose with that cracked branch, I realized. Weres were fully capable of moving silently. Did he taunt me? As I taunted him with my voice and songs earlier?

I grabbed the keys and cranked the engine, slammed the car into reverse, then as abruptly stepped on the brakes.

Shit.

They didn't know he was coming. None of them expected him—they wouldn't be ready. He'd—

Shit, shit, shit.

I stopped the car and banged my fist on my forehead as if to clear my thinking. I grabbed my phone, ready to call Sheila. Or Tim. Or Eliza. I aborted the plan before my finger hit a number, realizing—if the phones weren't in magical limbo—a ringing phone in the middle of the woods was as likely to alert enemies as to warn my team.

I had no choice.

And no gun. Dammit. I vowed to never, ever, ever leave the house again without a gun. Liberal politics be damned.

Cursing under my breath, I grabbed the sling and my sleeping baby. After a moment of thought, I slung him onto my back, snugged him tight, and made sure his head wasn't flopping around. This way, I'd have full range of motion with my arms and—hopefully— any attack would have to come through me before injuring my son. I firmly squashed the mental images that streamed through my brain with those thoughts. After I secured Carson, I took several deep breaths and threaded my way through the woods, thankfully clear of dense underbrush in this mostly pine-based forest. I tried to step lightly and found myself holding my breath as if that would allow me to hear better, to find the others. I cursed my woefully weak senses.

I smelled the smoke first and retched before getting myself under control. My pulse raced and I stopped, leaning my hand heavily against a nearby tree. I swallowed several times, shifted my shoulders to relieve the tension, reached back to check on Carson, and grimly proceeded. I caught movement from the corner of my eye and swung in that direction. Did those bushes just snap back? Was that a shadow or a darkness-wreathed Were? The motion didn't repeat, so I continued.

There.

Ahead of me on a slight upslope, I saw flames licking up the trunk of a tree. Leaves of red fire danced in the heat overhead. As I watched, Newt ran over and put his hand on the tree, right in the middle of the flames. The fire instantly tamped down, lingering near his hand as if in caress. He pulled his hand off the tree and the flame went with it, cupped in his palm. Then, he turned his back to me. I saw the concentration in the set of his spine and shoulders. The flames licked his hand and I watched in shock as they flickered into deep purple: beautiful indigo and blue flames wreathing his fingers. Newt drew back his arm and lobbed the flames at some target out of my sight.

"Wow," I breathed in awe.

"Newt," I called softly and walked a few steps toward him. I didn't move up the slope, instead choosing to stay where I was less visible.

Newt turned to me with a start. "Julie! What are you doing here? Tim said you were in the car." He kept turning his head frantically, dividing his attention between me and presumably, the other Salamanders.

"The black Were. Tony. He's here. He must have followed us," I said. "I needed to warn you."

A breeze spun up and ashes cascaded down from the recently burning tree as its leaves relinquished their forms.

"Okay, then—" Newt said. "Oh, shit."

A tree about forty feet away burst into a pillar of flame. I heard the pop and sizzle of its needles. I took one involuntary step backward, but stiffened my spine and stood my ground.

"Goddammit, I could fight better if I didn't have to keep the whole forest from burning down." Newt cursed and darted away in the direction of the new fire.

I crept up the slope for better visibility. Carson

shifted restlessly in his sleep, but gave a deep sigh and fell limp against me once more. His warm weight comforted me.

I watched as Newt snuffed out the pine tree, fire writhing back to the ground and then disappearing. Moments later, two fires started in opposite directions, quite spread out. I remembered Newt saying 'Manders could call fire better with touch and realized our enemies split up to keep him busy.

"There!" An exultant voice rang out and all of a sudden, Newt's running form was engulfed with fire. I closed my eyes involuntarily, then pried them open. A dazzling orange and red fireball resolved into Newt's form, dark against the light. He raised his arms, fingers spread wide. I watched as the fire drained into his hands; the orange flames concentrated into super-white then morphed into the purple flames I saw before. He flung the flames and I heard a scream in the direction of the earlier cry.

Fire tore through grass near a small rock outcrop about twenty feet to the left of me. I saw Tim leap up and crash into a figure I barely glimpsed, just enough to see he was the Salamander I'd labeled Surfer, the one with the bleach-blond hair. As the two of them struggled on the ground, Eliza stepped out from the shadows. Even from this distance, I saw her forehead crease with strain as she held her hands out in front of her. The flames on the ground guttered; the last red light glimmering on what I realized was water, called out of the ground by Eliza's link with the moon. Tim and Surfer 'Mander thrashed about, now kicking up mud. Bits of flame tried to erupt around the two, but immediately quelled with Eliza's water. I saw a flash of blood on Tim's muzzle and heard him growling, deeply resonant.

Wait. Not Tim.

"Eliza!" I yelled and pointed. Downwind from our Weres, the black wolf poised to spring.

Eliza's head whipped in my direction and I registered her look of surprise before her gaze followed my finger. She saw the other Were and—just like that—dropped into wolf form.

A scream rang out, followed by two gunshots. Sheila. I knew it was Sheila. So did Tim, because he was running before I could move, leaving the Salamander behind. I crashed after him, slower, much slower in my awkward non-Were body.

As I approached, Tim shifted to human form and cradled Sheila on the ground. At first, I didn't know why. Then I saw the burns, angry red and black. Flames had eaten deep into her skin on her right hand, up her arm, across her shoulder onto her collarbone. Blood-soaked and stiff, pieces of her blackened shirt stuck to the skin. Sheila's eyes closed; her face rigid with pain.

"Oh my God. Sheila!" I slid to a stop on my knees beside them, heedless of jouncing Carson on my back. Sheila bit back a moan. Her eyelids flickered and she fainted.

"We have to get her to a hospital." Tim's face remained impassive, his own anguish visible only in the way he held Sheila to him so desperately, yet careful not to touch her injuries. "And take care of the body."

Only at his words did I notice the dead Salamander scant paces from Sheila. The woman, the one I'd last seen with the cat eye sunglasses. She lay in a heap on the ground, two bullet wounds in her chest.

I heard sirens, wailing their way up Lithia Park, and realized the fire department was almost here. Certainly followed quickly by the police, unless we were lucky.

Newt appeared at my shoulder. "Crap. Third degree and bad," he said.

"Can you do anything?" I felt a sudden surge of hope, squashed as he shook his head. He laid one hand on her leg.

"I drew the heat out of her body so the burns won't get worse, but there's nothing else I can do. She needs a hospital. I can take care of the body, though." Newt jerked his head in the direction of the corpse.

"Tim! Do you need help carrying her?" Eliza reached us.

"No." Tim stood with Sheila in his arms and strode away without a glance at the rest of us. "Just take care of the body."

"Eliza!" The rest of the fight popped back into my head. "Where are the other two Salamanders? The black Were?"

"Fled. The blond one severely hurt. Not sure about the other. Tony took off after them."

"Probably because of the sirens," said Newt. Indeed, it sounded like the fire trucks arrived at the parking area and I heard shouts from that direction.

Newt moved over to the fallen Salamander and checked her pockets efficiently. He pulled out a wallet, then roughly stripped the body. I averted my gaze, feeling it was obscene. The reason for his search became apparent in a minute, however, as Newt said, "Look at this."

On the woman's left shoulder blade was a tattoo, a

stylized sun circled by a lizard. Eliza moved to study it.

"Eclipsers," said Newt. Then, seeing our blank looks, he waved his hand. "Later. Okay, hold on."

He heaped the clothes back onto the body, then extended his hands. He touched the pile of clothing and a white-hot tongue of flame descended onto the corpse. Light flashed and a smell of burning meat made me gag. Purple flames roared, and just seconds later, left behind a charred mass of ash, not even bones identifiable.

I stared at Newt, unable to muster up my usual foul-language response to shocking events. Eliza's eyes were wide and she let out a low whistle.

"Douse that? So it's not a pile of ash?"

Eliza took a minute to understand Newt, but then she nodded. A muscle twitched in her jaw as she called up a flood of water over the spot. The ashes swirled and settled into soggy earth.

I hear another shout and crashing, as someone—presumably firefighters—approached.

"Quick," Eliza said in a low voice.

She shifted form and darted through the trees, leading us smoothly around the firefighters and back to the car. She stopped and became human again before we approached the parking area. A fire engine idled there, with lights flashing. A firefighter hurried over to us as we emerged from the woods.

"Are you hurt?"

"No." I stepped forward. "We're okay. We ran into the woods to see what was happening, to see if we could help. There were some trees burning. Our friend—"

"At the hospital. I radioed for an ambulance, but

the guy wouldn't wait, put your friend in the backseat and left." The firefighter shook his head and grimaced. "She's bad off."

The reality of Sheila's injuries started to sink in. I swallowed hard.

"Is she going to be okay?" I asked, fighting the rising panic.

His forehead creased. "I'm not a doctor. But those were bad burns. Did you see anyone else in the woods?"

Newt spoke. "Yes—I saw two people, running away from the fire." He gave clear descriptions of the two remaining Salamanders, the one I'd called Surfer (shaggy blond hair, mid-twenties) and Mr. Average (middle-aged, dark hair, clean shaven).

The firefighter got out his radio and repeated the descriptions, then took down our names and contact information.

As soon as he let us go, I ran to the car and snapped Carson into his seat. He woke up and started to fuss, but we had no time. We had to get to the hospital *now*.

Chapter Twelve

The drive to Ashland Community Hospital only took eight minutes. Walking in almost seemed like a flashback: I'd never been to an emergency room before and now found myself at two in one week. My hands shook as I pried Carson from his car seat and we all rushed in. Carson fussed slightly and I knew he needed to nurse, but I shoved the pacifier in his mouth, bounced him on my shoulder, and hoped he could wait.

Tim paced back and forth in the waiting room and shot anxious glances at the swinging doors to the patient area.

"How is she?"

Tim tightened his lips before answering. "They're assessing. Critical burns. She's sedated so they can remove her shirt, clean and dress her arm. The doctor said he'd be out when they're done. She'll be hospitalized, maybe for weeks. Physical therapy to have full use of her hand. They're talking about flying her up to the burn center in Portland."

"Oh my God." I sank down into a chair and Eliza sat down next to me. She put her arm around me in silent commiseration. I swallowed past the lump in my throat.

Newt's face was pale under his freckles. "She's actually lucky." When we all looked at him, he dropped his voice and continued. "If they'd been more skilled at different types of flame, she'd be...I'm glad they weren't more powerful."

I couldn't find my voice.

Eliza asked, "That purple fire? Is that what you mean? What *was* that?"

Newt pulled a chair out of line to face us; Tim stood and watched the double doors, though I thought he listened.

"That's..." he paused and shrugged before continuing. "I guess it's not a state secret or anything. Skilled Salamanders can craft special fire. The purple flames burn only flesh. I used it to attack the others without burning down the forest."

"I've never heard of that," Eliza said.

"It's not common. Most Salamanders can't make it."

"But regular flame, can it hurt you? I saw..." I faltered at the memory of Newt's body consumed by a fireball.

Newt shook his head. "Not me. I can absorb it. Some can't."

Eliza looked at Newt with a very odd expression. After a moment, I decided it was respect. Even admiration.

Carson squawked loudly and jolted me back to awareness of his immediate needs. I nursed him as we waited to hear from Sheila's doctor.

Nearly an hour later, the double doors swung forcefully open and a middle-aged man wearing blue scrubs strode through. His gaze went immediately to Tim, then took in the rest of our group with a quick glance. We all jumped to our feet as he approached.

"Sheila's stabilized for now," he said. "We

removed the cloth from the wounds and dressed them. She's on IV fluids and antibiotics to prevent infection. She will be in a lot of pain when she wakes up, so we also started her on a painkiller. We need to transport her to the burn center in Portland for further care. Her burns are considered critical: third degree burns over nine percent of her body, encompassing her front and back of her shoulder, arm, and right hand. The hand is what we need to watch most carefully—if the skin heals improperly or scars too much, she could lose normal function. Most likely, the burn center will keep her inpatient for several weeks, after which she'll require intense physical therapy. Depending on how the hand heals or scars, she may need surgical procedures to remove some of the dead skin, but we hope to prevent that—that's why the best place for her is the burn center. We also need to watch for infection, but the prophylactic antibiotics will lower that risk."

The doctor's voice was kind, though clinical, and I found myself staring through his wire-framed glasses into his blue eyes, hoping to see some reflection of good news. Tears leaked down my face.

Tim cleared his throat and blinked several times. When he spoke, his voice came out steady. "Can we see her?"

The doctor assessed the four of us, five if Carson counted. "Two at a time," he said. "She's still sedated, but she'll wake up soon. She'll be in significant pain, she may be groggy from the narcotics, and she might be confused. It's vital you don't touch her bandages; the wounds need to remain sterile."

Tim looked at me. I nodded and handed Carson over to Eliza. Tim and I followed the doctor back into the patient area as he spoke.

The doctor continued, "Mercy Flights—that's the transport service—will be ready to transport her in about an hour. One person can accompany her."

Tim's eyes asked the question.

"You go," I said. "We'll follow by car."

He took a relieved breath. "Thank you."

When we stepped into the room with Sheila, I started sobbing in earnest, then tried to silence my crying so I didn't make her feel even worse. Gauzy bandages covered the entire right side of her body, from neck to waist. They had the head of her bed raised slightly and her arm—so thickly bandaged it looked like three arms—was elevated. An IV line ran into her left arm—the unburned one—near the wrist. All the color had drained from her face and lips until her skin nearly matched the white hospital bed. Even her blonde hair looked pale. A hospital gown covered the parts of her not bandaged, in turn overlain with a white sheet tucked around her legs. Her chest rose and fell, the only sign of life.

Immediately, Tim fell to his knees by the side of the bed and clutched her non-bandaged hand. Both of his dark hands wrapped around her slender fingers—as if he could pour energy, life, color back into her.

I blew my nose and dabbed my eyes with a tissue from the box conveniently located in the room. After I composed myself, I moved to stand next to Tim. I put my hand on her forehead, smoothing away an errant strand of hair.

Sheila's eyelids twitched.

Tim said, "We're here, Sheila. You're going to be okay." He kept repeating platitudes in a low, warm voice until her eyes came open.

She worked her mouth and closed her eyes again. A weak frown passed over her forehead and she looked at us again.

"Tim? Jules?"

"Yes. You're okay, sunshine."

I glanced at Tim, surprised by the nickname. I put my hand on Sheila's shoulder and said, "We're all here, Sheila, and they're taking good care of you."

"What...happened?"

Tim squeezed her hand. "You have some burns, some bad burns. But we're in the hospital and they're taking good care of you."

"My arm. Can't move it. Hurts."

"You're all bandaged up, sweetie. They're going to send you up to the burn center in Portland for the best treatment they have and you're going to be just fine," I said.

Her eyes opened wide in alarm and she moved her head slightly, trying to shake it. "No. Want to stay here."

"No, sunshine, you really need to go to the burn center."

"How. Bad?"

Tim and I shared a look and silently agreed.

"Bad, Sheila. It's pretty bad. You need to be in the hospital for a while. But everything should heal up fine, as long as you listen to the doctors and do your physical therapy and everything." I squeezed her shoulder.

"But." Sheila's lips were dry and started to crack. She tried to swallow.

"Hold on, sweetie, I'll get you some water." I stuck my head out the door and attracted a nurse who gave me permission to give Sheila a drink. The nurse also bustled into the room and checked Sheila's vitals, asked about her pain level, and said the doctor would be in soon. The nurse adjusted a dial on the IV to increase her pain medication.

Sheila took a small sip of water and a few ice chips during the nurse's ministrations. As soon as we were alone in the room again, she said, "Where's my phone?"

I found it in a stack of her possessions and held it up in her view.

"Call Tessa White. Tell her to come. Tell her everything."

A glance showed me Tim knew no more than I.

"Who's Tessa White? Sheila?"

Sheila's eyes fluttered shut again, perhaps because of the remnants of the sedative, perhaps the increased dose of painkiller. She rallied enough to say, "Coven in Salem. She can help."

Her eyes opened wide and she gazed wildly at Tim. "Don't call Mom. Yet."

A minute later, she slipped back into sleep.

"Why doesn't she want us to call her mom?" I asked. "She made me call after my house burned down."

Tim spread his hands to profess ignorance.

"Do I call this Tessa White?"

"Definitely. I'll wait until we're at the burn center to call her mom," Tim said. "Maybe I'll have more information by then."

A coven in Salem, Oregon. Was that some kind of Witch joke? I dialed the number and made a conscious effort not to pace while the phone rang.

"Second Sight Bookstore, can I help you?"

"Uh." I regrouped. "Is Tessa White there?"

"Yes, who shall I say is calling?"

"My name is Julie Hall. I'm friends with Sheila Martin."

"Hold on, please."

There was a pause, during which I heard faint strains of new age music.

"Hello, this is Tessa." The voice sounded—was there a feminine equivalent for avuncular? Because the tone of her voice evoked visions of the archetypal favorite aunt: a kind, doting voice that invited confidence and always had fresh-baked chocolate chip cookies.

"Hi. My name is Julie, Julie Hall and I'm good friends with Sheila Martin. Sheila told me to call you. She's, uh, had an accident?"

Tessa's voice sharpened, not in anger, but as if she'd put down knitting needles and given me her full attention.

"What happened?"

"She's in the hospital with critical burns over nine percent of her body—her right hand and arm and shoulder. It was from Salamanders?" I added the last with some hesitation, but Tessa responded with an emphatic sound, so I knew she understood. "The doctors here want to fly her up to the burn center in Portland, but—"

"Rightly so. I'll meet her there."

"Um, okay. Tim Rogers, her, uh, boyfriend, is flying up with her in the transport plane. They're leaving here within the hour."

I hung up the phone and told Tim, "She'll meet you

at the hospital in Portland."

"I heard."

"Do you think she can help?"

"She wouldn't come otherwise, right?"

We quickly stopped talking as the doctor knocked lightly on the door and walked in. After checking on Sheila, he told us Mercy Flights would be ready to transport her soon.

We both thanked him before he left the room.

****

When I walked out into the waiting room, Eliza and Newt sat sideways in their chairs facing each other. They paused in the middle of an animated conversation. Eliza stood, her arms full of Carson, somehow the picture of grace even when she made such a sudden move. Newt's face lost its characteristic trace of smile as he turned anxiously to me.

"How is she?" asked Eliza.

"Okay, I guess." I reached out for Carson, who cooed in excitement at the sight of me. "She was awake for a while, but she's dozing again now. They're flying her up to the burn center in half an hour. She asked me to call—" I looked around, suddenly aware of others in the waiting room. Choosing my words with care, I continued, "Her 'aunt Tessa' who's part of her, uh, sorority and might be able to help."

They both looked puzzled, then Newt broke into an eye-crinkling smile. "Oh, her *sorority*."

Eliza said, "I didn't know her sorority had a local branch."

"Her aunt Tessa lives in Salem, about four hours away, closer to Portland. She'll meet Tim and Sheila at the burn center." I took a seat across from the two of them and leaned as close as possible.

"Newt?" I said, trusting my low tone would keep the conversation private. "What did that tattoo mean?"

"They're Eclipsers." Newt's quiet voice matched mine. "A faction of Salamanders—you can think of them like a cult—who believe the solar eclipse in December will have severe negative consequences for us. This year will see the longest total eclipse in a hundred years and they're worried it will drain our powers."

"For good? Or while it happens?" I asked.

"For good."

"Is there any basis to that belief?" Eliza asked. "Any historical precedent?"

Newt shrugged and scrunched his freckled nose. "Hard to say. Certainly 'Manders are greatly weakened during an eclipse itself—much as your powers wane with the moon—but these Eclipsers have their own interpretation of oral history. They believe we've lessened over the centuries, that each total eclipse causes a demonstrated permanent loss of our abilities."

"Are there many who believe that?"

"Not openly. But maybe in secret."

"But how does this relate to Carson?" I asked.

"I'm not exactly sure, but my guess is the birth of such a strong Were makes them anxious Weres will gain power during the eclipse, at the expense of Salamanders. Some of our people—both Salamanders and Weres—think about our powers as a constant tug of war. Sun versus moon. I think we're more like complements, yin and yang."

Newt's gaze rested on Eliza as she spoke, but his words held no rancor. Eliza raised both eyebrows and nodded thoughtfully.

The strong Were in question, my baby, cooed happily while bouncing on my knees and didn't seem like much of a threat to anyone. I sighed and looked at the clock on the wall.

"Do you two want to go see Sheila before she's transported? Take turns?" I asked.

Eliza went first. I watched her disappear, long legs striding with confidence across the floor, back straight as a ballerina, fawn-colored ponytail swinging. I didn't know if her grace was due to being a Were, or if it was just her. I turned to speak to Newt.

"So," I said, then paused. "Seems like you and Eliza made up, anyway."

"Yes." Newt turned a serious face to me. "I'm really sorry about Sheila."

"Yeah. Me too."

We sat in companionable silence. I wasn't quite sure what went through Newt's mind, but I couldn't stop thinking how this was all my fault. Sheila jumped into a fight meant for me and now...

"She did really well, you know, held her own against them. I think she stopped focusing on the fight," Newt's voice dropped to a murmur, "and was working a spell to call rain when that woman attacked her."

I nodded. Sounded like Sheila.

"I'm sorry I wasn't there sooner to protect her."

I sighed. "Me, too. I mean, I'm sorry I wasn't there. You were busy fighting and putting out fires."

Carson was restless, so I walked him around the waiting room. A few minutes later, Eliza came out and told us Sheila still slept. Tim wouldn't leave her side, but Newt went in for a visit.

When Newt came out again, he walked over to me, as I bounced Carson in the corner.

"So tell me about this Were," he said.

With a start, I realized he didn't know anything about Dave Blythe or his brother Tony.

"It's a long story," I said.

Newt cocked an eyebrow at me and made a gesture to indicate we had time.

"Okay. Well, I guess it all started last winter when Carson's father Mac was murdered. After I found out a few months ago, Eliza and I headed to Vegas to try to see if we could figure out what happened. Not just for revenge, but also because the enemies were after me and Carson, too. They also killed another Were from Eliza's pack—a council investigator sent to look into Mac's murder. We discovered Dave Blythe from the Greybull pack had allied with the mafia and exposed secrets about Werewolves to the humans. The mafia tried to use bone marrow from the Weres to turn regular humans—their people—into Weres. They wanted Carson because he was so powerful and they hoped for better results from his bone marrow. That's where we met Tim; he was another council investigator on the same case. Sheila came to help us—that's when the two of them started dating."

I stopped and looked at Newt. "I'm not sure this is making much sense. This is the really abridged version."

"Enough sense I can follow it. So what happened to Dave?"

"The council executed him. Even though he was just a pup—just seventeen." I sat quiet for a minute. "I wasn't there, of course, but Eliza told me about what happened at the council. And about the execution. I—we should have been able to do something for him before it came to that. He was really troubled."

"So this Tony is his older brother?"

"Yes. But Tony left the pack about five years ago after a family tragedy ended with both their parents dead."

"Wait. Their parents died and Tony ran off and left Dave alone? At, what, the age of twelve?"

"No, Dave stayed with his older sister. She's a dark moon, though, not a Were."

Newt's freckles creased in concentration as he tried to figure that one out. He looked at me for confirmation and I nodded.

"Yeah, the sister had a different father—a human—that was part of what destroyed the whole family. Another long story."

"Tony has lived as a wolf ever since?"

"As far as we know," I said. "And I guess now he's back for revenge."

Newt let out a long, low whistle and shook his head.

After a minute, we moved back to the others, sat down, and waited for Sheila's transport to Portland.

Chapter Thirteen

Sheila's house seemed overly empty, even with me, Carson, Newt, and Eliza trying to fill in the silence. We arrived home at nearly eight, which seemed weird any way I looked at it: hard to believe we lost most of the day in the hospital, and yet I was so weary, our encounter with the Salamanders seemed to have taken place a week ago. Since Carson fell asleep on the way home, I put him into bed without even changing him into pajamas. I think he picked up on some of the strain and weariness of the group, because he had spent the last two hours being an incredibly cranky baby. Good thing he was cute.

Newt volunteered to cook dinner, so our trip home encompassed a quick stop at the food co-op. He brought his purchases into the kitchen as soon as we arrived and firmly shooed Eliza and me to the living room. Twenty minutes later, he called us in to what seemed—at least to culinary-challenged me—a veritable feast: fresh angel hair pasta tossed with garlic shrimp and broccoli in a creamy sauce. He also opened a bottle of pinot gris and poured us each a glass.

"After the day we had, I figure we deserve a glass of wine." Newt raised his glass with Eliza and I following suit. "To Sheila."

We murmured agreement and toasted together.

I ate a tremendous amount of pasta and drank only

two glasses of wine, but still felt a mild buzz by the end of dinner—just that hazy, warm-around-the-edges feeling that wine sometimes brings.

That's my only excuse for not noticing the wolf right away.

Eliza had excused herself right after dinner to take the first sleep shift, since she stayed up most of the previous night. She cast several long looks back at us on her way out of the kitchen, and I could tell she didn't want to leave the companionable group, but prudence won and she climbed the stairs. She'd been sleeping in the hall, in wolf form, and I imagined her curling up, sinking her nose into her paws, and falling fast asleep. Newt and I sat in the kitchen for a long time, finishing the last halves of those second glasses of wine and chatting about everything—movies, books, food—anything not related to Weres, Salamanders, Witches, or danger.

Finally, Newt stretched and said he was going to call the Salamander master to report more fully than he managed earlier in the day. I nodded and moved to do the dishes—only fair, since Newt had been our chef. After cleaning up, I decided to take out the garbage, since the smell of garlic and shrimp still filled the kitchen in a way that wasn't unappetizing now, but might be really gross in the morning.

I hoisted the trash bag and let myself out the back door. The waxing gibbous moon hadn't risen yet so only the light from the kitchen and one of the neighbor's side windows lessened the dark night. I paused on the steps to let my eyes adjust, then walked down the side of the house to the trash cans.

He rose to his feet as I approached. I saw his eyes

first, reflecting amber in the dark, then took in the black bulk of him standing mere feet from me.

I froze, all except for my heart, which galloped like crazy. The garbage bag slipped from my fingers and landed on the ground with a thump. I took a step backward, then another, at each moment expecting him to attack.

Instead, he sat down and watched me.

I stopped about fifteen feet away, halfway between him and the back door. My heart began to fall back into a normal rhythm, though every muscle in my body still screamed with tension. I stared at him. He blinked.

"What do you want?"

He didn't answer, of course, and I felt like a switch flipped inside of me from terror to anger.

"What do you want? What? Are you going to kill me? Kill me already." With no pre-thought, I closed part of the distance between us. My hands extended in frustration and only the neighbors kept me from yelling.

One of the wolf's ears twitched. I wanted to smack him.

"Listen, *Tony*." The wolf lifted his muzzle, lips curling slightly. "I've had a long day. My best friend is in the hospital and may never be able to use her right hand again. If you're here to take revenge, just do it now. Before anyone else gets hurt because of me."

As I spoke, I realized the words were true. The thought gave me some sort of peace and I pulled back my shoulders, waiting for the Were to lunge—surely, he'd attack now.

The night was dark, even though my eyes adjusted as much as possible for a human. Against the blackness, shadow crept in, a dense and roiling mass obscuring even those amber eyes. Then slowly, slowly, as if protesting, the heavy darkness dropped back and revealed a man.

He straightened. The light caught his face, a paler oval in the night, where deep-set eyes still reflected honey-brown. Dark hair coursed roughly down past his shoulders in tangled waves, matched by a long and uneven beard that should have looked awful, but instead increased his look of utter wildness. He was tall and lean, with a wiry musculature that echoed the wolf, as did his stance of alert readiness. He wore jeans ripped at the knees and tattered at the bottoms and a dark-colored t-shirt worn to shapelessness, tight at his shoulders and falling loose around his waist. His feet were bare. I wasn't a wolf, but I could somehow smell him—not the scent of soap, shampoo, or cologne, but a deeper, earthier scent that seemed to pull at me.

I swallowed hard through a blocked throat.

He didn't say anything, just stood there and looked at me, his face like a mask except for those startling eyes.

"Well?" I snapped, finally.

"I—" The man stopped and considered. "I do not intend to hurt you."

I actually laughed.

"Really? Well, you and your friends have been doing an awfully good job of it anyway."

His teeth flashed in the light and I braced myself so as not to flinch.

"Not my friends."

The back door crashed open behind me and I jumped.

Eliza and Newt, of course. Eliza loomed in wolf

form, hackles raised and teeth glinting. A deep growl crawled through the night. One step behind her and to the side, Newt stood with his hands wreathed in purple flame.

In front of me, the Were's expression didn't change. He slowly raised his hands, palms facing us in the universal gesture.

Newt broke the silence first. "What's going on here? What—?"

"I'm not sure. He says he doesn't want to hurt me. Us, I guess. And the Salamanders—the Eclipsers—aren't his friends."

"That is true." The Were—Tony, I guess I needed to think of him as Tony—looked at the buff-colored wolf. For the first time, a note of hesitation crept into his voice. "Eliza?"

Eliza stepped through shadow and emerged. "Yes." They studied each other before she continued. "What's going on, Tony? Where have you been? Everyone thought you died or truly turned wolf. Why *are* you here and why now, if not to take revenge?"

An expression crossed Tony's face too fast for me to catch it. He looked at me and my stomach leapt.

"I heard about Dave. What he did. What happened to him. I wanted to see—" He inclined his head in my direction.

I rubbed my forehead and pushed my curls behind my ears. I had a hard time looking at Tony for some reason, so I addressed the night air instead. "I'm sorry about your brother. I wish they hadn't—I wish there'd been some other way—I—"

He interrupted as my words petered out. "Dave was my responsibility and I abandoned him. My fault and no other."

Eliza spoke up, suddenly, and I jumped, almost as if I forgot anyone else were present. "The pack failed him, Tony."

"The pack didn't run away, forsaking everything and everyone, and try to drown its troubles in the wilderness. That was me."

I opened my mouth and closed it again. Tony's words weren't highly inflected, yet they carried a pain that silenced me. I wished Sheila could come lighten the mood somehow with one of her dramatic gestures. Actually, I just wanted Sheila—the memory of her pale face as the paramedics rolled her onto the plane lay close to the surface of my thoughts. I wasn't sure how much longer I could sustain this emotional intensity. I swallowed hard and felt my temples throb with a headache.

"Are all Weres this hung up on arguing who's at fault?" Newt struck a patently relaxed pose and started to juggle small balls of purple fire. "'Cause it seems to me we could stand out here and entertain the neighbors for hours with 'It was my fault,' 'No, my fault,' 'No, my fault.' Can we agree *Dave* was primarily at fault and move on? Preferably inside? Since we're not about to kill each other."

Eliza looked quickly at the neighboring townhouses, as if re-aware of our surroundings.

My words came slowly. "But were you?"

Everyone turned to me and I lifted my gaze to meet Tony's. I forced the words through a suddenly dry mouth. "Trying to kill me. Were you trying to kill me?"

His amber gaze held mine and I saw his mouth relax, move into a near smile.

"No," he said, his voice resonant in the darkness. "I saved your life."

Chapter Fourteen

We settled in the living room. I listened at the bottom of the stairs for Carson, but he slept soundly. Newt offered to make a pot of tea and disappeared into the kitchen. I sat in the rocking chair and tried not to be too obvious as I studied Tony. After a slight hesitation, Tony chose the armchair and settled himself into it gingerly.

"You've really been wolf for five years, yet not turned wolf completely?" Eliza leaned forward from her seat on the couch and fixed Tony with her full attention.

When he nodded, she shook her head slowly. "I'm...amazed you could come back."

"So am I. It feels," he lifted one shoulder, "strange."

"Is that why—" I stopped as both the Weres focused on me. A flush raced up my neck and I hoped no one noticed.

"Why what?" Eliza asked.

"Your eyes. Are they still part wolf?" I darted a look at those amber eyes, somehow dark, yet full of honey.

Eliza's brow wrinkled, then she snorted a laugh. "Nope, just Tony's eyes. Some Weres' eyes change between forms, some don't."

"Oh." Even my ears felt like they blushed and I

fought it down, tried to play it off as insignificant. "Just wondering."

Newt came into the room with mugs of chamomile tea for everyone and said, brightly, "So what'd I miss?"

The room felt somehow lighter with him there and some of the tension left my shoulders.

Newt took a seat next to Eliza, who said, "Not much. Tony's been in wolf form for the last five years, and I mentioned I was surprised he hadn't lost himself completely."

"Become a wolf in truth, you mean?"

"Yes. We refer to it as turning wolf. It happens."

Tony said, "Some of the packs I encountered assumed that was the case—that I'd turned wolf. They were kind to me."

Eliza nodded. "Of course they were."

"That's how you found out about what happened? From another pack?" I asked.

"Yes. I overheard them discussing Dave."

I broke our shared glance as he continued.

"I am deeply apologetic and shamed on behalf of my brother and my family. I—" He paused, and his expression displayed his search for words. "I wasn't ready to go back to Greybull, but after a while, I realized I slowly travelled in this direction. I wanted to see the pup, Mac's pup."

With a start, I remembered Tony and Mac had been friends—childhood friends and rivals, two of the full moon Weres in Greybull.

"He was a good Were," said Tony, now entirely focused on me. "He would have taken good care of you and your son."

I knew he meant it kindly. Or perhaps kindly

wasn't the word, but he didn't mean to give offense. Nonetheless, I felt myself straightening in my chair.

"I know I'm just a human." I paused and made sure no bitterness leaked into my voice. "But I am doing my best to take care of Carson. I do appreciate your help in waking us up on the night of the fire." I inclined my head to Tony formally.

He lifted an eyebrow and glanced at Eliza, who looked exasperated.

"Just ignore it, Tony."

But he didn't. He leaned forward in his chair. "You, mere human, stood in the wilderness and dared me to attack you. Ran into the woods in the middle of a fight to warn your friends about me." He ticked off points on his fingers. "Hunted murderers in Las Vegas. Faced the mafia. And—are you fleeing right now? Have I interrupted plans for you to run away and leave your friends here to deal with the Salamanders?"

"No," I said, stung, then realized I furthered his argument.

"So." He leaned back and folded his arms. "What I meant was: I am sorry my brother robbed you of Carson's father and your lover."

"Mac and I broke up." The blood rushed hotly to my face again and I took a deep breath over my tripping tongue. "I mean, Mac and I had broken up a long time ago. Before I even knew I was pregnant. We didn't work out as a couple. He was—I mean—I—actually, he didn't even know about Carson, which was all my fault. I didn't tell him."

Shut up, Julie. I closed my mouth against the wild babbling. What was *with* me tonight?

I wished I could read Tony's expression.

"Anyway. Um—excuse me, I think I hear Carson. I'll be right back."

I escaped up the stairs to regain my composure and check on my baby. Only after I reached the bedroom did I remember the two Weres knew it'd been an utter lie. Their hearing was much better than mine. Carson slept quietly.

****

When I came back to the living room, they talked about a safer topic: the Salamanders. Newt was in the middle of explaining Eclipsers to Tony, who nodded.

"I see. They fear the eclipse will upset the paranormal equilibrium, and they believe Carson's strength will tip the balance in favor of the Weres," Tony summarized, then turned to Eliza. "How strong is Carson, in your opinion?"

She spread her hands. "As strong as I've ever known. Calling water at six months old?"

"I agree. To me, he seems much stronger than a full moon Were as a full is to a half moon."

Full moon, waxing moon, half moon, waning moon, crescent moon. What was Carson, then? What were the people always going on about these days, the supermoon? Yeah. A supermoon. Whatever that was. I closed my eyes and wondered how I would handle him as he grew.

"Have they talked about containing his powers?"

My eyes flew open at Tony's question. "What do you mean? Eliza? What does he mean?"

"Calm down, Julie. No, Tony, not yet."

"Not yet what? What does he mean 'containing his powers'?" I said. Once again, the Weres kept something from me.

157

"Julie, remember before Dave's trial, I said the council could strip him of his powers instead of killing him?"

"The council could strip Carson's powers?" I jumped out of my chair and only realized I yelled when Eliza stood to face me.

"The council could strip his powers— temporarily—until he's older, until he can control himself better. They could reverse the process when he's older. Probably. But no one's talked about that yet. At least, I don't think they have. So just calm down, Julie."

"Probably? You mean they might not give his powers back. He's done nothing wrong. He's not a threat to anyone. He's just a baby."

Tony cut in. "He is just a baby—a baby who can call water and turn into a wolf. Who knows what power he'll demonstrate next? I'm concerned for his own safety."

I turned on him in fury, then lost my voice as he stood up and took half a step toward me. He held out one hand in my direction. "Julie," he said and I realized it was the first time he said my name. "I just asked the question. I wasn't recommending a course of action. No one's tried to do this—to temporarily strip someone's powers—for generations. The council wouldn't risk it unless they were sure of re-investing his powers when he's closer to maturity. Unless, he posed a real threat to his own safety."

I shoved my hands into my pockets and felt the adrenaline melt away.

"Sorry," I mumbled.

I took my seat and picked up my tea, now rather

cold, but the drink gave me something to focus on.

Eliza watched me. I gave her a half-smile and a shrug, then retreated behind my mug.

"On another note, I didn't have a chance to tell you about my conversation with the master," said Newt. I shot him a thankful look. He smiled back at me, with his freckles gleaming like copper. "I need to stay here and hunt the Eclipsers. I won't be able to go to Portland with you. I hope you'll give Sheila my best, though?"

I nodded. Eliza frowned, then slowly said, "That makes sense, I suppose, although the Eclipsers may follow us north."

"In that case, I'll be right behind them and I'll meet you there. The master's worried others will join the two Eclipsers we know about—the two still alive—so he's sending reinforcements of our own. They'll be here on Friday."

I had to do some mental calculations before I realized today was Wednesday. Two days 'til we could expect the other Salamanders.

"Great." Eliza lengthened the word into two syllables and rolled her eyes. "More Salamanders, just what we need."

Newt flashed her a grin, hearing the joking tone behind the words—words once filled with disgust.

"Well," he said, mock-modestly, "they won't all be as strong as I am, but I'm sure they'll do their best."

I snorted.

Tony followed our exchanges with a frown and I wondered if it was hard for him to catch all the interpersonal dynamics, after living so long as a wolf.

My cell phone rang and I jumped to rummage in my purse for it.

"Tim," I said, after swiping the screen. "Hello? How is she?"

Tim's voice sounded weary—a token of utter exhaustion, since I knew he usually achieved an even-keel demeanor no matter what the circumstances. I heard ambient noises behind him: someone talking, a beeping sound, the rattle of what was probably a cart moving down the hospital hall. I closed my eyes and listened to feel closer to Sheila.

"She's doing better. She's stable and on a lot of painkillers. Hopefully tomorrow, she'll be more of her normal self and able to talk to you. The facilities here are pretty amazing—top notch."

"What about Tessa White? She's there?"

"Yes, she was waiting for us when we arrived."

"Can she heal her?" I held my breath after asking the question.

"Not exactly." There was an odd catch in Tim's throat and he cleared his voice before continuing. "Tessa can't heal the injuries completely—witchcraft is more subtle than that—but she says she can aid the natural process and prevent Sheila's hand from losing normal function."

I fought against the wave of disappointment that passed through me. Finally, I said, "Well, that's good, anyway."

"Yes. It is." He paused slightly before continuing. "It's quite good. There are a lot of burn patients here and—from what I've seen…if Tessa can prevent some of the deep scarring and help the doctors, that will be—huge."

I held the phone so tightly my hand hurt, so I forced my fingers to loosen. I rubbed my forehead. Tim continued to talk, explaining Sheila would be in the burn center for at least three weeks and he planned to stay in Portland. He called the council to explain what happened and they granted him leave; Eliza should expect a call of her own soon to discuss the situation.

"Here, why don't you tell Eliza the details?" I said. "Um. Thanks for being there with her, Tim. We'll see you tomorrow, okay?"

"Thanks for—I know she's your best friend. So thanks."

"Yeah, she is. But she's your…" I couldn't find the right word. "Um, okay, see you tomorrow."

I handed the phone to Eliza.

"Hi, Tim," she said. "Listen, before you tell me whatever it is about the pack council, I need to tell you: we made contact with Tony Blythe and he's on our side."

Tim said something sharp on the other end of the phone, but Eliza lifted a hand and interrupted him.

"No, I'm sure. He's not in league with the Eclipsers. He heard about what happened with Dave and the story drew him here to see Carson. Julie too, I suppose." Eliza listened to Tim for a minute. "Yes, I do believe him. Okay, now tell me about the council."

I glanced sidelong at Tony and watched him under my lashes as Eliza finished her conversation.

To my side, Newt said in a low voice, "What did Tim say about Sheila?"

"Oh, sorry." I forgot he didn't have the Weres' preternatural hearing. "She's stable and he thinks the doctors are very competent. Tessa White is there to help—she can't heal Sheila completely, but at least she can help speed the natural healing and make sure Sheila can use her hand normally. Keep the scarring under control."

Newt nodded, mouth tight. He stood up and bounced on the balls of his feet for a minute, then rolled his shoulders.

I let out a deep breath. I'd been hoping Tessa would waltz in, cast a spell, and heal Sheila's injuries completely, as if they never happened. Most of me hadn't even grasped the enormity of her burns. When I thought about Sheila's arm, about the red and black flesh, about the pain lines on her face, the images seemed unreal. I was grateful witchcraft could help at all, I really was. I told myself that several times.

A yawn caught me unexpectedly and I blinked, eyes watering.

Eliza snapped the phone shut, reached over, and squeezed my arm. "Me, too. We should get some sleep if we're driving up to Portland tomorrow. It's, what, a five-hour drive?"

"Four and a half," I agreed. "Well, maybe longer with Carson."

Tony stood up, uncoiling lithely from the chair. "I will stand watch," he said. "That is, if you trust me."

I shared a glance with Eliza and Newt, who waited for me to give the verdict.

I nodded at Tony. "Thank you," I said and felt rewarded by his mouth curving in a smile. I swallowed hard and looked away, after realizing I stared at his mouth.

"Then tomorrow, while you two," he gestured at me and Eliza, "go to Portland to be with the Witch, I will help the Salamander with the hunt."

Tony stopped short. "But do you think—that is—

before standing watch, may I take a shower?"

****

I curled up in bed next to Carson who breathed deeply as if never damaged from the smoke. Even my human lungs felt easier today, I noticed, as I took a few experimental breaths of my own. Exhaustion overwhelmed me, but my mind wouldn't stop whirling. I thought about Sheila and Tim at the burn center, wondered if Tim would get any sleep tonight, if he'd be able to stay with Sheila, if they'd called her mom. I hadn't thought to ask.

The shower started across the hall. I listened to the white-noise hiss of the water and wondered if it had been five years since Tony took a shower. Five years as a wolf. Five years without human contact. The water ran a long time, while I stared at my dark room, gradually lightening as the waxing moon rose. The bathroom door opened, and I smelled the escaping humid air waft under my door along with the scent of soap. I listened to footsteps down the stairs and across the floor beneath me. I envisioned Tony's bare feet. Finally, I slept.

Chapter Fifteen

Newt and I were in the middle of our bowls of cereal—me on my third cup of coffee—when Eliza strode into the kitchen.

"Listen," she said, and turned on the radio sitting on the counter.

The local NPR station, Jefferson Public Radio.

"Approximately eighty acres west of Jacksonville near the Applegate river. Overnight, firefighters also responded to blazes south of Ashland near Highway 99, and in east Medford near Roxy Ann Peak. There's no official word yet about the causes of the fires or the extent of the damages, but authorities suspect arson. Firefighters have been called in from Klamath and Josephine counties. None of the fires are near containment at this point. Firefighters are focusing efforts on protecting the Grey Gable subdivision in East Medford and property south of Ashland."

Newt's mouth opened in surprise. He started to speak, but I waved him to silence so we could hear the rest of the report.

"In Ashland, Belleview Elementary school is closed due to concerns over smoke and Highway 99 is closed at Tolman Creek Road. No other public school closings have been announced at this time. Motorists in Medford are urged to avoid east McAndrews road and other areas near Roxy Ann Peak. Earlier this morning,

JPR's Melody Lin spoke with Chief Ron LeGrand, head of the Medford fire department."

Again, I held up a hand to indicate I wanted to hear the fire chief's statement. He spoke in a loud voice, nearly shouting over commotion in the background. "We've got good men—and women—on the ground here and hope to have the fire well on the way to containment in the next few hours. This fire came up quicker than most and the hot spots have jumped around, but we have the best firefighters in southern Oregon and I have confidence in our ability to contain the blaze. I ask the public to help by staying well clear of this area and reporting any suspicious activity they may have witnessed in the last twenty-four hours."

The anchor changed subjects, and I crossed to the radio and clicked it off. Carson banged on his high chair, but—for once—I ignored him.

"The Salamanders," I said. Not a question.

"Must be." Newt stood up. "Where's Tony? I need to get out there and help."

Eliza jerked her chin toward the stairs. "He's sleeping on Sheila's bed. I took the last shift early this morning."

The sound of a helicopter overhead nearly drowned out her last words. I yanked open the back door and we all stared at the helicopter, with its huge bucket full of water hanging below. I craned my neck in the direction of the blaze and saw a brownish smudge in the air.

"Holy crap. All this, for what?"

"To flush us out? To force us to bargain with them?" said Eliza.

"Like 'Surrender Dorothy?' " I asked. "Surrender Carson. Is that what they want? Because that's not going to happen."

Eliza looked back into the kitchen and I followed suit. The black wolf stood in the doorway to the living room. As I watched, he pulled on shadows and shifted to human form, a transformation that seemed quicker than last night.

He'd shaved, revealing a strong jawline. I jerked my gaze away from his mouth. Tony still wore the same ratty clothes, though they seemed considerably cleaner and I bet he used the washing machine sometime during the night. His dark brown hair, formerly tangled, was now clean and reached well below his shoulders. Strands curled around his face. He made an impatient face and reached up to pull his hair back.

"Did you sleep as a wolf?" Eliza's sudden question caught me by surprise.

Tony's eyebrows rose.

"Tony. Did you go to sleep as a wolf?" she asked again.

"No."

"But you woke in wolf form?"

He looked at Eliza for a long minute. "I believe there are more urgent things to discuss."

"Tony. Answer the question. Did you change back to wolf form while you slept? Unintentionally?"

The hairs on my arms prickled and I rubbed them before dropping my hands to my sides. I glanced between the two of them, both stretched to their full height. At six foot two or so Tony topped Eliza by a few inches. I wondered which was the stronger Were and if Tony was still considered part of Eliza's pack— the pack where she ranked second in command.

A gust of wind kicked across the backyard through the open kitchen door. I smelled smoke and choked down a fight-flight twitch in my muscles. Tony's hair whipped around his face and he frowned.

"Do you have a hair band or something?" he asked Eliza, whose ponytail hung sleekly behind her as usual.

"Tony."

A muscle in his jaw twitched before he spoke with exaggerated patience. "Eliza, your warning is duly noted. I am not going to lose my human form and turn wolf for good. I will be careful. Thank you for your concern, but I've been on my own for five years and managed quite nicely. Now, if you can't find me something to keep this hair out of my face, hand me a pair of scissors." He jerked his head toward the door. "Clearly, we don't have time to waste."

Eliza held his gaze for another second, then reached into her pocket and pulled out a ponytail holder. He managed to tug his hair back somewhat neatly and used the elastic to secure it, except for some shorter bits that fell out to hang near his chin.

Newt watched the whole scene with an amused expression. When he caught my eye, he winked and murmured, "All Alphas and no one to boss around, huh?"

Both Weres turned to glare at him and he laughed out loud.

"What's the situation?" Tony looked at me when he asked the question.

"The Salamanders started several wildfires—at least three: one in Jacksonville right near where," I faltered for a minute and searched for words that wouldn't inflame anyone, "near where we saw you yesterday, one just south of Ashland, one east of Medford."

"Anyone killed?"

"No." The question threw me for a momentary loop and I spoke my thoughts aloud. "I guess they're just trying to warn us—that they could do more if they wanted. The report said there'd been no loss of property so far. Or lives."

Tony nodded grimly. "Could be worse."

I pushed my own curls behind my ears and had a crazy urge to do the same for Tony. Because those little bits probably bothered him.

"So…is it going to get worse? I mean, are they going to…" I ran out of words and made an ambiguous gesture.

"Yes," said Newt, his voice flat and serious. "That's why we need to stop them. Now."

"Right." Eliza nodded. "Julie, you and Carson have to travel up to Portland alone. I need to stay here and help tackle the Eclipsers. We'll have more Salamanders as reinforcements tomorrow, right, Newt? The council's sending a team of four Weres; I talked to them last night. Julie, tell Sheila—"

I cut Eliza off. "No. We're staying, too. Sheila will be okay. Tim's with her and so is Tessa White. I can't do anything to help her. I can't let you all stay here and fight our fight—me and Carson, *our* fight—without helping."

Even if I wasn't sure what kind of help I could be, I added silently to myself, feeling a bitter twist inside.

I couldn't read Tony's face. Not that he got a vote; I didn't know why I looked at him, anyway.

Eliza sighed. "Okay, Julie. I knew you would say

that. And I definitely know it's not worth arguing with you."

"Nobody changes Julie's mind, once it's set." Newt grinned and I felt the warmth of his smile like a physical presence.

"All right then," I said. "I'm going to call Tim back. You guys talk strategy."

****

When I told Tim about the wildfires and our change in plans, I sensed his tension rise with tightness in his voice. He asked, "Should I come to help?"

His question revealed the torn loyalties he felt, because he asked for my opinion rather than making an executive decision. My response was firm.

"No. You stay with Sheila. She needs you. The council sent four Weres who'll arrive tomorrow—or maybe later this afternoon—and Newt's calling the Salamander master to get the other 'Manders here today if possible. There's no reason you need to come."

"Okay," said Tim, relief clear in his voice.

I got a detailed update on Sheila's condition, promised to call again in a couple of hours, and rejoined the others.

As I walked back into the kitchen, Newt played peek-a-boo with Carson, still in his highchair, and Eliza and Tony disagreed about something. I raised my eyebrows at the Salamander and indicated the Weres with a tilt of my head.

"Not sure what the all-powerful are arguing about," he said with a quirk of the mouth. "Doesn't matter to me, since I know what I'm doing today."

All conversation stopped as both Eliza and Tony turned to him.

"Uh, what are you doing today?" I asked, since someone had to.

"I'll start at the nearest fire and help contain it. Then I'll move to the Medford fire, since that's the closest to a population center. After that, the Applegate fire. If I see the other 'Manders, I'll kill them." His expression was implacable.

Tony studied him for a moment, then gave a sudden laugh. "Well, that's as good a plan as any," he said. "We'll be your support team—and if we find the other Salamanders, you need to promise that you'll share." His slow smile looked very much the wolf and made my stomach jump.

"Okay," said Eliza. She gestured to the kitchen table. "Fuel up, everyone. I'm calling the council to check in."

Tony sat down and devoured three bowls of cereal as if he fought fires and Salamanders every day. I choked down some more cereal and finished my coffee. I thought about another cup, but decided my nerves jangled enough without adding extra caffeine to the picture. Newt stood at the back door and studied the brown haze of smoke on the horizon.

"I'd forgotten how much I like coffee," Tony said, idly swirling a mug in his hand.

"I don't think I could live as a wolf for five years if it meant no coffee," I said.

Tony leaned back in his chair for a moment. "Being a wolf was…relaxing." I couldn't read his eyes, although his gaze was fixed on me. "Not to think. To just be. To follow the rhythm of life without worrying about the lyrics."

I turned the phrase over in my mind.

"Where did you go when you were a wolf?" I asked.

"I ranged north, mostly. All the way up to Alaska, for a while. Canada. I was in Alberta when I heard about Dave."

"In Alberta? They gossip about Greybull pack business in Alberta?" Eliza's voice sounded sharp. "Great. Lily will love hearing that."

Tony shrugged one shoulder. "Pretty big news, Eliza. A couple of Weres turning renegade and allying with the mafia? They probably heard about it in Europe."

"Newt." Tony turned to our Salamander, who still stared out the back door, though I bet he'd heard every word. "How did you get roped into this mission?"

Newt turned around, his freckles catching a glint of sunlight. "I've helped out before, when we've had a 'Mander problem. So has my sister."

"You have a sister?" Tony sounded surprised.

"Yes, a twin, actually."

"Your parents are very lucky," said Tony.

"Actually, they're dead. But you're right; we're lucky."

I looked from Newt to Tony, wondering what I missed.

Eliza said, "Salamanders usually have problems having kids, Julie. Viable offspring are rare, so having twins is especially lucky." She cracked a smile. "Which is a good thing, because Salamander powers are dominant—inherited from just one parent—so if they were really fertile, we'd be swimming in them."

Newt's back stiffened. "It's not much of a joke, watching people miscarry and babies die. Not funny at all."

Immediately, the smile dropped from Eliza's mouth. "I'm sorry, Newt. You're right, of course. I meant no offense."

"Apology accepted," Newt said.

After a minute, he broke the awkward silence in the kitchen. "Anyway, to get back to Tony's original question, the master likes to call on me for touchy situations because I'm likable, in case you hadn't noticed. Even to Werewolves, right?" He grinned at us and raised his eyebrows, dispelling the remaining tension from Eliza's remark.

Eliza snorted. Tony looked taken aback, but then said, "I think your powers are more important than your likability. You've a fair level of skill."

"A 'fair level'? Why, gee, thanks. Do I get a gold star?"

"Yes, yes, gold stars for everyone. Are we done with breakfast? Can we get started already?" I snapped.

Eliza turned worried eyes on me. "You okay, Julie?"

"Of course. I'm just ready to go. We're wasting time."

"Are you sure you don't want to stay here?" Eliza held up a hand to stop me. "Julie, I'm just asking. It might be hard for you to be near the fires, that's all."

"And it won't be hard for you guys? Just for the human?"

There was a pause, during which I saw Eliza attempting to find the right words. Newt spoke first.

"Well, not hard for me. I love fires." He quirked his eyebrows. "Eliza, stop bugging her. She wants to come? She comes. We can use all the help we've got."

Tony stayed silent and just watched me. I didn't know if he thought I would break under the pressure or explode in anger. I wasn't going to do either, of course.

Eliza finally said, "I wanted to make sure you completely thought through your decision, Julie; that's all."

"I have. Thank you for your concern."

"Jules," Newt started, then stopped as I shot a surprised look at him. "Am I allowed to call you Jules? Or is that only for Sheila?"

I shook my head, not even knowing what I meant by the gesture, and then said, "You can. That's fine."

"Okay. Anyway, is Carson coming with us?"

I opened my mouth to say he was, but then paused. "Would he be safe if I left him with someone? Eliza, what do you think?"

"The Salamanders are busy with the fires right now. I don't know. If you leave him behind, none of us can protect him. But if he comes with us, then you're bringing him right into the thick of things, within striking distance of the Salamanders," said Eliza.

"Julie." Tony waited until he had my full attention. I couldn't help wondering if he used my full name on purpose, and if so what that meant. Tony asked, "Do you have a safe place for him to stay?"

"Probably. If anywhere is safe."

Eliza said, "Is Carson still wearing the bracelet Sheila made?"

"Yes! Good point." My mind spun through possibilities and I came to a snap decision. "Okay, I'm not bringing him. Let me make a couple of calls."

****

When I came back to the kitchen twenty minutes

later, I'd arranged to drop Carson off at my friend Dana's *and* managed to pump six ounces of milk for him with the little pump Sheila bought for me. Along with some rice cereal and a banana, that should hold him for a while. I scrounged up a few toys, diapers, and a change of baby clothes, and Eliza and I hopped into Sheila's car to drop him off. Tony and Newt took the rental car and shadowed us. Two vehicles would be better in case we needed to split up to cover the multiple fires.

Drop-off took a bit longer than I hoped, because Dana wanted to assure herself we were really okay. I hadn't seen her since my house burned down and she had about a million questions. I also struggled to convince myself Carson would be safe without one of the mature Weres or our friendly Salamander to protect him. Luckily, he was in a happy mood: sitting up and staring at Dana's baby Ella while I said goodbye to him.

I blinked furiously on the way back to the car, but did not cry.

"Okay." I slammed the door shut and turned to Eliza. "Let's go. Day's a-wasting."

Her dark eyes looked at me for a few seconds, then she started the car.

Chapter Sixteen

We only went three blocks before my cell phone rang. I cursed under my breath and awkwardly fished it out of my pocket. Glancing at it, I saw a private number and frowned before answering.

"Yes?"

"Julie Hall. Next time, we'll set a hotel in flames. A tourist-filled hotel. If you refuse our demands, their deaths will be on your head."

Eliza slammed on the brakes, bringing our car to a stop on the side of the road. She put her hand out the window and gestured for Newt and Tony.

"Who are you? How did you get my number?" I asked. My hands clenched so tight my bones ached and my voice rose.

"Call me Ma'at. Egyptian goddess of balance." The woman's voice had an edge that made me want to rub my ear.

"Goddess? My, you have quite an opinion of yourself for someone who runs around trying to kill innocent people."

"If people are killed, it's by your choice."

"By your hands. Your fire. You would have killed me—and my baby—and we've done nothing to you."

"Your son is an abomination! I don't know what trickeries the wolves used, but a Were baby that strong is not natural. He is abhorrent. He threatens us all."

"He threatens no one. He's six months old." My voice shook with anger.

"He won't live another six months, unless his powers are stripped." The woman's voice dropped to a near whisper. "You have twenty-four hours, Julie Hall. Either the Weres strip his powers or we choose new targets for our fires. Targets that kill. Unless, of course, we find you before then."

The line clicked as she hung up. I looked at my phone as if it could explain this craziness.

"Carson's not an abomination," I said.

Eliza looked through the window at Tony before she answered me. "Of course he's not, Julie."

"He's not! He's just a normal baby! A normal Were baby!"

Again, the two Weres exchanged a look.

"He's *not* an abomination. There's nothing wrong with him."

Eliza squared her shoulders. "Julie, none of us thinks he's an abomination, okay? But he certainly is unusual—more than unusual." She held up a hand to stop me. "I'm *not* saying there's something wrong with him. But he's not just a normal Were baby."

"But no one used any…what did she say? Were trickeries. He was born this way. I didn't even know I was a dark moon. If the Salamanders are so worried about natural balance, well, Carson's part of that—he's a natural, regular Were who happens to be extra powerful. Maybe there's some equally strong baby Salamander out there, to balance him out. If they're so concerned with balance, they need to train their own babies to be powerful."

Newt stood outside my window. He said, "Jules,

Eclipsers are crazy. They're like religious fanatics. You can't reason with them."

"Great."

"I didn't catch everything she said," Newt prompted me.

I repeated the conversation nearly word for word, especially the "abomination" part.

"So we have twenty-four hours and then they start killing people," I concluded.

"I need to call the council," said Eliza. She slid gracefully out of the car and walked several steps away.

"Nice that she's calling herself after a goddess," I said. "Ma'at."

"Makes a certain kind of sense for them to use Egyptian mythology," said Newt. He leaned against my car door and talked through the window, his arms braced on top of the frame. "Re was a sun god, after all."

"Are you descended from him? A sun god?" I asked.

Newt burst into laughter. "Now that would be a good pickup line, wouldn't it?"

I rolled my eyes. "I'm serious. Tim told me Salamanders are descended from some creature that came from the sun or something."

Newt quirked his mouth to one side. "Or something. Who knows, it happened thousands of years ago."

All this time, Tony stood silently at Newt's side, looking at Eliza. In profile, his nose looked slightly too long for his face and I forced myself to focus on that, instead of his cheekbones. His mouth tensed and his eyes narrowed just enough to make faint lines at their corners.

"Tell them that won't work," Tony said. The next moment, he stood beside Eliza and grabbed her arm. She yanked away and shooed him like a fly.

I exchanged a look with Newt, but he held up his hands to express ignorance.

After a few more minutes of intense conversation, Eliza put her phone down and turned on Tony.

"Listen, Tony. You lived as a wolf for five years. You can't waltz back in and order the council around. Or me. Frankly, I worked hard to convince them you were really on our side—and weren't too much wolf to deal with rationally."

Tony abruptly seemed very tall, his fists clenched by his sides. I held my breath. After a very long minute, Tony gave a curt nod and I shot Newt a relieved glance. Newt winked at me.

"Fine," Tony said.

Eliza held his gaze for a moment, before turning to the rest of us. "All right. The council's discussing the situation with the Salamander master right now. They're coordinating a strike on probable Eclipser headquarters in southern California. Reinforcements for us—both types—will arrive later today. Our goal is to find and disable the Eclipsers in Southern Oregon, the ones responsible for the current fires."

"And?" I prompted, knowing there must be more to this plan for Tony to have reacted so strongly.

Eliza's eyes looked nearly black as she spoke. "If we can't stop them today, the council's taking Carson into their custody."

"What? What does that mean?"

"They will protect him, Julie. Not—anything else."

"Bullshit," Tony said.

I swung to him. "Then what? What does it mean, Tony?"

"They're considering it. The council might strip his powers. *That's* what it means. They want Carson readily available to them."

"Eliza?" I asked, begging for the truth.

She chose her words carefully. "Julie, they didn't say anything about stripping Carson's powers, just that the full power of the council Weres may be needed to adequately protect him." She looked at Tony, then back to me, before speaking again, reluctance clear in her voice. "It's possible, though. It's possible."

"Well, they can't take him. They have no legal right. I won't let the council have him. I *won't.*"

"I agree," said Tony. "We can't negotiate with the Salamanders. We can't give in to their demands and we can't do anything that might harm our most powerful Were."

I sucked in a quick breath at his last words. He was right, of course. Carson was the most powerful Were. I just wasn't used to considering him in those terms: as a potential asset to the whole community of Werewolves.

"Well." Newt drawled out the word to at least two syllables, gathering all of our attention. "We stop the Eclipsers right now, right here, while the others raid their headquarters. Then we don't need to worry about their twenty-four-hour ultimatum."

"Yes," said Eliza. I thought she sounded not just determined, but also relieved—probably happy to have a course of action with no conflict of loyalties.

I wondered if the council agreed on what to do with Carson—had the entire council discussed it? Or the inner council? One hundred and eleven packs across the country meant one hundred and eleven pack Fulls who liked to throw around their power and lead their own Werewolves. That was a lot of strong Weres to wrangle into agreement, even to get a simple majority. More probably, the inner council was in control, the elite group of twelve Weres who made most of the real decisions. I knew any twenty percent of the representatives could demand a whole council vote. Perhaps even now factions within the council argued about whether Carson's powers should be stripped. Or maybe everyone agreed. But if so what had they resolved?

"Newt?" I paused for a minute, not sure if I wanted to bring this up, but then continued with the words tripping over each other on their way out. "Why are you doing this? Why are you on our side? Why is the Salamander master working with the Weres against your own kind? Even if they have some wacky ideas? I mean, why are you—all of you Salamanders—working to protect Carson?"

Newt's face turned serious. "First of all, no Salamanders who use their powers to kill or hurt innocents are 'my kind.' Second, some of us believe Salamanders and Weres should be allies. We're alike in many ways, you know. We should work together— focus our strength to fight the things out there that want to devour us all, Weres, 'Manders, and humans alike."

"Devour—what—" I started, then shook my head. "Forget it—I'm not even asking. I don't want to know right now."

"Good idea. Let's focus on the present fight," Newt said. "Besides, I forgot the most important reason. I like you guys. Plus, I like testing my skills."

I smiled at him. "No offense meant, you know. With the question."

"None taken."

Tony watched our exchange with an intent expression that made me flush slightly. I turned away from him to hide my face.

"Allies," said Eliza. A note in her voice sounded suspiciously like embarrassment and I remembered her earlier derisive comments about firebugs.

"Hell, yeah, wolf." Newt raised his hand and waited. Eliza chuckled and high-fived him. "So let's go get those Eclipsers."

Chapter Seventeen

Tackling the closest blaze first, we drove to the intersection of Tolmon Creek Road and Siskiyou Boulevard, the main drag they'd closed because of the fire. We parked at Belleview Elementary School, where classes had been cancelled for the day. Police blockaded the road just past the school, with their cars parked near those white-striped orange barrels used in construction. One officer stood waving people to the detour.

I touched the bracelet still tied on my left wrist and mentally urged on that don't-notice-me spell. Then I checked the gun I'd shoved in my jacket pocket. I didn't need a jacket in this weather, of course, but I needed to conceal the weapon somehow and didn't want to rely on the spell. Especially since it was Sheila's gun, not mine, and I didn't exactly have a permit to carry it around. Which wouldn't be a problem, because we were going avoid attracting the notice of anyone official, I told myself.

Tony, Eliza, and Newt had no need for weapons. They *were* weapons.

We parked in the corner of the lot, making it fairly easy to walk the edge of the school fields and bypass the police officers, who weren't focused on pedestrian traffic, anyway. Eliza called on the moon and pulled shifting shadows around us, just to make extra sure we escaped detection. We walked in the tree line just off the road, crossing people's gravel driveways every so often. The air started to get heavier and we were close enough that the smoke burned my lungs.

"How many acres did they say were burning?" I asked.

"Nearly a hundred, last I heard," said Eliza.

Of course, I didn't have much concept of the size of an acre. But the smoke pouring into the sky and the massive array of fire trucks on the site proved this was a considerable fire.

An airplane droned overhead, low enough to make my heart race, and passed us on its way to the fire.

Something brushed against my side and I startled, then looked down and realized it was the black Were—Tony. His fur twitched and I snatched my hand back, as if shocked. He turned to look at me with amber eyes and darted slightly ahead.

"Tony," Eliza called, in a quiet voice, nonetheless loud enough for any Were.

The wolf checked his stride for a moment and glanced back at the group. I saw the fur on the back of his neck stood at high alert. He visibly hesitated, then swung his head toward the fire and gave a low snarl that brought goosebumps to my arms. The next moment, he was gone.

I stopped. "Eliza?"

"Dammit."

"Eliza."

"He smells them, Julie. So do I. There's at least two 'Manders and he's gone after them. Dammit, he's more wolf than human. He'll lose himself completely if he's not careful."

Newt's eyes seemed to lose focus for a moment. "One's nearby. I can barely read the second."

I glanced around wildly and put my hand on the gun in my pocket.

"How nearby?" I asked, proud to hear no fear in my voice.

"Not that close. At least one hundred fifty feet. Probably right near the fire line." Newt reached out and touched me on the shoulder. The warmth of his hand coursed through me and lowered tension I hadn't even felt in my shoulders.

"Okay. So Tony's gone after him."

"Her," said Newt and Eliza at the same time.

"But—we killed her, the one with the cat eye glasses," I said, then winced at the baldness of my statement.

"I don't recognize this one's scent," said Eliza. "Must be reinforcements."

She wheeled toward the two of us and pointed. "You two stay here. Newt, the fire's yours—get it under control. Take the nearest Salamander if you can. I'm betting Tony's gone after the far one, from the direction he took. I'm going after him. I'll try to draw up whatever moisture I can as I run around the perimeter. That'll help the firefighters."

"We need to get rid of the Eclipsers. *That* will help the firefighters," said Newt.

I nodded, pulled out my gun, and made a show of nonchalantly checking it.

"Be safe," said Eliza, then slipped into wolf form and disappeared from my sight.

I realized we were no longer cloaked in darkness. The thought must have been transparent, because Newt said, "Hey, we've got the bracelets. I can also play with the light a bit, if we need it. No worries, Jules."

"Right."

We stayed close to cover and worked our way forward.

"How many more Salamanders do you think there are?" I asked.

"Doesn't matter," said Newt, "I can take them."

An edge in his voice surprised me and I glanced up at him, then stared. A nimbus of light surrounded him and his freckles looked like burnished copper. His spiky hair stood up, so distorted by heat-shimmer that it almost seemed crafted from flame. The expression on his face looked both labored and exalted.

"Um, Newt? What are you doing?" I asked.

He looked at me with eyes like sunlight on moving water. He smiled—his normal grin immensely relieving at that moment—and said, "I'm pulling heat from the fire and sinking it into the ground. Helps the firefighters. Will be easier when we're closer."

"Shouldn't you wait until we get closer, then? So you don't exhaust yourself?" I said.

He shook his head and I half-expected to see drops of sunlight thrown off his hair. "No, it feels good. Like stretching. Besides, I need to sink the heat a distance from the fire line so the hot ground doesn't prevent containment."

He pointed to the right, away from a fire brigade we glimpsed through the scrub. We climbed the slope of the Cascades now, just outside of town where houses were scant. I spared a moment to be thankful the Salamanders hadn't started by hitting a major population center, but had thrown these fires toward the outskirts. Although that would change by tomorrow, if we weren't successful.

Newt grabbed my arm—his hand hot through my jean jacket—and pointed. I squinted, but couldn't make anything out, just a brown miasma of smoke rising into the air and bright flames piercing the woods. I swallowed hard.

"She's there," Newt said. "In that bright spot."

I looked again and thought I might see a figure.

"Okay." I switched the grip on my gun and wiped my hand against my jeans before taking hold of it again. "What now?"

"Jules?"

Newt's eyes seemed to lose that uncanny light as he studied me.

"What?"

"You okay? You're shaking."

I tightened my mouth and met his gaze levelly. "I'm fine."

"Hey. You're not fine and that's understandable. Not weakness." He reached out and rested both his hands on my shoulders. Warmth from his touch trickled through my body. "It's just fire, okay? You need to respect it, but you don't need to fear it. Fire can't hurt you while I'm here, while I'm right next to you. I promise."

I nodded, but he wasn't satisfied with whatever he saw on my face.

"Look." He kept his left hand on my shoulder and cupped his right hand in front of me. His eyes slid out and back into focus and his fingers danced with flames, little orange flames that played over his hand.

I didn't realize I'd tried to step backward until I felt

his fingers on my shoulder holding me still.

"It can't even burn you. I've pulled the heat away—this is just the flame."

I saw the flickering flames, cradled in his hand. In my mind's eye, I saw my house, engulfed in fire, and felt the remembered panic rising. Desperation when I couldn't get through the hall to Carson's room. The blackness, the searing flames, the heat, the crushing noise. Sheila's arm, the skin blackened and bubbled.

Newt snapped me back to reality by drawing his hand down my arm until he clasped my hand, forcing my fingers to ease and open. His mouth relaxed in a smile, his gaze fixed on mine, and he brought my fingers to the dancing flames on his palm. I moved to jerk away, and he shushed me, the way I'd quiet Carson.

"The flames can't burn you. Trust me."

Our joined hands moved to the orange fire. I braced myself, ready to cry out and snatch my hand back, but I felt nothing—no burn. Barely heat. Just the flames themselves.

My face must have been full of wonder, because Newt laughed; his loose and ready merriment unexpected in the middle of everything.

"You see?" He dropped my hand, although I continued to pass my fingers through the fire. "That's what I can do when I'm nearby. The fire can't hurt you with me here. At all."

A shadow crossed his face and his jaw tightened. "Just wish I'd been closer to Sheila yesterday."

The flames snapped out on his hand.

"Okay?"

"Okay," I said. I couldn't think about Sheila right

then, had to clear my head for this fight. I squared my shoulders and gave Newt a decisive nod. "Game on."

Newt and I skirted the edge of the fire zone, staying well away from the firefighters. Luckily, the Eclipser must have had the same idea, so we were able to move close to her without being near any of the crews. Or at least, Newt assured me we were close and the glaring shaft of sunlight hid her from my view.

"I'd rather not have to kill her," said Newt, a grim note in his voice indicating he was nonetheless ready for the possibility.

"Okay. So what's the plan?"

Newt tightened his lips in thought while staring at the Salamander. "I'm going to call flames around her, like a cage. Make it clear she can't get away. Try to capture her that way."

I nodded and didn't ask the obvious questions: how could we keep a fire-calling creature captive for long? Wouldn't she burn anyone who came near her? If we imprisoned her somewhere, wouldn't she ignite the building? I full-heartedly agreed—in concept—we shouldn't kill every enemy we ran up against, but I just didn't know if we'd have the luxury of allowing her to live.

Newt's plan would have gone smoothly, if this Salamander hadn't been more skilled than the others we'd fought.

We closed within thirty feet and still escaped detection, either because of Sheila's bracelets or because the 'Mander focused on the blaze. Newt gave me a nod, his eyes once again brilliant blue-white, and called up vivid purple flames to encircle the 'Mander. In the midst of the fire, I saw her: a dark shadow suddenly apparent against the glare. She froze within the flickering prison, then moved to face us. The noise of the fire surrounded us, and more distantly, the fire crews working—background to our confrontation.

Newt grinned. Beads of sweat stood out on his forehead and the air danced around him, but he stood there with arms relaxed at his sides and a keen look on his face. He walked forward and I made haste to follow him with my gun up and ready.

We approached the fiery cage. Heat leapt from the flames to batter me and I fought trembling muscles tensed to flee. Newt wouldn't let the fire hurt me, I reminded myself and remembered the tickle of those small orange flames on my fingers. Only the most skilled Salamanders could call this type of flesh-searing blaze, so I tried to take comfort in the demonstration of his skill.

This close, I saw the 'Mander plainly. She appeared to be in her sixties, with gorgeous steel-gray hair cut short: sleek and stylish. Her eyes were dark and outlined with a strong line, her lips painted a clear red, and everything about her exuded confidence.

Newt spoke in a voice pitched to carry. "I don't want to kill you. But I will."

The corners of the Salamander's mouth curved up in a smile, and I felt my heartbeat speed in response.

Newt continued. "If you pledge on the sun not to harm us, I will drop the fire."

"Not necessary, dog-lover." Her voice rang out deep and rich; she wasn't our so-called Ma'at.

Almost before she finished spitting the last words, she raised her hands and threw fire—purple fire, hers nearly fluorescent. The flames streamed in a blinding bundle straight at Newt.

"Shit!" I yelled. I leapt away from Newt, crashed right into a nearby tree, and fell. Pain lanced through me as I landed. Everything happened at once: I looked at Newt just as the fire reached him.

He held up his hands and caught the purple flames. I gasped, waiting for him to scream. The woman's fire wreathed his hands then slowly, slowly blanched to white and bled into orange flickers that raced up and down his arms and disappeared.

I picked up my gun and spun around to focus on the woman. Newt's cage of fire had disappeared—he must have lost concentration—and I looked around wildly to find the Eclipser.

Fire bloomed in the branches near me and I screamed, scrabbling in the pine needles to push myself away. The fire guttered and Newt stood at my side. He put one hand on my shoulder, heat radiating from his skin into me.

"You're okay." He gave me the smallest of shakes. "*Jules.*"

I pushed myself up on my knees and took a deep breath. His body was warm beside me, like a hearth in the winter. It quelled some of the shaking in my gut.

"Where did she go?" I asked, once again steadying my gun.

His eyes narrowed and purple flames shot up to our left. I trained my gun on the area.

"You're good," Newt called in a strong voice. "I'll give you that. But I'm better. And this is your last chance."

She lobbed flames and fire fountained in the tree next to us: orange and red. Newt gestured impatiently and snuffed the fire down. The flames around the other Salamander rose taller and deepened into indigo.

Purple fire spat out in our direction and I realized the woman could only call flames with a touch; that was why she threw it at us, while Newt could call fire at a distance to appear around her. As he drained the new flesh-searing flames—this time not losing focus on the prison he created—the other Salamander lobbed bright globes of white fire over our heads. I heard a tremendous crack and roar. I twisted and saw dark, rushing movement framed by white flames. I think I shot my gun. Then Newt was there, sweat pouring down his face. He pushed me *hard* and then something slammed me into the ground.

Chapter Eighteen

I groaned myself awake. My entire body ached. A thundering sound in my ears slowly resolved into my own heartbeat. I opened my eyes and saw darkness, light, movement. I blinked several times.

"Jules?"

Newt.

He put a hand on my forehead and I looked up at him. His face was grim.

"Are you okay?"

I swallowed several times to get enough moisture in my mouth to answer him.

"I think so. What happened?"

"The tree fell. It clipped you. I think you have a concussion, but I don't think there are any broken bones."

I lifted my head to look around, then closed my eyes as everything swam fuzzily around me. I waited while the vertigo passed.

"Eclipser?"

"Dead."

I waited for Newt to elaborate.

"Capturing her would take too long. I was worried about you and—well, really angry. So I killed her. She's dead."

"I want to sit up."

Newt helped me. I sat still for a minute, waiting for

my vision to stop spinning.

Oh shit. I fought off the nausea by focusing on the ground right in front of me. Old pine needles, sere grasses. I stared as if memorizing each blade. I breathed in and out. Finally, when I was fairly sure I wouldn't throw up, I looked at Newt.

His forehead creased with concern. He reached out to feel the back of my head and I jerked away as he hit the tender spot.

"Sorry I wasn't a little bit quicker," he said. "I knocked you out of the way, but a stray branch hit you. She threw those flames at the tree on purpose, must have wanted it to fall on us and cover her escape."

I blinked several times to get my eyes properly in focus before answering him. "Well, thank you."

Newt nodded. "If you're okay to sit here for a moment, I want to pull some major heat off the fire so it gets put out quickly. There aren't any Eclipsers around."

"Anything from Eliza and uh, Tony?"

"Not yet."

I reached up to feel my head and winced as I probed the extent of the damage. Just behind my right ear, I felt a large bump, raised and wetly warm. I looked at my bloody fingertips for a moment, then wiped them on the ground. Realizing Newt still looked at me expectantly, I cast back to what he just said.

"I'll be fine," I said. "You deal with the fire. I'm just going to…sit here."

"Okay. I'm not going far."

As Newt strode in the direction of the wildfire, his whole body began to shimmer with heat mirage. He stopped several yards from the fire line and spread his arms wide. Canting his face toward the sky, he stood motionless, his face taut with focus. The reaction of the fire proved he did *something*. The flames nearest him danced and faded; the roar of the blaze abruptly muffled. After a few more minutes, sweat trickled down my back and I shifted uncomfortably, only then realizing the very ground beneath me grew hot to the touch—hotter than usual even in late summer. I wondered how far his influence reached, how much of the fire would tamp down at his call, how much of the heat could be pulled from its source.

Newt stood there for what seemed like a long time. I glanced at my watch—10:27—and then realized I had absolutely no idea when any of this had started.

After another ten minutes, Newt dropped his arms. He rolled his shoulders and stretched his neck to either side before turning to me. I saw a grin on his face and took a deep breath of my own, feeling some of my stress ebb. He scrubbed his hands through his hair, leaving it more tousled than ever, and came back toward me with his lanky, bouncing stride. As he approached, the unnatural play of light on his hair and skin faded.

"Well?" I asked, as soon as he was close enough.

"That'll help, anyway. They should have the fire under control soon. This part's nearly out—just burning enough to seem normal—and I calmed down this whole quadrant quite a bit."

"Should we—I don't know, circle to a different area and do the same thing?"

Newt cocked his head. "Can you stand up?"

"Of course!" I said, stung, and moved quickly to prove my toughness. The effect was slightly marred when Newt had to reach out and grab my arm to steady me.

"I'm fine, really." A lie, of course, and one I'd repeated a lot these last few days. My head pounded and standing left me with a vague sick feeling in my gut. Newt looked at me as if he knew how I felt, but let my words pass.

"Okay, then. Let's start walking. We'll go slowly so Eliza and Tony can catch up." He didn't add the other obvious reason to take our time: he didn't want me falling on my face. Instead, he swooped a mock-bow and extended a crooked arm, somehow knowing I'd be less reluctant to accept his help if we disguised it as a game. I wound my arm through his and we wended our way through the brush.

We only walked for a few minutes before Newt paused, and a split second later, I heard branches crack off to the side. Newt pulled me around to face that direction, just as the two wolves emerged.

They both shifted form, stepping through darkness to emerge as their human selves. I noticed Tony's transformation this time was nearly as fluid as Eliza's. Almost before he fully changed, he strode toward me. Half of his hair hung loose, his clean-shaven jaw set in a hard line, and his eyebrows lowered in concern. I started to take a step backward, just from the sheer intensity of him.

Newt dropped his arm from mine.

"What happened?" Tony aimed the question at Newt, but his gaze locked on me.

I straightened my shoulders and raised my chin. "I'm fine. Really."

Tony hissed a low breath as he reached me. His

hand rose to push away my hair and his fingers unerringly found the bruised spot on my head. I shivered, perhaps because I'd been braced for pain, but his touch was so light it didn't hurt me. I swallowed hard and found Eliza to focus on.

"Did you find the other Salamander?" I asked.

"Yes, he's dead. Didn't put up too much of a fight, wasn't skilled. We threw his body into the fire, so hopefully there won't be any traces of us, even once he's found." Eliza frowned, but I couldn't tell if she was upset with me for being injured, or with Tony. Though, I couldn't imagine why she'd frown at him.

"What happened here?" Eliza asked.

Newt answered. "We were trying to capture our Eclipser and a tree fell on Julie."

"Well, the tree *would* have fallen on me, but Newt pushed me out of the way. I guess a branch just caught me on its way down."

Tony's hand lingered on the back of my head, and I steeled myself not to move away. He looked past me, at Newt. "The Eclipser got away?"

"No, I killed her."

"You should have killed her in the first place, instead of trying to capture her. Julie could have been killed."

I cleared my throat and both of them looked at me. "I wasn't killed and it was a good plan—a *wise*—plan to try to capture the Eclipser. If we can win this fight without killing everyone in sight, we should."

Newt's voice sounded studiously light. "I agree, Jules. Guess it's up to you and me to calm down our bloodthirsty wolves." He winked at me.

Tony looked at me, then jerked his hand away from

my head as if he'd forgotten he still touched me. He stood with his hand up, my blood on his fingers. His face moved with a strange expression and for a fleeting moment, I actually thought he was going to lick his fingers. My stomach jumped and I bit my lip.

Tony cleared his throat. "You're still bleeding."

"Just a little bit. I'm fine."

"Okay, folks," Eliza said, calling us all to attention. She walked toward us and took hold of my shoulders. She peered into my eyes, and evidently reassured by what she saw, nodded and drew me away from both Tony and Newt. "Let's get back to the car and regroup. Julie, do you think you need to see a doctor?"

"No." My vision didn't spin anymore and I thought my headache could be managed with some ibuprofen. My stomach still felt a little funny—which I told myself was because of the head injury and not because of the way Tony looked at me.

"Okay." Eliza set the pace, with me by her side and one hand on my arm. "Newt, you dampened the fire as much as possible, yes?"

"Right-o." Newt followed us closely, while Tony lagged behind.

"As we circled the blaze, Tony and I tried to call up moisture near the fire line, so that should help, too."

"Then let's move on to the other fires," said Newt.

"Without Julie," said Tony and my spine stiffened in response. "She should stay behind. She might have a concussion."

Eliza's face didn't reflect her thoughts. "Julie?" she asked.

"I'm not staying behind."

"You're being foolish. Carson needs you. For his

sake, if not your own, you need to try harder to stay out of harm's way," Tony said.

I opened my mouth to make an angry retort, but Newt beat me to it.

"Ya know, Tony," Newt said, "Julie can make her own decisions. She's proved herself fully competent. Besides, she's not some member of your pack you can order around. If she wants to come, she comes. Unless you're planning on physically restraining her? Right, Jules?"

I nodded, unable to find the right words.

Eliza's hand tightened slightly on my arm. "Right. Back off, Tony. You've lived the wolf too long."

His response proved her point: a black wolf with hackles raised raced by my side and disappeared in front of us. The rest of us walked back to the cars.

Chapter Nineteen

As we reached the parking lot, Tony leaned against the side of Eliza's rental car and waited for us. His expression revealed no tension and I gave a small sigh as I relaxed in response.

"Took you long enough," he said as we approached.

"Two feet are slower than four," Newt said.

Eliza and Newt spent the walk back planning our approach to the Salamanders at the Medford fire. They agreed we should all work together to capture one of the Eclipsers before dealing with the blaze itself. We needed more information: how many Eclipsers in the area, the location of their headquarters, and their targets for tomorrow if this conflict wasn't resolved. Newt reminded us friendly Salamander reinforcements should arrive any time and could help with fire control. As Eliza briefed Tony on the plan, I walked away to make a quick phone call and check on Carson.

Dana reported he took a bottle, ate a quarter of a banana, and lapsed into a food coma, so all seemed well. I reminded her my phone was on silent—since we were allegedly in meetings with the insurance company over rebuilding my house—and told her I'd check in again soon.

When I re-approached the group, everyone seemed in fine spirits, so I guessed Tony hadn't put up any fuss over the plan. He seemed to have a hard time remembering Eliza was in charge, but I hoped we'd avoid an actual fight for dominance.

"We ready?" I asked.

"Yup," said Newt. "Bring it."

I smiled back at him. We piled into the cars, me and Eliza in Sheila's car and Newt and Tony in the rental, and headed to Medford.

****

Eliza turned on the radio to hear the latest on the blaze they'd named the Roxy Ann fire. No closer to containment, which proved Eclipsers were at the scene egging on the flames. Roads in the vicinity remained closed. I pulled a local map out of Sheila's glove box and tried to find an alternate route that might get us closest to the blaze without detection. Eliza detoured through a coffee kiosk while I figured things out, so we stocked up on lattes and muffins. I was lucky enough to find a bottle of ibuprofen in Sheila's glove box and helped myself to three.

"Julie," Eliza said, "the way Tony looked at you back there…"

I shot her a look meant to stop her. "I have no idea what you're talking about."

"And the way he talked to Newt. Possessive."

I shook my head in denial.

"He's strong, you know. Powerful. The latent wolf in you—your dark moon side—well, I understand why you're drawn to him."

"Wow," I said. "I am not having this conversation."

Eliza frowned at the road and shot me a glance.

"I mean it. We are not having this conversation.

There's nothing to talk about, because I'm not some lovesick idiot controlled by her latent dark moon wolf."

We lapsed into uncomfortable silence and I forced myself to focus on the task at hand.

"Turn here," I said. "Okay, this road winds around some orchards and takes us close to the far side of the fire."

Eliza rolled down her window, even though it was in the upper nineties, even though the air hung with the brown haze of smoke.

"Let's skirt as much of the fire as we can, while I try to scent an Eclipser," she said. "If we can't sense one from the road, Tony and I will scout as wolves, but I'd rather get us all close enough for an ambush."

"Right," I said.

I pored over the maps, trying to find roads that came as close to the fire as possible—not the easiest thing in the world, since roads were sparse in the area and the firefighters closed some to the public. The Eclipsers had thankfully avoided major population centers when they set the blaze. That wouldn't hold true for the next fire they set, if we could believe Ma'at's threats. At the thought, I glanced at the clock and saw half the day was gone. Tonight, the council wanted to take Carson into their custody. By tomorrow morning, if his powers weren't stripped, people would start dying.

My phone rang. I fished it out of my purse and answered eagerly when I saw Tim's name.

"Hi!"

"Hi," Tim said, sounding tired.

"How is she?"

"She's doing well, considering."

"What does that mean? Is she in pain? Is she awake?"

"I'm sure she's in pain, but you know Sheila: she's not complaining. I'm out in the hall right now. She's awake and I know she wants to talk to you, but I wanted to warn you that she's still a little out of it."

I nodded. "I'd like to talk to her anyway."

"Okay, hold on."

After a moment's pause and some muffled noises, I heard Sheila. The sound of her voice forced tears to my eyes—I knew her well enough to hear the pain behind her words.

"Jules?"

"Hey, Sheila. It's me. How are you feeling?"

"Okay. They're taking good care of me."

I winced. "I'm sorry I'm not there with you. I'll be there as soon as I can."

"It's okay, Jules. I know you're...busy. Tim told me." Her voice cracked slightly and I heard her taking a sip of water.

"Yeah. We should have things cleared up by tomorrow, though." God, I hoped that was the truth. "I'll come up to Portland then, for sure."

"All right."

There was a pause. Too much to say and no words to say it.

"You're being careful, right?"

I dashed tears from my eyes. "Of course, you idiot. Really careful. Eliza, Newt, and...uh, Tony are all here, too."

After a moment of silence, Sheila said, "Tony. Dave's brother. Do you think we can really trust him?"

"Yeah, I do."

I'm not sure what emotion she heard behind my simple sentence, but her voice suddenly rose, became clearer through the haze of pain, exhaustion, and drugs.

"Julie Hall?" Sheila drew out my name with particular emphasis. "Tell me about Tony."

"Jesus, Sheila, nothing to tell."

"What's he like?"

"He's—I don't know. I think we can trust him and you don't need to worry about *any* of this right now. We'll take care of the Salamanders and get up to Portland as soon as we can. You just need to listen to the doctors, do everything they tell you, let Tessa White do her thing, rest as much as possible, and get better. Okay?"

I glanced over at Eliza. She smiled, damn her.

"Okay," said Sheila. "Just don't—don't do anything stupid, Jules."

"I promise I won't do anything stupid."

"Yeah, right," said Eliza. "That'll be the day."

I gestured for her to shut up and turned my back to her as much as possible in the confines of the car.

"Sheila? You go rest and take care of yourself. Okay?"

"Okay."

"I'll talk to you soon, BFF."

I stared at the phone for a minute and wiped my eyes again.

"Hey," Eliza said, gently. "She's strong. She's going to be all right."

"I know that. But I—" I shook my head to clear it and pushed my hair behind my ears. "Let's just do this."

Chapter Twenty

In the end, we lucked out. As we drove down the two-lane county road, Eliza suddenly slammed on the brakes and came to a stop on the gravel shoulder.

"Got one," she said with narrowed eyes. "One of the Eclipsers from the woods near the reservoir. Not the blond one, the other one."

"Mr. Average? Where is he?"

"Not close, but between here and the fire."

I stared in that direction. From the road, we couldn't see any flames, just dark smoke billowing up from the back side of the wooded peak a good distance from the road. Newt and Tony pulled off the road behind us.

Eliza and I got out of the car as they approached.

"Okay," said Eliza. "Tony, call darkness for you and Newt. I'll cover Julie. You two get behind the Salamander on the peak side. Julie and I will hang toward the left flank. If that rocky bluff there," she pointed, "is twelve o'clock, he's at the eleven, probably half a mile in."

I took a bearing and nodded. Eliza went through the plan and assigned tasks, while the rest of us listened attentively. With no debate, we moved.

****

I stood with my gun ready, wreathed in Eliza's darkness. En route from the road to our current position, I realized Newt wasn't by my side to siphon heat away from a fire attack. I fought away the resultant terror and banished the image of Sheila's charred flesh dancing behind my eyes. I would be just fine.

Eliza led in wolf form, ears cocked and muscles taut with anticipation. We both focused on the Salamander thirty feet in front of us. Eliza's Were senses had been right, of course. He was the one I'd called Mr. Average: clean cut, dark hair, middle-aged, and nondescript. We were at least a hundred feet from the true blaze and Mr. Average was in the process of burning a wide swath of trees. He walked quickly and touched each trunk, leaving gouts of fire snaking up into the branches in his wake. I frowned: he was probably creating a new hot spot for the fire to jump containment. Hopefully, his actions proved he couldn't call fire without a physical link. The Salamander paused for a moment to watch a plane circle the area before it moved farther toward the fire line and dumped a load of...something. Some fire-fighting chemical, I guessed, because it wasn't water. From the serious look on Mr. Average's face, he calculated how quickly he ought to move on to another area.

Suddenly, fire blossomed on Mr. Average's far side: not called by him, but purple flames called by Newt. Mr. Average whirled with a shout I barely heard over the roar of the fire.

The signal!

I moved in quickly, darting between trees. Eliza became a blur of speed as her buff-colored body hurtled through the brush to close on the Eclipser. Right before she reached him, she disappeared into a writhing mass of shadow and then emerged in human form to crash into the Salamander. I trained my gun on the two of them.

Newt and Tony emerged from the shadows. Purple flames wreathed Newt's hands and Tony's dark wolf form drew my gaze like a black hole, like barely covered danger. I pulled my gaze away from him to watch Eliza and the Salamander.

I held my breath, finger on the trigger, Newt and Tony equally ready to spring.

Eliza rolled off the Eclipser and rose to her knees. One of her hands firmly grasped Mr. Average's forearm.

"Okay," she said, her voice strained. "Got him."

We all approached the strange pair: Eliza with body taut and sweat on her brow, the Salamander lying on the ground and blinking.

He hiccupped and waved a hand at us. "Joining the party! Join the party! Come on in." The Salamander started to giggle. "No dogs allowed, though, sorry."

Newt walked right up to the man and stood there with dark flames still dancing in his hands. For once, no trace of humor etched his face.

"What's your name?" Newt asked.

"What's in a name? Smells so sweet. Should have known." The man gave a lopsided smile and hummed for a minute before saying, "Name of the rose, rosemary, sage, thyme."

I kept my gun trained on the man, just in case. He seemed pretty crazy, though.

"How many Eclipsers are here?" Newt tried again.

"Here, there, everywhere a quack, quack."

"How many?"

The man started picking his nose with complete

absorption.

Newt gave an irritated sigh. "So this is what happens when you Weres call on the moon to make someone insane?"

Tony said, "One of Eliza's strongest skills: making people crazy. Sometimes, she doesn't even need to call the moon."

I shot a glance at him. Was that a joke? Tony, joking? Judging from the smile that quirked his lips, yes. Eliza grimaced in return, but otherwise remained focused on the Salamander.

"I'm glad he's not trying to burn us to a crisp," I said. "But I'm not sure we'll get anything useful out of him in this state."

Newt tried again. "How many Eclipsers are here?"

The man started humming again. This time I recognized it as "One Little, Two Little, Three Little Indians"—though they probably called it something else these days? Was that a disrespectful song? Dammit, I wrenched my mind back on task.

"Do you think that means there are ten? Ten Eclipsers?" I said.

"Could mean anything. Or nothing at all, which is most likely." Newt ran his hand through his hair and tugged in irritation, which caused even more spikes.

I took a step closer to the Eclipser with my gun still aimed at his chest. The man gave me a loopy smile.

"Hey, I know you," he said.

"Eliza, can you back off slightly on the crazy stuff for just a minute? Without him attacking us?" I asked.

"I'll try."

"What's your target tomorrow? Where will you set fires, if we don't give you Carson?" I tried to keep my voice friendly.

A moment of clarity passed over the man's face like a cloud moved. "Dog-lover," he said and tried to spit at me. He furrowed his brow.

Newt yelled, "Watch out!"

Eliza gritted her teeth and pressed both hands to the man's arm. I saw the exact moment when her powers prevailed, because the Eclipser's head lolled to one side. The pine needles near his hands smoked; Newt scuffed the area clear.

Tony said, "This is not useful. We might as well kill him."

A shiver ran up my spine from his voice.

"Dammit," said Newt and took several steps away as if to clear his head.

"Okay, so when he's insane, he makes no sense. When Eliza releases him, he tries to kill us." Somehow, cataloguing the obvious helped me. "Newt could imprison him with fire, but that wouldn't necessarily make him talk, either. Plus, we don't know exactly how strong he is, so we should avoid a fight if possible."

Newt started to speak, but I cut him off to continue. "Yes, I'm sure you could take him, Newt, especially with the rest of us for backup. But we won't learn anything that way."

"So." Obviously, the Salamander wouldn't shake off Eliza's called-insanity, because Mr. Average babbled animatedly to a large pine cone. I lowered my gun and alternated rubbing each hand on my jeans to dry the sweat off my palms. "We resort to normal human methods of investigation."

"What do you mean?" asked Newt.

"Here." I held out my gun, grip first, and Tony

took it from me. Then I knelt by the Eclipser and went through his pockets. I tossed his wallet to Newt, who caught it smoothly. Mr. Average's other pocket was pay dirt: his cell phone.

I checked the contact list first. Many unknown names, half of them probably non-Eclipser friends and completely irrelevant to the current situation. Too bad he hadn't added some code to everyone's contact information, "Eclps" or "bad guy" would have been helpful. I looked at the call record and saw multiple recent calls to Paula Davidson, Tim Wheaton, Johnny Browne, and "Mary."

"His name is Mr. Average," said Newt, with the wallet thumbed open.

"What?" I said. Even Tony did a double take.

"Just kidding." Newt grinned. "His name is Mike Hollis and he's from Grover Beach, California. I wonder if that's near the suspected Eclipser headquarters."

"Do you know any of these names?" I rattled off a bunch of contacts from the recent call log.

Newt shook his head. "No, but someone might. We'll run them past the master."

"Okay."

I clicked through the cell phone menu again and went to his text messages. He seemed to be a compulsive delete-er—anyone who looked through my texts would have found things from months ago, but Mike Hollis only had two texts in his inbox, which seemed completely bizarre. The most recent from Paula Davidson: *Unless other news, ASH @ 7. Team is M, R, Ts.* The other text was sent yesterday by Mary and read: *Billy home and fine, call tonight? Love you!*

Mary must be his wife. I looked down at Mike Hollis, who seemed happy enough under the veil of insanity. What were we going to do with him? I didn't like the idea of killing anybody, but somehow knowing he had a family made me feel even worse.

"Anything?" asked Newt.

"Maybe." I read them the text from Paula Davidson.

"Ash? Like Ashland? The town?"

"It's capitalized. Capital A, capital S, capital H." After a minute, I shrugged. "I don't know; maybe it does just mean Ashland."

"This Paula Davidson must be involved," Newt said.

"She could be our Ma'at." I looked at the phone, and after a second's hesitation, pocketed it.

Tony growled and darkness dropped over him. Newt's body stiffened with a jerk and he swung wildly to look through the trees in the direction of Roxy Ann Peak, toward the fire.

"What?" I asked.

"Salamanders. Three of them." Newt's eyes started to gleam—literally—as he gathered power.

I couldn't see Tony; didn't know if he'd already sprung into the woods in pursuit of our enemies.

Shit.

"Tony," I said, through clenched teeth. "My gun. You have my gun."

For a brief moment, I thought I'd be left once more with no real weapon in the midst of a paranormal fight. The air beside me roiled and Tony appeared.

"Here," he said, holding out my gun. When I reached for it, he brought his other hand up to cover mine, his skin hot against me. "Be safe."

I nodded, not trusting my voice, and pulled away from him.

"Newt, I'll circle them and attack from the rear, while you have them distracted from this side." Tony looked around our position, then frowned as he caught sight of Eliza, teeth bared in concentration on our captive 'Mander. "Give me back that gun for a second," he said and held out his hand peremptorily.

After a moment of reluctance, I handed it over, upon which Tony walked over to where Eliza held Mike Hollis insane. Tony raised the gun high and brought it smashing down on Mike's head. Mike collapsed to the ground unconscious.

"Dammit, about time," snapped Eliza and jumped to her feet. She rubbed sweat from her brow and rolled her shoulders. "Tony, circle to the rear as you said. Remember you don't have one of Sheila's bracelets and the rest of us do. Julie and Newt, attack from this direction. I'll take the flank. One long bark followed by two short means fall back to the cars. Got it?"

I grabbed my gun back from Tony before he changed into a wolf and forgot again. I checked over the pistol: five shots left and one clip in my pocket. That would have to be enough. When I looked up again, Tony and Eliza had both slipped away.

Even now, excitement underlay the grim look on Newt's face.

"Three coming from that direction," he said, pointing. "Two men and a woman; no one we know. They may be close enough to call fire soon."

"Strong?"

"Hard to say. Hopefully, not too strong."

I found cover behind a nearby tree and took a stance, holding my gun steady with both hands. Newt would take care of the fire; I'd shoot anything I saw. That was all the plan I needed.

With a roar that made me jump and sent my heart into rapid pounding, flames leapt up at Newt's feet—regular fire, not flesh-searing purple. It guttered with a small gesture from Newt. I risked a short glance at our Salamander and saw his eyes narrowed in concentration as he scanned the tree-laden slope in front of us. I grounded myself on the tree trunk and took a deep breath to force the trembling out of my muscles.

I heard a wild crash and glimpsed a blur of motion through a tangle of blackberry bushes. Our wolves in action? Then purple fire erupted where Newt had stood—blindingly bright. I cursed. He'd be okay. He could handle it, I told myself. There was nothing I could do about fire. He was okay. I scanned frantically for the Salamanders.

Then—that patch of sunlight, had that been there before? Was that—?

I shot. The recoil jolted me and caused my head to pulse, stabbing pain radiating from behind my ear where the tree hit me. Relax, I told myself and huffed a breath. I forced my muscles to loosen, took aim, and fired again. The sunlight flickered and I saw a figure in its midst. I aimed at the torso and shot again. The Salamander jerked and then searing light streamed into the spot, so bright my eyes teared and I had to blink. The white-hot light consolidated into a stream of fire that arced toward me and deepened in color as it came—white to red, then flickers of blue and indigo.

The beautiful brilliance of the colors, of the fire

itself, nearly paralyzed me and only at the last minute did I yell something—who knows what—with the full realization that purple flesh-searing fire hurtled at me. I flung myself to the side, hit the ground hard, and rolled into a nearby Manzanita shrub. Pain blossomed in my leg. I looked down in horror to see my jeans burning near the ankle. I smashed my leg into the ground and tried to rub out the flames, even as they tried to climb and devour me. I somehow fumbled off my jacket and beat at the fire, even as the flames disappeared with a slight popping noise.

Panting, I looked up and saw Newt.

"You okay?" He asked in a terse voice. "Jules?"

"Yes."

Before the word cleared my lips, he whirled and disappeared into a shaft of light that streaked through the trees. Indigo flames blossomed in a swath twenty feet from us, but then as quickly tamped down. Smoke lay heavy in the air. My leg *hurt*, but I couldn't stop to feel it. My head swam with dizziness, but I pushed it aside. A confusion of light, flames, noise: I blinked my stinging eyes and forced panic to the side while I scanned the brightest spots. There. I took a breath, exhaled, and pulled the trigger.

The sunlight winked out as the Salamander I glimpsed spun around and fell heavily to the ground, exactly the way people do in movies. I needed a moment—needed the world to stop, the way it does in film sometimes, to stop and pan to me as I realized the enormity of what just happened. I killed someone. Again. Instead, a heavy body tackled me and drove me to the ground, pushed the air out of my lungs. My gun went off and spun from my hand. The world darkened for a moment and I swam back to myself to see Mike Hollis's face inches from my own, his body holding me down. His hands clamped around my throat and I struggled to breathe past the crushing pressure.

"Where is the baby?" He ground out the words through gritted teeth.

My mouth opened and closed, not because I would tell him, but because I gasped for air. My hands scrabbled weakly at his wrists, trying to pull him off me. No use. Gun, where was my gun? I felt on the ground.

"Tell me! Where is he?"

I tried to throw him off me, but couldn't, no matter how hard I thrashed. My hand closed on something. Not the gun. A rock? I tried to pick it up, but it stuck to the earth. I pried and tugged, all the while flailing with my other arm and hitting Hollis around the head and shoulders. He cursed and used one hand to pin my right arm above my head, as he kept his other hand around my neck. I sucked in a breath as he squeezed tighter.

"Tell me!" He lifted my head up and thumped it back to the ground. Waves of pain flashed through my skull. The world grew black and fuzzy around the edges. All I saw was his face; all I felt was the damned rock, embedded in the baked Oregon soil.

"Tell me!" Suddenly, fire danced in front of me, called by him and held there as a threat. I made a whining noise as I tried to scrabble away but couldn't. I tried to nod, tried to show with my eyes that I'd tell him, if only he'd let me talk. His hand loosened a fraction and I sucked in a long gulp of air.

"Where is he?"

I panted and choked out the words. "He—is—

he—"

The rock loosened. I fumbled it into my hand and threw all my strength into my arm as I smashed into Hollis's head. He grunted and lost hold of me with the impact, and I flung myself over and hit him again and again and again while I screamed in fury.

When I finally stopped, I was covered in his blood and his head—

I dropped the rock, dragged myself off his body, and threw up. My throat was so raw and swollen I could barely vomit; the retching made my skull pulse like it might explode; all I could see was the man's broken, bloody face.

"Julie!" Newt. I became dimly aware he'd been calling my name for a while; he was yelling and running toward me.

"We've got to go!"

What?

As I watched, Newt spun around and picked fire out of the air: purple fire streaming toward the two of us. He grabbed it and winced as it touched him. The flames faded very slowly. Newt panted heavily by the time the fire disappeared and sweat streamed down his face.

"Back to the cars! We've got to get out of here!"

I tried to stand up and staggered. Newt moved to catch me, but a whirring mass of dark fur rushed near my face and Tony grabbed me as I collapsed. The world swooshed dizzily as he swung me into his arms and held me close to his chest, as if I weighed nothing at all. I heard Tony command, "Guard the rear!" as he set off quickly through the woods. Everything bounced: a confused play of light and shapes, which made me shut my eyes in the hope I wouldn't vomit again.

Tony said, "You're going to be okay. Julie! Hang on."

I felt the words as a deep rumble against me as much as I heard them, and I allowed myself to be comforted by his voice.

Chapter Twenty-One

We regrouped miles away in a pull-off leading to someone's pasture. My whole body felt boneless and bruised; I'd been barely conscious as Tony piled me into the backseat of the car. When Eliza and Newt pulled up, I roused myself enough to focus.

"What happened?" I asked and winced at the way my voice sounded: rough and croaky. Then I bolted upright in my seat and gasped. "Newt? You're bleeding!"

Newt had wrapped his t-shirt, now soaked with blood, around his left arm. His arms and chest were red around his freckles with what looked like deep sunburn.

"I'll be okay, but I need to see a medic. I got grazed by a bullet."

"By...by me?" I asked.

"No. One of the Salamanders had a gun, too."

"We definitely need medical care, for both you and Julie," Eliza said. She studied me and moved to hold my chin, tilting my head this way and that to look in my eyes. Because she was my friend, I did my best and managed not to puke on her. Eliza's face and arms were covered with scratch marks that healed as I watched; after a moment, I realized she must have fought in the midst of blackberry bushes, which, for some reason, struck me as extremely funny.

Eliza looked at me like I was crazy when I started

to giggle. "Julie?" she asked.

I waved my hand to say I was okay. When my laughing fit didn't subside, Newt said, "I thought *I* was supposed to be the comic relief."

"Julie?" Eliza frowned at me and I tried to stop giggling—I really did—but laughter seemed to well out of me in convulsions, until my eyes watered and I had a really, really hard time breathing. "Julie! Settle down, take a deep breath."

I couldn't. The laughter turned to strange hiccupping sounds and my whole body shook. I went to wipe the tears from my eyes, but then stopped in horror, staring at my hands, covered in blood. Mike Hollis's blood. The nails on my left hand were black with dirt and one was ripped off to the quick. That must have happened while I scrabbled for the rock.

I dimly heard Eliza say, "Should I slap her?"

"That can't be a good idea with her concussion." Newt sounded worried.

Tony twisted in the driver's seat and took hold of both my shoulders, his touch running through me like electricity, giving me something to focus on.

"Julie." A note in his voice reached me and I caught my breath. His amber eyes fixed on mine, imposing some sort of calm on the sea of emotion that tossed me back and forth. I took several breaths in and out, staring at his wolf eyes.

"I'm okay," I finally said and meant it, at least partially.

"Well, you're not okay, exactly." Newt was in the backseat now, leaning close to me while Eliza hung through my window. "You have a concussion and burns on your leg, you were nearly choked to death, and you're probably covered in other bruises and scrapes. But at least you're not hysterical anymore."

I took another quick breath to stave off more giggles. "What happened back there? We…lost?"

"We strategically retreated," said Eliza.

I snorted and barely controlled the impulse to laugh again.

"We were outnumbered," Eliza continued. "I thought we had the upper hand, but then three more Salamanders poured out of the fire—out of the fire itself; they'd been in the blaze which messed up their scents, I think. We accounted for several of them. Newt?"

"Julie shot one, and uh, killed Mike Hollis. I dueled with another Eclipser when we pulled out. He was strong, really strong. I think I could have taken him, though."

Tony's voice was matter-of-fact. "I hamstrung another. Took her out of the fight."

Without meaning to, I glanced at his mouth, at his lips. Tony caught my gaze and smiled, causing my stomach to flip as a surge of heat ran through me.

God, I really was in shock.

"How bad is your leg, Julie?" Eliza asked. She opened the car door and motioned for me to swing my feet out. She pulled up my pants and I peered down at my leg, scorched red with a wide swath of blisters.

"Well, I don't think it's too bad. I was lucky."

"Lucky and brave, I'd say, Jules." I heard the grin in Newt's voice and reflexively smiled back.

"Oh my God, I lost my gun," I said, as I remembered.

"I picked it up. Here." Newt pulled the gun out of

the waistband of his jeans and handed it up to me. I frowned at his arms, noticing how his skin looked sunburned.

"Did you get burned?" I asked.

Newt looked down at himself, at his arms and shirtless torso, and I did, too. He was quite muscular, especially considering clothed he looked lanky. Freckles covered his shoulders and scattered across his chest. He shrugged.

"I absorbed an awful lot of heat out there, drained it from the fire aimed at you and the others. I'll be fine; it's just superficial. Could get worse from a day at the beach. Well, I couldn't, but you humans could."

I remembered how easily he sucked the heat out of the flesh-searing flames in the past, thought about the way he drew down the wildfire in Ashland earlier today, and wondered just how much energy he used during our fight. Everything swam fuzzily in my memory; I didn't even know how many Eclipsers we fought.

"I'm more worried about the bullet wound," said Eliza.

"Let me take a look at it," Tony said, and got out of the car to go to Newt. "Do we have a Were-friendly doctor in the area? Or, I guess, a Salamander-friendly doctor? Someone we can trust?"

"No packs close by." Eliza tapped her forehead in thought. "I'm calling the council." She walked a few steps away and took out her phone.

I had nothing to offer. My family doctor was fantastic, but I'm not sure she was up to dealing with burns, bullet wounds, and paranormal creatures, and Newt certainly couldn't waltz into a hospital with an unexplained gunshot injury.

"Why don't you heal quickly like a Were?" I asked.

Tony unwound the shirt from Newt's arm. Newt winced as the shirt caught on some clotted blood.

"Because I'm *not* a Were. I'm a Salamander. That's not one of our powers."

When Tony reached the wound, fresh blood started oozing out, startlingly bright against Newt's skin, and I had to look away.

"The bullet just clipped you. You're lucky. I think you'll be fine if we can get it cleaned out and bandaged properly. You should probably have some antibiotics. Painkillers, too." Tony said.

His voice seemed to come from far away and I realized I was fading out again. I made the effort to keep my eyes open, but everything around me moved jerkily, like bad film editing. Tony wrapped Newt's arm; Eliza yelled into her phone; Tony had his hand on Eliza's shoulder, as if to shake her; Newt stared at me; the car engine revved, reminiscent of the fire's roar.

****

I tried to jerk away from the light shining in my eye, but my head spun. Adrenaline surged through me, yet my body wouldn't respond. The light moved and my left eye tracked it as the rest of me groggily came to grips with the situation. I lay on a bed. Someone held my eyelid open, even as I winced against the brightness. The warm, dry hand moved to my other eye and the light—it must be a flashlight—followed. I licked parched lips so I could voice a protest.

"Julie? Are you awake?"

Tony.

Both my eyes opened and I searched for him in the middling darkness beyond the flashlight. The light clicked off and I sighed in relief, blinking several times to flush away the bluish afterimage and bring the room into focus.

The guy leaning over me, flashlight in his hand, was not Tony. Close cropped hair, deadpan blue eyes, square face framed equally by cheekbones and jaw. His short-sleeved white t-shirt perfectly set off bulging arms. Even his neck had muscles.

I knew this guy.

Who the hell was he?

"Ms. Hall," he said, in a voice so courteous I couldn't be sure I read the irony correctly. "If I didn't know better, I'd suspect you make trouble for real Werewolves on purpose."

Oh.

"Chris Usher." I tried to coax more moisture in my mouth. "Guess you're just sorry the council didn't decide to 'silence us' after our work in Las Vegas. So sorry to trouble you."

Tony growled. Literally.

Chris Usher the council goon snorted. He glanced over his shoulder at Tony, who stood with his whole body canted toward our exchange. Tony's eyes gleamed in the dim room and his hair was loose. My body, which possessed a world of aches and pains, felt alive to see him. Looking around, I learned we were in some mid-grade hotel room: two queen beds, one of which I lay on, a large flat screen television, prints of generic pastoral paintings spotting the otherwise bare yellow walls. On the other bed sat a woman with red-highlighted, black spiky hair and dark eyes. She wore a plain blank tank top and what looked like army surplus shorts, complete with lace-up black boots. She studied me intently.

"Always happy to do my job," said Chris, standing up. "You'll be fine. Should have iced that bump after you got it, though."

"Next time I run around after wildfires and Salamanders, I'll remember to bring an ice pack." Good. If my attitude was intact, I must be fine.

"Does she need to stay awake?" Tony asked. "After a concussion like that?"

"No, we don't give that advice anymore."

"You're...a doctor?" I looked at Chris in doubt.

He scowled at me. "Medic. Trained in the Navy. Embedded with the Marines for eight years."

Ah, now *that* made more sense than medical school. "Is Newt okay? Where's Eliza?"

Tony answered me. "Newt's fine; Chris saw him first and bandaged his arm. Eliza and Newt are in the next room arguing with James, who's in charge of this council group."

Arguing? My gaze flicked back to Chris. I'd assumed he was in charge, since that had been the case when his squad of council Weres swept into Las Vegas a few months ago. From the look on his face, he didn't much enjoy not being head honcho.

I turned my head, wincing a bit when the movement put pressure on the lovely goose egg behind my ear. "And who are you?" I asked the female Were on the other bed.

She leaned closer. "Yuko Kinashita. Council Special Ops."

"Special Ops?" I echoed.

She nodded. "Yep, we're here to deal with the Salamanders and take custody of your son."

Like hell they were.

My spine stiffened and I pushed myself up to a sitting position. I shot a look at Tony, noted his grim face. My leg, bandaged in gauze, hurt as the burns slid against the bed, but didn't seem too bad. Considering. Actually, when I thought about some of the alternatives, I felt positively dandy. Someone had even washed the blood off my hands. I wondered if Chris had done that, or Tony. I tried to focus my whirling thoughts, suddenly sure I needed all my reserves to deal with this so-called Special Ops force who expected to take my son into their "custody."

"Tony?"

Tony held out my cell phone, as if expecting my request, and I took it quickly. I watched Chris Usher with narrowed eyes while I dialed.

Dana answered on the first ring. "Julie! I'm glad it's you. Listen, Carson's been mostly okay, but he's pretty whiny right now and I think he's hungry."

"Okay. I'll be there in—" Shit, I wasn't even sure where we were. Tony flashed all his fingers at me twice and I finished my sentence. "Twenty minutes. Try giving him some more rice cereal."

"Okay, see you then!" Before Dana hung up, I heard Carson fuss in the background and I quickly pressed my arms against my breasts. The absolute last thing I needed right now was big wet milk spots on my shirt, dammit. I tightened my lips and thought about something else. Unfortunately, the first "something else" that crossed my mind was the look of Mike Hollis's crushed face, covered in blood. I fought to banish the image, locking my gaze on Tony's face as if he were a lifeline. His eyebrows drew together; his eyes looked like honey. His mouth was relaxed, lips soft, and I wondered how he'd taste, sweet and warm against me.

Oh shit.

Well, at least I wasn't thinking about Carson anymore.

I swung my feet over the edge of the bed, and after that seemed just fine, stood up.

"Let's go get him," I said with a nod at Tony. To Chris, I announced, "I appreciate your help with the Salamanders, but you won't need to take my son anywhere."

Chapter Twenty-Two

Chris and Yuko made no move to either stop us or
accompany us, so I offered some awkward thanks, and
Tony and I left the room. As soon as we stepped into
the hall, Tony caught my arm.

A shiver crept up my spine and I flushed, hoping
he wouldn't notice under the florescent lights.

"I'm glad you're okay," he said, in a voice pitched
so low I strained to hear him. Totally reasonable to take
a half step closer until we stood close enough I felt his
body heat. "I don't trust them." His eyebrows rose and I
knew he meant the whole council. "Eliza and Newt are
negotiating right now, asking that the four of us
accompany Carson. James wants Carson in their 'care'
right away and says 'our assistance' is not needed."

"When did they get here? I'm fuzzy about the end,
there."

"Eliza called the council to ask about medical
options and learned the Special Ops were driving into
town right at that moment. We met them at the hotel
and Eliza promptly started butting heads with James—I
think they have a history." Tony nodded at the door
next to the room we'd been in. Ah, he spoke quietly so
not even the other Weres could overhear; I cursed
myself for being slow on the uptake.

I started to brush past Tony, but he grabbed my
arm and drew me to a halt. His hand stayed tight, but

not uncomfortable, on my forearm and he didn't let go even after I looked up at him.

"It's dangerous, being a Were," he said.

"I know. I could die from the bite." I gave the correct response and began to move on.

"No. That's not what I mean."

I paused, my curiosity piqued.

"Being born a Were. It's not…simple. You can lose…your humanity, for lack of a better word. We can become hyperaware of what separates us. Isolated. Too focused on our power and our little world."

"Yeah. I've noticed."

Tony frowned.

"Carson needs me. Now. Should we tell them we're going?" I asked.

Tony considered for a moment, then gave a wicked grin that made my stomach lurch again. He walked over to the door and knocked three times, decisively.

The door opened inward to reveal a smartly-dressed woman in her thirties, shoulder-length reddish brown hair held out of her eyes by the sunglasses perched on her head.

"Up and moving already, huh?" she said, squinting at the two of us.

In response to something said within the room, she stood back and made a sweeping gesture with one hand. I strengthened my spine and walked in, determined to make a good impression on this James guy. Tony followed closely, providing me with absurd comfort.

Two more Weres—at least, I assumed they were Weres—occupied the room. One guy, gray hair shot with black, sallow cheeks pitted with old acne marks, and sporting silver wire-framed glasses, leaned against the wall. He straightened as we entered and gave me an assessing look. I took him in with a glance, my attention more occupied by the other Were.

This had to be James: a middle-aged black man, with a shaved head and an immaculately groomed goatee as if to compensate. He reclined in the leather desk chair, the picture of ease and command.

"Julie Hall," he said. "James Robinson, in charge of this mission." He nodded at me and I gave a quick bob of my head in return.

"Glad to see you're feeling better. I've just been discussing with Eliza, here, when to take Carson into protective custody." He paused and gave a genial smile. "Of course, you're welcome to join your son as our guest."

He said it like he granted a favor by allowing me to accompany my own baby, as if he could conceptualize taking Carson *without* me. A wave of anger filled me, causing my heart to beat faster and blood to rise to my cheeks.

"And as *I* was saying, James," Eliza interjected before I could do something damaging. "Carson and Julie will not enter your custody without me. I represent Carson's pack and we have the right to be included in any decisions regarding his welfare."

Eliza looked outwardly unperturbed, but because I knew her so well, I saw the lines at the corner of her mouth that meant she seethed with fury.

"Carson's pack." James leaned farther back in his chair and bounced a bit, as if in thought. An act, of course. "I wasn't aware we were in Greybull." He smiled at me, showing all his teeth. "Julie, have you formalized Carson's place in the Greybull pack?"

Eliza's jaw clenched so tight my own ached in sympathy.

I attempted nonchalance. "Well, James, since the Greybull pack is part of Carson's birthright, I don't believe any other acknowledgement of his status is needed."

"You argue he's not a rogue Were subject to council disciplinary action?"

What? Crap, he was playing hardball.

"I hardly think a six-month-old baby could be considered a rogue Werewolf." I smiled and shook my head slightly, like I thought he misunderstood.

"Hmm. If Carson is part of the Greybull pack, I assume you plan to move to Wyoming? Especially, since you no longer have a home here in Oregon?"

Holy crap. Eliza looked shocked, caught between rage and hope. Her brown eyes stared at me in mute appeal, as if James had articulated her own desires. I fought down a surge of anger at her.

Tony took a step forward to stand by my side.

"Or what?" Tony said.

Prickles erupted violently as energy spewed from Tony and I clenched my fists to keep from rubbing my arms in reaction. All the Weres in the room—except James—stood up straight and the air nearly crackled with power.

"I wasn't talking to you, wolf," James said, a twist of disdain coloring his voice.

"If you're making a threat, make it." Tony's words rang loud in the room.

"Tony." Eliza warned.

"No threat, wolf. It's simple logic. If Carson is part of the Greybull pack, then the pack has input on decisions regarding his care. And if he's part of their pack, then he needs to live in Greybull. If he's not part of the Greybull pack, then he's a rogue Were and falls under direct council jurisdiction. The council will make all decisions regarding his welfare."

Anger surged through me at James's complete dismissal of me, Carson's mother. A mere human. I sucked in a slow breath of air while I tried not to yell.

Tony turned to me, his gaze asking a question I couldn't interpret. I gave a tight smile to reassure him, then reached out to touch him lightly on the arm. A jolt of coiled energy jumped between us, causing me to startle and snatch away my hand, fingers tingling. I swallowed hard.

James cleared his throat and I felt myself blush. Dammit.

"Julie?" James prompted, as if I might have forgotten why we were all in the room.

"You know." Newt spoke for the first time, a lazy drawl in his voice. I'd nearly forgotten he was there. He stood past Eliza, near the far wall, dressed in someone's loaner t-shirt with a bandage wrapped around his upper arm, just visible below the sleeve. He shrugged with his good shoulder and gave me the shadow of a wink in reassurance. "I know this is Were business and not mine, but I'd say any discussion of who's living where could wait until after we're sure everyone will continue *living*. Meaning, after we deal with the Eclipsers."

"You're right," said James, without looking in Newt's direction. "It is none of your business."

"I don't know why everyone's making such a fuss," I said, lightly. "Of course we're moving to Greybull, just as soon as we get everything cleared up."

Hand by my side, I crossed my fingers like a ten year old, as if that would make the lie acceptable. Although I didn't specify the "everything" to clear up. Surely I'd be able to argue that, if need be?

Eliza looked down quickly, but I saw her broad smile. Damn her, I knew she thought it was for our own good, but for a brief moment I hated her. Even though she was my friend. I hated not having choices. Like a cat backed into a corner.

"Fine, then. Glad to have that settled. Eliza, you may accompany Julie and Carson. Bring the baby back to us here by six o'clock."

Tony tensed next to me. I tried to send him a psychic message: Don't do anything stupid.

"Salamander." With a start, I realized James addressed Newt. "Go with Chris and Stacy to liaise with the other Were team at the Medford fire. Unless you're hurt too badly?"

Newt answered hotly, "I'm fine, thanks for your concern." He stalked out of the room, pausing only to squeeze my shoulder on the way past. The female Were who must be Stacy followed him out.

"See you by six, Julie. All of you," said James in dismissal.

Newt waited for us in the hall, which didn't seem nearly as dim now that our agitated Salamander paced the flowered carpet like a living flame. He grabbed my arm and leaned down to look in my face.

"Are you okay? I don't like these people." Newt did *not* lower his voice, seeming not to care whether the Weres heard him.

"I'm fine. I need to go get Carson. He's hungry." Urgency spiked with fear flashed over me as I uttered the words.

"Everything will be okay, Julie. The council's only trying to protect Carson," said Eliza, though she spoiled her confident statement by muttering, "Just wish they'd sent someone else to do it."

"Let's go. I need to go *now*." I looked up at Newt. "Be careful. Don't let the Weres push you around."

He laughed, though his usual carefree tone was colored with something else I couldn't interpret. "No worries, Jules. Besides the other Salamanders will be here in less than an hour. I'll call you later, okay?"

I nodded, not sure what else to say.

****

Eliza drove and I fidgeted in the front seat, checking my watch. I talked to Dana only a short time ago, but somehow I was convinced something would happen—we'd reach Carson too late, not because he was hungry, but because the Eclipsers would find him first. Tony followed us in Sheila's car.

As soon as we pulled up in front of Dana's house, I sprang out of the car and ran halfway to the front step before anyone else opened their car door. I knocked, but then opened the door and yelled, "It's me!" My nerves shot ice cold as my voice rang in the house, but then I heard Dana call, "We're in the back." My whole body flushed with relief as I stumbled through the house to get to my baby.

Carson didn't look any worse for wear: he sat on Dana's lap with her long necklace grasped firmly in his chubby fist. Dana's baby Ella balanced on her other knee and drooled on a teether. When Carson saw me, he pumped his arms up and down in excitement and I swooped him up. Almost immediately, he made little hungry noises and I sat down to nurse him. The connection soothed me and I fell into a level of relaxation I hadn't felt all day. I stroked his little cheek and he gave me a milky grin, wadding both of his fists in my shirt.

"Oh my God! Julie, what happened to you?" Dana said.

I froze and attempted a smile. "What do you mean?"

"Your neck! What happened?"

One hand flew to my neck and I winced as I touched the tender area. I hadn't spared a minute to look at myself. Now, I wondered if I had a deep ring of bruises. The smile stuck on my face and I didn't know what to say. I swallowed, feeling the aching pull and tightness in my throat.

Another knock sounded on the front door.

"That's probably Eliza," I said. With a narrow look, Dana hoisted Ella onto her hip and went to answer the door. She returned with both Eliza and Tony in tow.

"Dana Saxton, nice to meet you," Dana said to Tony, as they entered the family room.

I glanced down quickly and adjusted my shirt. Not that I was embarrassed about feeding Carson in front of people. Usually.

"Julie was just about to tell me what happened to her," Dana said. Her gaze darted to Tony and back to me; clearly, she wondered if he'd been the one to choke me. She edged slightly farther away from him.

"Uh..." I looked at Tony and Eliza for help.

"You were at the insurance company?" Dana asked.

I stared at her for a minute, before I remembered

our cover story for the day's excursion. "Oh! Yes, it was fine, really. Lots of forms to fill out."

"And…" She frowned at me.

"And…I fell? Um. Or…" I stared at her for a long moment after I stumbled to a halt. Finally, I shrugged. "The truth is so strange you wouldn't believe it, Dana, and I can't tell you. Long story. But…the person who did this won't bother me again."

Dana shook her head. "Listen, Julie, I don't know what you've gotten yourself into, but I think you need help."

"Thanks, but I'm okay."

"Do you need me to call the police?"

"No! No police. I promise we don't need the police."

"Are you safe?" Dana looked at Tony again.

"Yes, I am. The guy who did this to me is gone. Won't hurt me anymore."

Dead. In the woods. With his head bashed in. By me.

Carson started to fall asleep and I cradled him to me. "I think Carson's ready for another nap."

"Should we get him in the car before he falls asleep here?" asked Eliza.

"Yes, definitely. Then we can all get out of Dana's hair." I fiddled with my shirt for a minute, then stood up with Carson nestled against my shoulder. Picking up his things, I thanked Dana again and attempted to make small talk while heading toward the door as quickly as possible. When she watched us pull out of her driveway, I still saw the frown of anxiety on her face.

Chapter Twenty-Three

I surveyed the wrapper from my sub sandwich and gave a long sigh. I crumpled the empty chip bag, took the last sip of my soda, and leaned back in my chair. Tony had finished his sub, too, and Eliza took her final bites.

"Next time we're hunting Salamanders all day, let's remember to take a lunch break," I said.

Eliza smiled at me, and I got up from Sheila's kitchen table and walked to the base of the stairs just to make sure Carson wasn't making any noise. Still sleeping soundly.

When I rejoined the others, Eliza cleared the garbage from the table. I paced around the kitchen to release my jittery energy.

"Anyone heard from Newt?" I asked, though I knew the answer. I looked at the clock. "The other Salamanders ought to be here by now. They're probably getting the fires under control."

"Do you want me to turn on the radio?" Eliza offered.

"No. No, I don't." I ran my fingers over the countertop, not sure what I *did* want.

"Are we going to talk about it?" Tony asked.

Eliza watched me.

"About what?" I stalled for time.

"About the Council Special Ops ordering us to

bring them Carson by six o'clock."

I looked at the clock again, even though the time hadn't changed. Four forty-five.

"What's to talk about?" Eliza's voice sounded strangely flat.

The words burst out of me. "There's nothing to talk about because I won't bring Carson to them. Not even if they 'allow' me and Eliza to accompany him. No way. I don't trust Chris Usher and I don't trust James whatever-his-name-is."

Tony nodded approval.

"Robinson," said Eliza. When I turned to her, she clarified, "James Robinson."

"Whatever. I don't trust him and I'm not sure you do, either."

"He's extremely competent. He *will* protect Carson."

"No, he won't. Because I'm not turning my baby over to the council. Who knows what they'll decide to do? I will *not* have him used as a pawn in some Werewolf power struggle."

Eliza opened her mouth, closed it, and rubbed her forehead. Finally, she said, "I'm not sure you two realize the full ramifications of what you're saying."

"Really?" Tony asked. "I'm fairly sure I understand the situation."

"You'll be labeled rogue, you know. A rogue wolf, Tony. You *and* Carson. You might be strong, but can you fight off the full might of the council when they come for you?"

"Have to catch me, first."

"Dammit, Tony!" Eliza shouted. "You want to atone for your sins? To make up for running out on

Dave? You turned your back on the pack and now you're Carson's savior? Tony against the council? *You're* the only one who cares about his welfare? You think I'm not looking out for his best interests? You think I can't protect him better than you?"

Tony leapt to his feet and I thought he would punch Eliza in the face. The room roiled with energy.

"Stop it!" I yelled. I pushed my way between the two of them. "Just stop it."

When they both turned their attention to me, I ran my hands through my hair and tugged on the ends in frustration. "We can figure this out. No blaming and no yelling. We're all on the same team here, right?"

"Right," said Eliza.

Tony jerked his shoulders in quasi-agreement.

"But we're out of choices," Eliza pushed.

"We always have choices. Okay. Okay. Let's think. If we take Carson to them, they might strip his powers," I said. "They're unlikely to negotiate with the Eclipsers, but I think the council is already uncomfortable with me. They want Carson under the control of a formal pack structure." I held up a hand to stop Eliza. "Yes, I know. That's something I can remedy right now—James made that all too clear."

"You promised. You promised to move to Greybull and bring Carson fully into the pack. You promised," said Eliza.

"I remember." A surge of anger shot through me.

I walked the length of the kitchen, while formulating my next thoughts. "All right. The council might decide to strip Carson's powers, because he's too dangerous even under supervision. Or maybe because they fear a rash of Salamander arsons will draw too much human attention? Maybe they worry about the paranormal connection becoming public somehow?"

"Could be," said Tony.

"Or maybe the council's worried the Weres can't defeat the Eclipsers?"

"A bunch of rogue Salamanders wouldn't worry the council," Eliza said. "We've no reason to be afraid of them. Besides, I still think the council won't strip his powers. We *need* strong Weres. They *want* Carson. I think they really want to protect him." Eliza gestured earnestly with her hands.

I grimaced. "I just don't trust them. They—Chris and James—they treat me like I'm barely worth their notice. A lowly human. Like the only important thing about me is my son." My hand moved involuntarily to the bruises on my neck. "They probably wish I were dead. Then they could just take Carson and do what they want." I looked at Eliza. "Why couldn't they have sent someone else? Someone reasonable?"

Her mouth twisted. "James is supposed to be the best."

"But you don't like him either. I can tell."

"No, but I don't have to like him to know he'll do everything in his power to follow the orders of the council. You don't want to make him an enemy."

"*He's* making *me* an enemy," I grumbled, meaning it, sort of.

Dammit. I knew Eliza was right. What she said was logical. We didn't want the full strength of the council after us. But I just couldn't do it. I couldn't bring myself to trust James Robinson with the welfare of my son—not when the Special Ops force considered me a second-class citizen. I didn't want Carson under the control of people like that.

Something I hadn't recognized before suddenly crystallized for me.

I didn't want Carson to grow up in a pack.

I froze, shocked by my own thoughts, and quickly turned to stare out the window, unwilling to look at Eliza or Tony while my mind sped.

Tony was right, what he said to me earlier. Weres *could* lose their humanity. I saw it in the way Chris Usher devalued my existence, in the way so many of the Weres I knew—good Weres and my friends—were preoccupied with issues of dominance, continually throwing around their paranormal weight. They might have powers I didn't have, but they also had their share of weaknesses, one of which was their inability to see the true worth of non-Weres—humans, Salamanders, Witches. I didn't want Carson to be like that. I wanted him to respect all peoples, regardless of their difference, regardless of their powers or strength. He wouldn't learn that in a pack.

Carson was the strongest Were. If I didn't help him temper such power with wisdom, compassion, and tolerance, he could be the most brutal. I needed to make sure that didn't happen. Me. His human mother.

I could cede control over his future to no one. Not the Greybull pack, not the council, not James Robinson.

When I turned around and faced the two Weres, I knew my voice was steady. I made my decision; now Eliza and Tony would make theirs.

Chapter Twenty-Four

Eliza rocked back on her heels at the force of my declaration.

"If you don't want to be part of this," I said into the silence, "leave now. If you stay, we do things my way, no matter what the council says."

Tony grinned and I had to avert my gaze from the look on his face, even as my heart raced in response.

"I'm in," he said, just as I knew he would.

Eliza stood mute. A muscle in her jaw twitched with tension. "Can I have a minute to think about this?" she asked, finally.

"Of course." My heart hurt to see her in such conflict, but she needed to find her own way through this one.

"I'll be outside on the porch," Eliza said.

As the door closed behind her, Tony said, "She's not coming with us."

"What?"

"She can't do it, regardless of your friendship. She honestly believes the council knows best. She's too caught up in pack structure to see anything else. You know that."

Shit.

I did know that. I just didn't want to believe it. I wanted Eliza to understand—maybe even to make the council understand—why Carson wasn't just something to control.

Tony and I stared at each other. At nearly the same moment, we both turned and raced for the stairs—ridiculous, because I didn't believe Eliza would actually take Carson, but my heart pounded nonetheless.

Carson was fine, of course. When I wrenched open the door, he stirred on the bed and looked at me with a delighted grin. He pushed up on his elbows and kicked his feet, completely unmarked by any thought of Eclipsers or defying the entire council. I wished I could change places with him.

I crossed the room quickly and sat on the bed next to him, patting him on his soft diaper-covered bottom. He spread his arms and airplaned on the bed, rocking on his little belly. The rightness of my decision settled into me viscerally. Carson needed to grow up without the constant pressure of being the strongest Were, without others always seeking to use him or ingratiate themselves with him. He needed to grow into himself fully and humbly. His powers gave him a responsibility not just to other Weres, not just to ensure Were supremacy in the paranormal world, but to fight for what's right for Weres, Salamanders, humans, Witches—and whatever else was out there. All of us.

I remembered something Newt said, when I asked him why he was on our side against the Eclipsers: *We should work together—focus our strength on fighting the things out there that want to devour us all, Weres, 'Manders, and humans alike.*

Tony's head jerked and he moved in a blur to the window.

"She's leaving."

"Eliza's leaving? Without even saying anything?" I

crossed to stand next to him.

Her rental car was halfway down the street.

"What's she going to say? 'Hey, Julie, I decided to go to the council and let them know you're defying them?' "

I let out a long breath. "Well, at least she didn't try to...I don't know. To take Carson from us."

"I doubt she wants to sever your friendship. If I know Eliza, she's punishing herself right now, wallowing in guilt and conflicted feelings." Tony's voice sounded so even—I envied him.

"What's our plan?" he asked, and I jolted back to the moment, aware I'd just been staring at him.

Our plan.

Right. I'd firmly declared myself in control of this mutiny and I needed a plan.

"Special Ops will be here soon, especially if Eliza calls them from the car," Tony said.

"Okay. So first order of business, we need to find a place safe from both the council and the Eclipsers." I bit my lip in thought, focusing my gaze on Carson. "We can't stay here, we can't go to any of my friends' houses—Eliza's met some of them, plus I don't want to drag anyone else into danger. A hotel? Or do we just flee the area?"

Neither of those latter options appealed to me. Running away seemed cowardly. The Eclipsers were still here, ready and willing to kill people because of my son, and I wouldn't leave that fight to others. Even if I didn't know how we could fight the Salamanders without giving ourselves up to the council. I'd worry about those details after we had a safe place to hide. Also, fleeing the council felt like granting them the higher ground, as if we were truly fugitives instead of...rebels. Not rogue wolves, not fugitives. Rebels. I tried the word on for size and liked its weight, its import. We were rebels.

"Wait." A thought darted like a slippery fish through my mind and I closed my eyes to follow it. "Don's house."

I grabbed my baby sling from where it lay strewn across Sheila's desk chair and settled Carson against me, even as I hurried downstairs. Tony followed me.

I explained while rummaging in Sheila's junk drawer next to the refrigerator. "Sheila said she was watering plants for her colleague Don who's out of town for another few weeks. She has to have the keys here...ah ha!" I held up the key ring triumphantly. "We can camp out at his house. Eliza wasn't there when Sheila mentioned it. At least, I'm pretty sure she wasn't, but even if she was, she doesn't know who Don is or where he lives."

The two keys chimed against each other as I waved them at Tony. "Eliza can't know where Don lives, because *I* don't even know where Don lives. But I know how to find out." I tossed Tony the keys and he caught them casually with one hand. Then, with a "just watch this" grin, I turned back to the kitchen drawer and pulled out the Southern Oregon University phone directory. First, I thumbed to the listing for the Department of Communication, because I couldn't remember Don's last name. Sosa. Next, I found his entry, complete with home phone number and address: 1127 Greenmeadows Way. I wasn't familiar with the street, so had to find it on my phone.

"Okay," I said. "It's off Tolmon Creek Road on the

up-mountain side, bordering the woods, west of the wildfire we were at this morning. Let's go."

****

I was willing to bet Don Sosa either came from money or had another career before becoming a university professor, because his home exuded taste and elegance. The house sat on the side of the mountain with a great view of the valley to the east and the wooded hills of the Cascades, now partially obscured by the brown pall of smoke still curling up from the dwindling, contained fire. An upper-story deck wrapped around two sides and wood siding somehow gave the impression the home sprang organically from the surrounding landscape. Inside, high ceilings and walls painted in shades of cream and coffee, accented with azure blue and pale yellow greeted us. The wood floors alone looked equal to the entire worth of my house. What had been my house. Plants filled the rooms with variegated shades of green and the earthy smell of growing things; ferns trailed from plant shelves above head height and small orange trees fronted the glass doors to the deck. I bet Sheila had to spend quite a while watering everything.

I opened the garage door for Tony to pull in Sheila's car. We took a circuitous route here and Tony assured me we wouldn't be tracked by scent, but we shouldn't take chances and leave the car in the driveway.

Five-forty. James Robinson must know by now we weren't bringing Carson to the Special Ops force.

I went into the living room, turned on the flat-screen television, and flipped channels to find the local news.

When Tony came in, I updated him. "The Ashland fire's completely contained and they project it will be out by morning. The Roxy Ann Peak fire is eighty percent contained and hasn't destroyed any homes or personal property, and the fire in Applegate is nearly out."

"Sounds like the other Salamanders arrived and they've been busy," Tony said. "Hopefully, they also made progress finding the Eclipsers."

"With a team of Were Special Ops and a bunch of Salamanders, maybe they'll get all the Eclipsers rounded up before nightfall and we won't have to worry about their damned ultimatum."

"Perhaps." Tony didn't sound convinced.

He stood in the doorway of the living room, looking in at Carson and me. We were alone in the house. The first time we'd been alone. A strange shiver ran along the base of my spine and I rubbed my palms on my jeans before shoving them in my pockets, as if they might touch something without my permission.

Carson sat on the area rug in the living room, straining to reach a tempting pile of books on the coffee table. I shifted my attention to him and swooped him up, holding him in front of me as if he were a shield. As if he could save me from thinking about the look on Tony's face, the way he moved his lips slightly to moisten them, the way his hair fell in disarray around his chin and ears. I exhaled and forced a bright smile.

"Well," I said. "I guess we might as well look around the house."

Tony followed me from room to room as we took a survey: three bedrooms, three full baths, living room, family room in the finished, walk-out basement,

gorgeous kitchen full of stainless steel and marble—
what they'd advertise as "a cook's delight" if the home
were on the market. Front door, side kitchen door,
sliding glass doors, door to the garage. I saw Tony
making a mental note of each exit and window as he
assessed security concerns. I felt very weird prowling
around someone's house like this, claiming it as our
base of operations. Lucky for us, Don Sosa and his
family didn't have any close neighbors, so hopefully no
one would ever know about our intrusion. Including the
Eclipsers and the council.

"I guess Carson and I will sleep in the blue
bedroom?" Somehow, that choice seemed less
obnoxious than using the master bedroom.

"Whatever makes you comfortable. I plan to sleep
in the hallway."

I remembered what a big deal Eliza made about
Tony still choosing—or not choosing, but lapsing
into—sleeping as a wolf and I opened my mouth to say
something. But after a sidelong look at Tony's face, I
silently shrugged it away. He could take care of
himself; he'd done it for five years.

"Julie?"

His voice saying my name made my stomach flip
and I settled Carson more firmly on my hip before
answering. I *had* to get control of myself. He was
gorgeous, but this was ridiculous.

"Yes?"

"Do you think you could find a pair of scissors in
this place?"

"Scissors?" I stared at him.

He shrugged one shoulder. "I know it should be the
last thing on my mind, given the situation. But if I have

to go one more day with all this hair, I may just go insane." He slipped off the hair band and let the dark strands fall. "Could you cut it for me?"

As I hesitated, he said, "If not, I'll hack it off myself just to keep it out of the way."

"Uh." I fidgeted for a minute. "I don't really know what I'm doing. But I could try to cut it for you, I guess."

"That would be great. Thanks." Tony's eyes crinkled at the corners as he smiled.

Almost wishing I could renege on my offer, I gave a semblance of a smile in return. "They probably have scissors in the office."

I walked there quickly and rummaged in the desk drawers until I found a pair that looked both sharp and smallish, not huge shears. Of course, his hair bothered him, falling in his face all the time. A simple request, really. Nothing to read into it. No big deal. If I cut it short for him, he could have it fixed by someone professional later, when we weren't on the run from every paranormal creature ever. I cut my own bangs sometimes and I'd cut my friend's son's hair once: this was no different.

"All right. Are you sure you trust me with these?" I *snip snipped* the scissors, then cursed myself for sounding flirty. Carson reached for the shiny metal scissors and gave a squeal of frustration as I jerked them out of his reach.

"I trust you."

I cleared my throat. "Let's go into the kitchen so it's easier to clean up."

I put Carson on the floor, gave him his pacifier, and scrounged up a few plastic containers and spoons for him to play with. Tony sat sideways on a kitchen chair with his back to me. His hair lay in waves, falling down his neck and onto his shoulder blades. When I looked closely, I saw lighter strands among the dark brown, catching the light just like his eyes.

"Hold on, let me find a comb." I escaped into the nearest bathroom, closed my own eyes, and gave myself a stern pep talk. Comb in hand, I returned and gave Tony a smile. "Okay, you realize I'm a complete amateur here, right?"

"Right."

"I'll do my best. How do you want it cut?"

"Short. Out of my way. Other than that, I don't care."

I moved in front of him and studied his face impersonally, trying to imagine him with short hair. "I don't want to make it too short. I'll leave enough length so someone else can fix it later. Besides with the waves in your hair, I think it would look nice a bit longer anyway."

His hair was soft as it caught around my fingers and the comb, snapping with static as I worked. I gathered the top of it up and fastened it out of the way with his borrowed hair band. Kind of a shame to cut his hair, even though I actually didn't usually like long hair on men. All combed and smooth, it really was beautiful—thick and glossy like his wolf coat, but lightened just a shade or two to an espresso color. Of their own accord, my fingers lingered for a moment on Tony's neck, feeling the warmth of his skin.

Focus, Julie.

I started cutting, trimming the back to lay just a bit down his neck and then snipping each layer. As the length fell, his hair curled slightly at the nape of his neck and the other layers followed, creating a tousled look. A just out of bed look. I moved through his hair, working on each section and trying to ignore the closeness of our bodies, the feel of his hair and skin under my fingers. My hands shook slightly. I moved to the front.

Tony's gaze fixed on me, darker than usual. I wasn't sure of his thoughts.

"Can you tilt your head up?"

He complied, but not the way I wanted. I reached out put my hand on his chin, raised his head. My fingers paused a moment and ran along his jaw, feeling the rough hint of stubble under his smooth skin, the contrast in textures sending tingles up my arm.

I snatched my hand back and cleared my throat. Behind me, Carson banged a spoon on the floor and I startled, giving him a quick look to make sure he was still happy. And hadn't noticed his mother acting like an idiot.

I gave Tony a tight smile as he sat there, so quiet and still, just watching me. I focused on his bangs, not his face, as I leaned over him.

"Shit!" I dropped the scissors and popped my finger in my mouth, tasting the tang of blood from where I cut myself.

Tony's eyes darkened further and his eyebrows lowered in concern. "Is it deep?"

I looked. I'd cut my left index finger somehow. Not bad, but it really stung, even after everything else I'd been through today.

"It's fine," I said.

Tony took my hand and drew it to him. Suddenly,

the pain seemed very far off and I stood motionless as he looked at my finger.

"You'll be okay. Probably needs a Band-Aid."

As he let go of my hand, I took a step back. "Right."

On cue, Carson squawked and I turned to deal with him, grateful for the distraction from the intensity of my reaction to Tony. He'd done nothing to encourage me, but I couldn't seem to shake off the mad attraction I felt.

Carson managed to scatter the plastic containers across the tile floor out of his grasp, so I collected them all again for his drumming practice. By the time I finished, Tony found a Band-Aid in the bathroom. He handed it to me and I fumbled it on, happy he hadn't taken my hand again to perform the first aid. I could do this myself.

"Okay." I took a deep breath and let it out. "Almost finished, just need to shape up your bangs."

I snipped more carefully this time. After a few more cuts here and there to clean things up, I declared myself done.

"That's the best this amateur hairdresser can do, anyway," I said.

"Looks good—and it's out of my way, which is even more important. Thank you."

"You're welcome."

Actually, I agreed with him. His hair looked quite good, especially considering my level of skill. The wave in his hair gave a nice shape against his neck and the layers I'd cut looked more artfully disarranged than inexpertly styled. Tony's eyes stood out even more with the shorter style—as if attention really needed to be drawn to them, with their arresting color. His jawline looked stronger, too.

His nose was a shade too long, I reminded myself. Plus, he was a Were. And not interested in me. He was probably embarrassed by me making such a fool of myself. God, I hoped I wasn't making a fool of myself.

Carson banged on the floor again, having lost his plastic containers under the kitchen table.

I ran fingers through my own hair and pushed it behind my ears, thrusting away the sensory memory of Tony's hair against my hands.

My cell phone rang and I crossed to it, eager for the distraction. As I pulled it out of my bag, I hoped it wasn't Tim. I wanted to hear how Sheila was, of course, but I didn't want to put Tim in the same position as Eliza—didn't want him to have to choose between me and the Were status-quo, between his love for Sheila and his allegiance to the council.

"It's Newt," I said and eagerly answered the phone.

Chapter Twenty-Five

"Julie?"

Not Newt. Eliza.

"Eliza? What are you doing with Newt's phone? What do you want?" My back stiffened and Tony jumped to his feet, standing behind me.

"Listen, Julie, I know you're upset with me and you don't understand. But Newt's hurt, he's really hurt, and he's asking for you." Eliza's voice sounded odd.

"What do you mean? What happened?" My heart raced and I reached out to hold onto the wall for support.

"The Eclipsers set a trap and he walked right into it—well, we all did—"

"Eliza! What happened?"

She was wrong. She had to be. Newt couldn't be hurt by fire. I'd seen his strength, the casual way he'd fought all the Eclipsers, the way he shrugged off even the flesh-searing flames.

"They rigged a bunch of explosives. When we came after them, they lured us there." Eliza paused as if to give me time to say something, but I found nothing but silence. Her words came slowly, awkward to my ear as if she felt uncomfortable talking to me. "They called flames and set off the explosions. They killed two Weres and one of the other Salamanders on our side. Lots of injuries. Newt—he's the worst. He figured it out, right before the explosives went off, and rushed toward the nearest cluster of bombs—says he was going to throw it down the ravine before it exploded."

I closed my eyes, envisioning the scene all too well: Newt running toward the danger, trying to save everyone else.

Tony moved as if to take the phone from me, but I snatched it closer and scowled at him. *He* could use his Were senses to hear the conversation. I couldn't.

"How is he hurt?"

I heard the grimace in Eliza's voice. "Broken ribs and collarbone. His left arm is shattered. He's in surgery now. Uh, one of his lungs was punctured."

"Is he…burned?" Newt's freckled skin, scorched black and peeling.

"No. Somehow, he absorbed the heat. Just not the force and shrapnel."

I rubbed my forehead, hard. "Right. Well. That's good, I guess. You're hurt, too?" I probed cautiously, not clear of this new balance, now that our friendship was so fragile, our alliances broken.

"I'm fine." Eliza's voice revealed no emotion. "Newt asked for you. We're at the hospital."

I looked at Tony, who spread his hands to indicate it was my call.

Eliza said, "If you want to come, James promised he won't take Carson while you're at the hospital."

"Hold on." I covered the phone, then realized she'd hear me anyway and further realized I didn't give a damn. "Tony, can we trust them?"

Did I trust *her*? How was it possible that within the space of a few days, I twice faced that question about one of my best friends?

He weighed his words carefully. "If you were a Were, I'd say absolutely. They wouldn't break their word to you. Since you're a human, I'm not convinced James will view his word as binding."

"Dammit, let me talk to Tony," Eliza snapped.

"No. If you have something to say, say it to me."

Tony's eyebrows rose, but he stayed quiet.

"Julie. Do you really think the council wants to destroy our strongest Were?" Her words held passion, but something about her tone rang flat.

"He's not *your Were.*"

"That's not what I meant! Do you think we want to hurt Carson?"

"I don't know, Eliza. A week ago, I would have laughed at anyone who suggested it. But now, I just don't know."

"Julie—"

"Controlling him is as bad as hurting him, Eliza. He's not some tool for the council to use."

"It's not like that."

"Really? Then what is it like?"

Eliza let out an angry breath. "You're not even open to understanding what's at stake."

"My son is at stake. *Carson's* at stake. His whole future. Everything he might be, if the council will just let him grow into someone with...with humanity." Goosebumps erupted on my arms as I said the words; I meant them that strongly.

I looked down at my little boy on the kitchen floor, perfect in every way. He breathed as if his lungs had never been filled with smoke and smiled slightly, as if wrapped in sweet thoughts that contained no danger. I loved him beyond all reason. I would do anything to protect him, to make sure he became the person I knew he could be.

"We all want what's best for Carson, Julie."

"*You* don't get to decide what's best for him." I knew she heard the anger in my voice and I didn't care. Dammit, I wanted her to understand.

"Right. Well, then I'm not sure what else to say."

"Me neither." There was a long pause. I gripped the phone hard. "Tell Newt...tell Newt I'm thinking of him. To call if he wants to. That I wish..."

God, did I wish.

"Sure, Julie. I'll tell him." The cordiality in Eliza's tone felt like a blow. "Bye, now."

The connection dropped.

****

I knew when Tony came back in the room, before he said a word. He'd been ranging around the property to become familiar with the land, just in case. I stopped rubbing my eyes, gritty from fatigue and recent tears, and sat up on the couch.

"Are you all right?"

"Yes, I'm fine." I looked at Tony as he sat down next to me, but quickly glanced away again.

"Carson?"

"He's sleeping. He's fine. I don't know. Maybe I *should* trust the council to know what's right." My voice caught slightly on the sentence.

"No." Tony's gaze fixed on me. "Too much risk."

I searched Tony's face as if he might have the answer: his cheekbones a strong frame, his mouth set in a gentle line. His amber eyes looked like his wolf, almost back-lit. A faint smudge of soot stood out on his forehead; I'd noticed it earlier when I cut his hair.

"Do you know I'm a librarian?" I said abruptly.

"What?"

"I'm a librarian. That's what I do. Master's in Library Science. I work at one of the county branch libraries in Jacksonville."

Tony looked puzzled.

"A librarian." I shook my head slightly and looked away. "I killed two people today. I killed another in Las Vegas a few months ago. A mafia guy who shot Tim and intended to finish him off. I shot him first, though, right in the head. I shot that Salamander today, too, but Mike Hollis—I—did you see what I did to him?"

At first, I thought Tony wouldn't respond. He kept glancing at me and I couldn't tell if he was uncomfortable or if he thought I was an idiot.

Just as I was about to make some silly joke to downplay my comments, Tony cleared his throat.

"I haven't killed a lot of people either, though you may think we Weres are a bloodthirsty lot. But"—his voice suddenly dropped in volume while gaining intensity, causing me lean closer—"I don't have a problem killing when it's necessary."

"Necessary," I repeated.

I sat there thinking for a moment. The day's events had been so momentous I couldn't wrap my mind around them.

"Now I'm fighting the Eclipsers *and* the council. No matter how this turns out, you're in big trouble. Why are you on our side, anyway?" I said.

Tony shrugged, a fluid motion that reminded me of Newt. God. Newt. "I've lived without the council for five years. I suppose I'm out of the habit of blind obedience."

I looked at him, sitting close enough to touch. My fingers tingled.

No.

I was not going to—

I—

Was I—

I leaned over and kissed him. A soft kiss that turned passionate, as Tony's arms wrapped around me. We kissed with a mounting fervor that sent heat through my body and led me to gasp against him. I felt his breath catch in his throat, smelled musk and ash on his skin.

The next moment, he pushed me away. He sprang up, stared at me with wild eyes, and moved in a blur to the front door. He wrenched it open, and with nary a backward glance, sprang into wolf form and disappeared into the darkness.

Oh, shit.

I scrunched down into the couch. My breathing was rapid, almost spasmodic, and I couldn't tell if I wanted to scream or cry. My muscles tensed painfully and I ached all over in some strong emotion I didn't have words to name.

Shit, shit, shit.

I waited in the living room for a long time, but he didn't come back. I didn't know what I'd say to him, anyway. Finally, I made my way upstairs and let myself fall into sleep.

Chapter Twenty-Six

I bolted upright in bed and panted for several minutes while my brain sorted itself.

"Tony," I yelled.

"What is it?" His dark form materialized in the doorway. I knew he'd be in the hall, just as he said earlier before—well, I wasn't going to think about before. I was done thinking about that.

"A-S-H. Ashland Springs Hotel. They're going to burn down Ashland Springs Hotel. That's what the text meant, the one on Mike Hollis's phone."

"Where's your cell? We need to call Eliza, get the Special Ops on it."

"Uh, in the pocket of my jean jacket, I think. Hollis's phone is there, too, if we need to check it again." I got out of bed and felt very naked in the t-shirt I'd been sleeping in. I'd neglected to pack pajamas with the other things I grabbed from Sheila's house. I wore a long shirt, though, and it didn't matter. He wasn't interested and I would *not* waste any more time on stupid fantasies.

He canted away from me as I crossed the room. I blinked hard as tears flooded my eyes from rejection or embarrassment—I wasn't sure which and I couldn't spend time on it because more serious things were at stake.

I paused to pull on my jeans before grabbing the

phone.

Eliza picked up on the first ring. "Hello? Julie?" Her voice came across frantic.

"We're fine. The Eclipsers are going to burn down Ashland Springs Hotel. It's the big one on Siskiyou Avenue, right downtown—that tall one with the colonial British feel that looks like it should be in an old movie. That's what the A-S-H meant in the text. Ashland Springs Hotel." I looked at the clock. "In ninety minutes, they're going to burn it down. Seven a.m."

"Okay. Okay. Ashland Springs Hotel. Got it. Let me tell James."

"Wait. How's Newt?"

Eliza didn't answer.

"Eliza! How is Newt?"

"Not good. He's in a lot of pain. He has another surgery scheduled for today. He keeps asking for you," she finally said. "I have to go tell them about the hotel."

"Right." The connection cut before I even said the word.

I crossed my arms across my chest to hug myself after I slipped the phone back in my pocket. One of my hands slipped up to my neck and I winced as I touched the still-sore bruises. Time for more painkillers.

"Did you catch all of that?" I asked Tony. I didn't need to look at him to know he stood in the doorway. I hoped my painful awareness of him faded quickly now that I knew he wasn't interested.

"Yes."

I looked back at Carson, still asleep sprawled on the bed.

"I hate this. I hate not helping. I hate not being

there for Newt. I don't want the council to fight my fight. Especially when I made it quite clear I don't want their help protecting and raising Carson."

Tony considered for a moment. "A rogue group of Salamanders like this threatens everyone," he said. "They're not just fighting for Carson. And there's nothing you can do to help Newt, you know. He's getting medical care. I'm sure he understands why you're not there."

"Eliza says he keeps asking for me."

Tony didn't say anything.

"I know, I know. He'll be okay." I stopped myself from fidgeting with my hair. "I also know I can't run and join this fight—or go to the hospital—if I want to keep Carson safe."

I looked at the clock again.

"I guess I'll go make coffee. I'm not going to get back to sleep."

"You should. You need the rest."

I bit back my first angry reply and retreated to polite formality. "I'll be fine, thank you."

As I pushed past him in the doorway, Tony reached out to touch my arm. I flinched.

"Julie."

Oh God, I did not want to have this talk. No, no, no.

"You're doing the right thing, you know."

"What?"

"You want Carson to grow up as a person, not a tool of the council, not a Were-shaped weapon, not an arrogant bastard who thinks he's better than everyone else because he's so full of power."

I glanced back at my baby. "Yes."

Tony gestured with one hand and I nodded, preceding him down the stairs and into the kitchen. He settled at the kitchen table, in the same chair where I cut his hair. I shook the memory out of my head and busied myself by finding the coffee supplies. Thankfully, Don Sosa had some decent beans in the freezer—if he'd been anti-coffee, I might have had to go out and purchase some regardless of the risk.

Picking up the thread of the conversation, Tony said, "Look at what happened to my family."

I glanced at him, unsure where this headed.

"My mother loved a…a human her whole life. Not my father." Tony's voice sounded flat, revealing no emotion. I didn't know how to respond, so I kept quiet and filled the coffeemaker with water while he talked.

"She didn't marry him, though. Peter. His name was Peter Ramirez. She couldn't face the pack, what they'd say and think if she chose to mate with a non-Were. So she married my dad, who'd been crazy about her since they were in middle school."

I already knew how this story ended, but I waited.

"When my father found out she'd been seeing Peter for many years, for the entire length of their marriage, he lost it. My sister Rebecca is Peter's child. She's four years younger than me, six years older than Dave…was. She's a dark moon wolf and when she reached eighteen without changing, the whole marriage fell like a house made of straw. You probably know what happened."

I nodded, but he continued anyway. "My father murdered Peter Ramirez in a fit of rage—about more than my mom having an affair. Because she chose Peter, a human, over him, rejecting everything about pack life. That's how my father saw it. My mother killed herself. I—I found her." His voice caught and I clenched my hands into fists so I didn't reach out to him. He would have been twenty-three at the time, five years ago. Werewolves didn't die easily; I could only imagine what he found. "I was with her when my dad came home and saw...then he tore away. Drove off a cliff."

The kitchen counter pressed into my back so hard it hurt, but I relished the focus, needed to feel anything besides the emotion evoked by what I saw on Tony's face.

"Rebecca hates the pack, because they forced my mom—and my father, too, I suppose—to make such choices. She hates the pack for the contempt she saw in every Were's eyes once they realized she's a dark moon."

I nodded in complete understanding.

"Dave loathes—loathed—all humans because he found it easier to blame Peter Ramirez than my parents or the pack. I think he helped the mafia with those twisted experiments to turn regular humans into Weres because he actually thought that was the right thing to do. Like missionaries who kill heathens in their best interest."

I'd seen the pitiful creatures that resulted from those experiments; I still saw them sometimes in my dreams. I'd also heard the fervor in Dave's voice when he tried to convince us he'd been doing the right thing, that human lives had no inherent worth, that the larger goal of creating Weres was worth any cost.

After a moment, I asked, "What about you?"

Tony's mouth twisted bitterly, but when he spoke,

his voice was clear. "I spent five years as a wolf in order not to think about any of it. Something has to change, Julie."

What he said supported my choices, my desire for Carson to bridge the gap between Were and human. But I heard something else behind his words: Weres didn't marry someone who wasn't pack. No matter what the personal cost. Better not to love in the first place, because a relationship between a Were and a human could never work out. I wasn't sure if he intended me to hear the message, but it came through loud and clear, and spiked the rejection swirling inside of me with a dash of anger.

We drank our coffee in silence, mostly because we found nothing left to say. I kept glancing at the clock, very aware of our seven a.m. deadline, wondering if the Salamanders and Special Ops even now surrounded the hotel, if any tourists would die this morning because of my stubbornness.

I set down my mug and stood up. "I can't take this. The waiting is worse than anything else."

"What do you propose? A game of Scrabble?"

I had to glance at Tony before I knew he joked. Even then, it felt more like mockery than anything else. I couldn't trust any of my emotional reactions where he was concerned.

"I need to call Sheila."

Tim answered the phone on the second ring. "Julie? Where the hell are you and what the hell are you doing? Why are you calling at six thirty in the morning?"

That quickly, my anger drained, leaving a residue of exhaustion, worry, and fear. Six-thirty. Thirty more minutes before a hotel full of Shakespeare Festival tourists either burned to the ground or didn't.

"I'm fine. I'm all by myself—well, almost—defying the entire Were structure and a bunch of crazy Eclipsers about to burn down a hotel. I know it's crazy, but it's *right*."

There was a beat. "That's exactly what Sheila says. Eliza called us last night."

"Oh my God, can I talk to her? How is she?"

"She's good, Julie. She's doing really, really well. The doctors are amazed at how well she's healing, thanks to Tessa White."

I sent silent thanks up to the universe. "I'm so glad." An understatement.

"You know what she said after Eliza tried to convince us to talk sense into you? She said—and this is a quote—'That's our Jules. Damn, I love that girl.' " Tim's voice sounded bewildered, but the affection for Sheila shone through.

"Can I talk to her?"

"She's asleep, but I can have her call you later."

"Oh. Okay." I tried to shrug off my disappointment.

I finished my coffee, glanced up at Tony who sat on the other side of the kitchen table. I found myself unable to break the silence, which seemed like a tangible object between us in the room. When Carson stirred upstairs, I jumped up, happy for the excuse.

Chapter Twenty-Seven

"It's seven o'clock," I said, when I came back downstairs with Carson.

"Yes," said Tony.

"I feel like a coward."

"I don't."

When I glanced at him, he elaborated. "We'd be very little help in the fight at the hotel. They already have a combined force of Weres and Salamanders at the scene. We need to focus on the larger battle: protecting Carson and changing the council's attitude on Weres and non-Weres alike."

"Oh, is that all?" I glanced down at Carson, nestled on my hip. "Dammit, I know you're right. We're not going to be able to do this by ourselves. We need allies. We can't stay underground forever."

"We can't hide from the council, it's linked to most government agencies. Unless…unless you'd like Carson to hide as a wolf. With me."

I nearly laughed. "No. For so many reasons."

Tony nodded, as if he expected that answer. "Then we need to find more allies."

"Newt will be on our side. I think. When he's better."

"Right. He would be. I imagine many Salamanders would like to see the council lose power. As things stand, Weres are far more influential than 'Manders."

"The trick will be to find other Weres to join us— Weres who believe prejudice against non-Weres hurts us all."

We sat in the living room. Or, at least, Tony sat. Almost immediately, I sprang up and paced the room, my whole body jittery, partly from remembering what a fool I'd made of myself the previous evening on that very couch, partly out of my anxiety over what might happen at the Ashland Springs Hotel.

Carson practiced sitting up, while Tony and I discussed possible Were allies. I argued that Carson's MacGregor relatives—Mac's parents Erin, Liam, and his brother Ian—might join with us, both out of a sense of loyalty and because Erin had been close with Tony's mother, hence affected personally by their family tragedy. Tony was noncommittal, but thought of a few younger Weres he knew in other packs who seemed dissatisfied with the status quo.

As our brainstorming petered out, I tapped the pen on the pad where I'd scribbled a list of possibilities.

"I guess that's a start," I said, dubiously surveying the double handful of names we'd come up with.

Tony jerked his head, a sudden frown on his face.

"What?"

After a minute, he shrugged. "Nothing. I just thought—"

He jumped to his feet and chills broke out on my skin. In the same moment, I heard a roar and flames shot up the rear of the house. The sliding glass door exploded, flinging shards across the room. I dove toward Carson, grabbed him to me, and turned back to the door, searching for an exit through the sudden wall of flames. Fire leapt the length of the house and consumed each window. The wrap-around deck burned, as well as the wood siding.

Carson writhed in my arms, like an electric eel covered with fur.

"No!" I yelled. "No!"

Too late. He sprang from me and landed on the floor: a small gray wolf with hackles raised and little fangs gleaming. He barked, though I could barely hear him over the fire. His small body tensed as if he wanted to run, to fight.

"Carson! Stay here!" I screamed, just as he leapt toward the hall, away from the wall of fire that used to be the back of the house.

Tony grabbed my arm so hard I knew I'd have bruises the next day. If we were still alive. He shouted in my ear, "Come on!"

The air shimmered with darkness and distortion, resolved into the huge black wolf. He ran after Carson.

I grabbed my gun off the mantel, checked it, and shoved it into the back of my jeans. Dropping to the ground to escape the choking gusts of smoke, I crawled after the wolves. Terror spiked through me, but I forced myself to breathe evenly and focus. I survived this once. I could do it again.

Flames engulfed the front hallway. The door. The windows. I looked frantically through the smoke, searching for an exit, for Carson and Tony. I crawled into the kitchen and found the two wolves on the tiles. Carson lay on his back, with one of Tony's paws on his chest, Tony's muzzle inches from Carson's neck. My heart skipped a beat, then settled back into its rapid pounding as Tony nosed Carson to his feet.

Tony swung his black head in my direction.

"Take him," I shouted. "Get him out of here!"

Tony's ears pressed back and he shook his head like a human.

Flames roared at the side door of the kitchen. The room was dark from smoke and I knew we didn't have much time.

"I'll be okay. I'll be right behind you."

I didn't wait for Tony to agree. I scrambled to the kitchen sink, opened the water full force, and grabbed the sprayer. I turned the hose on the two wolves. Tony flinched inadvertently before he realized my intention and stepped into the spray to soak his fur. Carson nosed closer—goddammit, in the midst of all this, he looked excited by the commotion, by the chance to fight. Tony grabbed Carson by the scruff of his neck and dragged him into the water. I doused the two wolves as much as possible, then soaked a nearby kitchen towel.

"Get him out," I yelled at Tony.

Tony hesitated. Carson squirmed and Tony gave the pup a short shake until he lay quiet. Tony's amber eyes bored into me for a long second.

"Go! Go, damn you!"

I dropped as close to the ground as possible and turned the spray on myself, holding the wet towel to my face.

Tony whirled and ran toward the side door. Flames leapt outside; the small windows had shattered into sharp bits that Tony ran through without heed. At the last moment, he turned his head—protecting Carson—and slammed his shoulder into the fire-weakened door. The door crashed open and the wolves disappeared into the flames.

My whole body shook with adrenaline.

They'd be okay. Carson would be okay. Weres healed quickly, even from burns, and I did all I could by soaking their fur. Tony would call darkness, would somehow avoid all the Salamanders waiting for us...

I needed to worry about myself, to get out.

Flames climbed the wall above the broken kitchen door, spread to the cabinets.

I crawled a few feet in that direction, but stopped. I couldn't do it. I wasn't a Were and I just couldn't force myself through the flames. Even if clear air existed on the other side—which I didn't know for sure. I didn't know how big the fire was, how long it would take to run through it, and my whole body fought against the part of my brain that said I should just do it, just dart after the Weres.

Maybe there was another way. There had to be another way.

I scuttled down the hall toward the door into the garage. I put my hand on the connecting door and it was warm. Warm, but not hot. There must be fire in the garage—but how much? And where? Could I get through?

The entire far side of the house near the kitchen was filled with flames now and I cursed myself for the earlier indecision. I looked wildly in all directions: a wall of flame against the shattered sliding doors, fire at the front windows. Every second I was separated from Carson made me more desperate and my mind tortured me with images of him on fire, surrounded by Salamanders, dead. My God—how many Eclipsers were out there?

I lay flat on the ground near the garage door and tried to smell the air drafting through. How smoky was it? I had to try.

Wait.

I reached into my pocket and grabbed my phone, called Eliza. It rang once, twice, and I cursed. I nearly hung up, but then she answered. I couldn't hear her over the flames, over the blood pounding in my ears, but I didn't need to.

"Eliza," I shouted, "we're on Greenmeadows Way. We need help now!"

I didn't wait for an answer, but shoved the phone in my pocket. I held the wet towel to my face, braced myself, and opened the door to the garage.

Heat smacked me in the face and I flinched before realizing it wasn't fire. Just heat. I pulled the door toward me and half-crawled half-fell down the few stairs onto the concrete floor of the garage. Smoke filled the space, but not as bad as the house. A side door to the yard. Charred black. But not on fire? I couldn't see. The wooden garage doors burned; flames licked the blackened ceiling.

Which way?

I scraped my way across the garage floor toward the door leading to the yard. A roaring boom made me scream and I swung around. A gas tank near the front of the garage had exploded, sending up a gout of flame and choking black cloud. I crawled quicker, suddenly very aware of Sheila's car in the garage—it could catch at any minute, the gas tank—

I reached the side door and didn't pause because at this point it didn't matter if there was fire outside or not; this was my last chance and I'd fully committed. The doorknob burned my hand and I yanked it back.

"Fuck!"

I crouched on my feet, wrapped my hand in the wet towel, held my breath, and opened the door. I darted out, ran through and beside the small flames. I missed my step on the irregular ground and fell heavily, then crawled to a group of trees. My body screamed. I expected at every step to feel fire on my skin.

I made it. Somehow. I crashed to the ground behind a pine tree and lay there for the space of several breaths, my body spasming. I breathed in and out, conscious of each lungful of air so dearly won. The noise of the fire rolled over me, punctuated by a sound that drove me to my feet: someone yelling from the other side of the house.

Carson.

I slipped the gun out from the back of my jeans and thumbed off the safety, checking to make sure it was loaded. Six shots, no extra ammunition. Eliza would come; I knew it in my core. Tony and I had to hold the Eclipsers off until then.

I crouched behind the brush and took stock of the area. Across the grass in front of me, the house still burned. The fire had spread to the roof, sending a plume of black smoke into the air that would surely have someone calling 911 any moment. The house was surrounded by a lawn of well-irrigated grass, some of which burned with a line of red tracing outward. Near the back corner, just out of the fire's reach, a man stood, looking across the yard toward the other side of the house, the direction taken by Tony and Carson. I gave silent thanks he wasn't facing me, even as I wondered what captured his attention. I didn't see any other Salamanders—which didn't mean they weren't hiding in plain sight, covered by a shaft of sunlight. The woods surrounding the house were sparse nearest the lawn, but I thought if I were careful, I should be able to stay under cover and make my way closer to the Weres. To my son.

I knelt and raised my gun, brought the Eclipser into my site and steeled myself with a grimace. I braced for a shot and exhaled, but didn't squeeze the trigger, finally lowering the gun to my side.

Shit. A long shot and I'd only have one chance. The noise of the fire might not cover a gunshot; as soon as I fired, my cover was blown. If I killed him, it would be one less enemy, but others might surround me in seconds. If I missed, I'd surely find myself consumed by flesh-searing fire. Better to maneuver across the back of the yard and assess the situation before I lost surprise as my only advantage.

Keeping my gun in hand, I skirted the yard and crept from tree to tree. At first, I tried to be as quiet as possible, freezing each time a stick snapped, but I soon realized such small noises weren't audible over the sound of the blaze—and that most, if not all, of the Eclipsers were solidly occupied by something. Even the Salamander standing at the corner and presumably set to guard this side of the house neglected his duty, standing with his whole body turned away from me. As I moved down the length of the yard, I glanced in that direction as my angle of vision changed. Purple flames leapt up, moved, a dance of bright lights and shadows, barely glimpsed figures. Suddenly, someone shouted at the Eclipser near me and he abandoned his post, sprinting away.

I cursed under my breath and hurried as much as I dared, finally rounding the corner and making my way behind the yard. A crash sounded from the woods and I saw flames in that direction—dark indigo flames. I looked down at my wrist, where the woven bracelet from Sheila still lay. I touched it for luck, hoping it still worked to make me less noticeable. Letting out a breath to calm my nerves, I crept my way toward the fight, staying as low as I could, using every bit of cover, gun held at the ready.

"I see him," someone yelled and came crashing through the woods near me.

I shrank back into a blackberry bush, heedless of the sharp tear of its thorns, and froze. Were they coming for me?

The man came to a stop next to a tree about ten feet from me. He scanned the woods ahead of us and I let out a silent, shaky breath.

"There," he shouted.

I followed the direction he pointed and frowned, seeing only—wait, that knot of shadows—

The Eclipser made a motion and a ball of purple fire appeared in his hand. As he raised his arm, I shot him in the back. He jerked and I shot again. Several voices shouted, even as the man fell to the ground. I scrambled out of the brush and launched myself pell-mell in the direction the Eclipser had aimed, hoping I had a few seconds as the 'Manders realized what had happened. A tree branch whipped me in the face. Fire blossomed just inches behind me and I felt the blistering heat through my jeans.

Then a cloud seemed to cover the sun, somehow— a confusing pattern of shadows and suddenly gray air. Tony called darkness to cover me, I realized, even as I skidded to a stop next to his wolf form, behind a pile of dead branches. Static electricity hung heavily in the air and resolved as Tony shifted shape.

"Come on," he said, and took off at a run down a slope. I followed, silently, though I wanted to yell, to scream, to shake him.

Tony crashed to a halt in a deep cluster of Manzanita trees, taking advantage of their shade to enhance the called darkness. I slid to a halt next to him and grabbed his arm.

"Where is Carson?" I hissed the words instead of shouting.

His face twisted in a grimace.

"I hid him."

"What the fuck does that mean? You hid him?"

"Look. He's six months old. He wouldn't listen to me. He tried to jump out and attack the Salamanders. I knocked him unconscious."

"What?"

"I knocked him unconscious and hid him in a pile of leaves and brush."

I couldn't breathe. Couldn't say a word. Just stood there with my mouth open like I'd been struck by lightning—which is what I felt like, burned to my core, and rooted to the ground in shock.

"He's going to be okay, Julie. He will."

Tony sounded adamant, but I wondered who the hell he tried to convince. Me? Or himself?

"He has that bracelet. He's well-hidden. I'm distracting the Eclipsers, drawing them away from him."

Finally, I found my voice. "You knocked my six-month-old baby unconscious. You hid him in a pile of leaves. Unconscious. In a pile of leaves."

Tony shook me. "Quiet. Julie, there might be twenty Salamanders and it's just you and me. Quiet."

I held my breath until the urge to scream passed. Then I punched Tony as hard as I could. At the last second, he dodged, so my fist hit him in the shoulder, instead of the face.

"Julie!" His voice was hoarse in its urgency. "He's a Were, he'll heal, and *I had no choice.*"

I panted, silent sobs shaking me. Tony held up his hands in some meaningless gesture. I wrapped my arms around my shoulders, hugged myself tightly, gun digging into my shoulder. The pain of that felt good, felt right. For a second, Tony looked like he would put his arms around me, but I shook my head, took a step away from him. The line of his mouth tightened and he jerked a shoulder in response before turning to scan the area.

"You with me?" he asked, sparing me a quick glance.

I nodded. My teeth hurt from the tension in my jaw.

"We should circle that way, find an outlying 'Mander and attack. Keep their attention this direction." Tony pointed back the way I came.

"No. I want to get Carson."

"We go back to Carson and we risk drawing the Eclipsers with us. I've killed two, injured several. You shot one—I think we're still dealing with at least a dozen. Maybe more."

Shit.

"Okay, you're right. I called Eliza, when I was still in the house." I had no idea how much time had passed since then—probably five minutes, though it seemed like hours.

Tony grimaced. "No alternative, I guess. We need the help if we're going to make it out of this. Follow me."

Shadow twisted and goosebumps erupted on my arms; the black wolf stood beside me. My hand moved to his shoulder, touched the warm fur without my volition. He swung his head around to look at me and I took my hand away quickly.

We moved fast and found a target: a young, female Eclipser, brow creased, corners of her mouth turned down as she concentrated and scanned the woods. I thought she might have sensed our presence—at least, she turned in our direction, though her gaze passed right over us. Her hands guttered with flame, as if ready at a moment's notice. I reminded myself she was the enemy; she'd kill Carson without hesitation and we needed to even the odds. Tony signaled the plan with his eyes and a tilt of the head before he slipped to the other side of the Eclipser.

When he dropped the darkness covering me, I was ready.

"Looking for me?" I said with my gun raised, as the woman startled at my sudden appearance, raising her fire-laced hands instinctively.

Before she could respond further, Tony sprang, knocked her down and tore out her throat with a horrible crunch. He rose and shook his head, blood flying from his muzzle, as I stood frozen. He ran to me, then nipped my jeans when I didn't respond, snapping me back to myself. When he saw I was capable of movement, he loped into the woods with a backward glance to make sure I followed.

I did. Followed him. There was nothing else to do, after all. I tried to compartmentalize—to lock away any part of me that quailed from our actions. This fight would only get bloodier before the end and I'd do anything to make sure it wasn't Carson's blood being spilled.

The next few minutes passed in a series of horrible flashes too quick for my conscious mind to interpret. I moved on pure instinct. We ran through the woods. I slipped on a layer of pine needles and slammed into a tree so hard my head reeled. Tony attacked an Eclipser from behind and his fur was suddenly aflame, then extinguished with a quick roll as I distracted the Salamander with a shot, leaving him for Tony to finish off with a tearing snap. We hid, panting, down a gully to avoid a group of several enemies. Smoke billowed from the house, from the woods. Salamanders yelled. I clung to the thought that we led the Eclipsers farther and farther from Carson, deeper into the woods.

We came up the gully to see a wall of purple flames in our path.

"Shit!" I scrambled back down the slope with Tony crouched at my side. He panted with mouth open and I couldn't tell if it was sheer exhaustion or pain from the burns running along his left side. His fur lay curled and singed from the heat—I kept expecting to see wounds visibly healing, but they weren't. Perhaps because he expended so much power to keep us hidden, to call madness and confusion wherever possible.

I followed Tony along the gully, thankful the smoke gusted away from us. We pushed up and over the slope, only to see more indigo flames blocking our path.

Tony crouched on his belly, head raised. His ears plastered to his skull, his fur splattered with blood.

I finally said, "That way?" and gestured with my head across the gully, away from the flames that seemed to dog our steps.

He pulled on darkness and emerged in human form, lying by my side in jeans torn and singed, his t-shirt stained by blood and flame, his left side and neck marked with red burns. One sleeve hung in shreds and I saw a gash on his shoulder—I hadn't noticed it when he was a wolf. His hair streaked with sweat, a smear of blood on one cheek. He looked at me, those honey-brown eyes shining with some contained emotion.

After he didn't speak, I asked again, "Should we go that way?"

He tightened his lips. Looking away from me, he rubbed his mouth on one arm violently and cleared his throat.

"No use," he finally said. "They've surrounded us. A circle of fire. Coming closer every second."

I pushed up on my elbows and looked around in panic.

Sure enough, I saw flashes of purple down the slope, smoke pouring off the trees toward the house, flames creeping toward the edge of the gully.

"What do we do? Tony, what do we do?"

He shook his head.

"No. No! There has to be something—there has to be some way…we can break through the circle."

Tony pulled me to the very bottom of the gully, where we lay on the ground over leaf and needle-covered rocks.

"It's a massive wall of fire," he said. He grabbed

my face with both hands, rolling his body closer to mine. This close, I could smell his scent, overlain with sweat and the copper tang of blood. "You wouldn't survive. I might not survive. It's over, Julie. We surrender or we die."

"No," I said, hearing the lie in my voice. "They'll—Carson—"

"Certain death or possible death. You chose."

"I—I—"

Tony kissed me, savagely, demanding a response. I pressed myself to him, opened my mouth to taste his lips, his tongue. I wrapped my arms around him, heedless of the rocks that dug into my back, feeling only his body on mine, his lips moving to trace a line of fire on my neck.

"Julie," he breathed in my ear. "We lost this fight."

I kissed his neck and tasted blood. He buried his face against me, then bit my shoulder, gently—just hard enough to draw a sound from me, but not to hurt.

Tony pulled away to look at me. His breath came fast, his eyes darkened with lust that made me move against him, wrap my foot around his. He raised himself up on his hands and moved away slightly, waiting for me to say something.

"Right," I said, after swallowing a few times. I licked my still-tingling lips. "Okay. We surrender and hope they don't kill us."

Or Carson.

Tony nodded and sat up, took my hand and drew me to stand beside him. His face looked grim, all traces of passion fled. We climbed up the lip of the gully; at least we could surrender on high ground. I pushed back my hair, removing a few pine needles, and Tony straightened his shirt. He gave me a nod, then waited until I was ready. This side of the fire loomed twenty feet away and closing, its heat buffeting us.

"We surrender," I yelled as loud as I could.

Tony's hand closed harder on mine. I wasn't sure why—why he kissed me, why any of it, perhaps just a response to near death and no more—but I took strength from the warmth of his hand in mine, the tingle of his power on my skin.

I tried again. "Eclipsers! Salamanders, we surrender." The top of a nearby tree burst into flames and I flinched. "Ma'at. You win. Let's talk."

Chapter Twenty-Eight

A woman walked through the wall of flame in front of us. The fire licked her like a corona, gave her up with reluctance as she approached.

"Drop your gun," she said.

I swore as the metal of the gun seared my palm and I flung it to the ground where it sent wisps of smoke into the air.

"Change form and you die, Were."

She was middle-aged, sturdy rather than svelte, with chin-length brown hair and eyes that assessed us narrowly.

"Where's the baby? Tell me and I might let you live."

"Are you Ma'at?" I asked.

"Yes. But all you need to know is I'm the one who can have you burned to death, right here, right now." She gave a tight smile. "Or you can live. In exchange for the baby."

"He's…" God, was there any way out of this? "Are you going to kill him?"

She lifted a well-shaped brow. "You're not in position to bargain, Julie Hall. I wonder which would be more entertaining. To see how long it takes a Were to die from fire? Play with the balance so he heals even as we burn him? Or to watch his face as the fire slowly consumes you, as you beg for us to kill your baby instead?"

I felt the rage building inside Tony, his hand gripping mine so strongly it hurt my bones. Or maybe it was me, holding him too tight. Through the purple flames now surrounding us, I glimpsed figures, other Eclipsers waiting.

"He's not an abomination," I said. "He's not. He's just an ordinary Werewolf—no threat to you. He's just a baby."

"He *is* an abomination and he must be destroyed. You had your chance, but you refused to have his powers stripped, so you left us no alternative. You shouldn't have gambled with your son's life."

"How did you find us?"

I stalled and her smile said she knew it. A ball of fire appeared in her hand and she tossed it idly in the air.

"GPS on Mike Hollis's phone. Last chance."

"We'll strip his powers. Give us an hour and I'll have his powers stripped—you can keep us as hostages—I can call the Were council right now and have it done. Then you win, right?"

"No."

Fire roared and engulfed Tony's right hand, the one not holding mine. He wrenched away from me with an incoherent yell of pain until he clamped his jaw and stood there, just stood there while sweat ran down his face, every muscle in his body hard as stone, while his hand burned.

Tears blurred my eyes and I screamed, "Stop! Stop it! Okay!"

Just like that, the fire snuffed out.

Tony's hand was black, charred to the bone in

places, with thick red blisters up his arm. I went to touch him, but he jerked back, body rigid.

"I'll be fine." His voice grated harshly.

"The baby?"

"Over near the house. He's hidden." I nearly stuttered in my desperation. We could still get out of this. There must be a way. I shot a glance at my gun, at Tony's stony profile, at the fire-rimmed shapes of Eclipsers.

"Take us to him," said Ma'at. At a gesture, the ring of flames surrounding us guttered to black ash and revealed nearly a dozen Salamanders, perhaps others I couldn't see.

I looked at Tony, who gave me a grim nod, and started back toward the house. The Eclipsers fell in around us.

After we walked for half a minute, without warning, Tony yanked me to a halt. Chaos erupted as several Salamanders yelled and flames popped up, in our midst, in the woods, seemingly everywhere. Ma'at's hand snaked out and grabbed my arm, her grip so hot my skin blistered. The world exploded.

Tony shifted; the black wolf sprang at Ma'at on his three good legs. Water poured up from the ground under my feet, just as the air itself seemed to burn. I screamed and hit at Ma'at with my hand, kicked with my feet, trying to get free of her. We landed in the mud and my vision distorted with the impact, but I hung on to consciousness. Scrabbling for purchase on the suddenly wet earth, I wrestled with the Eclipser, while hearing Tony growl and attack. Then I was on fire and I screamed, not a sound of pain—though, God, it hurt— so much as utter, desperate anger. The flames disappeared, only to spring back, then douse again, in a flickering cycle.

A gray wolf slammed into me and knocked Ma'at away. Purple fire flashed on the wolf's back and the smell of burning fur choked me. People screamed; knots of furious fighting crashed through the woods; I thought I saw—but it couldn't be. Everything was so confused. Several figures darted away into the trees. I didn't know if they were Eclipsers or friendly, and all I could think about was Carson, lying somewhere in the woods. With Salamanders running everywhere, someone was bound to find him and soon. Or he would burn to a crisp by accident in all this chaos.

I rose to my feet, stumbled as bruises and burns sang with pain. Holding my left side tightly as my ribs stabbed with agony, I crouched and managed a stumbling run toward the area where Tony hid Carson. I swerved around several burning trees, nearly crashed into a wolf who turned and snapped at me before drawing back in recognition. Above all the confusion, I heard sirens as firefighters responded to the blazing house.

I saw the edge of the woods and the lawn beyond. Noises from the fight and fire engines roaring closer all rolled past me, as my focus narrowed to any sign of my baby. Frustrated tears ran down my face, as I lurched from one bush to another, searching in piles of leaves and debris.

"Jules!"

I swung around in shock.

"Newt?"

"Are you okay?" He strode toward me, put both his hands on my shoulders, and stared down at me intently.

I straightened slowly and pushed my hair out of my eyes, only then aware the ends were singed rough. My ear throbbed with pain as I touched it; that side of my face stiff with a scalding burn.

"Shit, Jules." A look of intense dismay crossed his face, followed by cold anger utterly unlike his usual self.

"Newt! But how…"

Newt whirled and purple fire flared through a group of trees behind him. He grabbed my hand and tugged me along with him, deeper into the trees.

"Wait!"

He stopped, his fingers closing more tightly over mine, his skin warm as always. "Jules, we've got to get out of here. The fight's turned in our favor, but—"

"Carson. I need to find Carson. He's around here somewhere. He has to be."

"What?" Newt's eyebrows knitted in confusion.

"Tony hid him. I need to find him before someone else does."

Newt ran his thumb across my knuckles. "Okay. Okay." He closed his eyes for a minute. "Dammit. I can't sense him."

God, that didn't mean he was dead or something, did it?

He saw the panic in my eyes. "No, no, Jules, Sheila's charm still works, that's all. That's a good thing—means the Eclipsers can't find him, either. Okay. Where did Tony leave him?"

"He knocked him unconscious and hid him in a pile of leaves and debris. That's all he said."

"Knocked him—are you fucking kidding me?"

"No, that's what he said." I'd never heard Newt

swear before; it shocked me.

Newt's hand clamped down on mine and he jerked me behind him, shielding me with his body before abruptly relaxing.

"Newt. I thought it was you." Tony's voice didn't sound entirely pleased.

"Tony! Where's Carson? Where is he?" I asked.

"This way." Tony reached out to take my arm, but I jerked away from both him and Newt. Flakes of blackened skin covered Tony's other hand, the one that hung at his side. I thought I saw a thin layer of pink flesh forming underneath the burned crust. None of his other injuries seemed to be healing, though they were minor in comparison. Were energy spilled off him, raising the hairs on my arms, and I wished he could somehow direct it into me—to heal the thousand aches that covered my own body.

Tony grimaced and led us to a dense cluster of pine trees. At his gesture, I fell to my knees and pushed through the branches into the dark center. Carson lay there, half-covered with pine needles and I brushed them off, murmured meaningless words, and felt him from head to toe, the warmth of his body proving he was alive. He would be okay.

I gathered him to me and held him tightly, sinking my nose into his hair. His head had a reddened bump on it, still not completely healed, and I tried not to think how hard Tony must have hit him to knock him unconscious for this long—although it had probably been less than fifteen minutes? My sense of time utterly distorted. Yes, Carson would heal, but would he be scarred in other ways? I tamped down my anger, reminded myself Tony had been out of options. Or he'd thought so. I curled around Carson. He was all right and that was almost the only thing that mattered. I brushed tears off my cheeks and looked up. Both Tony and Newt stood alert and focused on our surroundings.

"Eliza said you were hurt," I said. "She said you were in the hospital with serious injuries, that you were in a lot of pain, you asked for me. You had surgery."

"What?" Newt said.

"She called me from your cell phone."

"I lost my phone during the fight yesterday. Or...I thought it was lost...that's why I didn't call you—I told you I would call. And I couldn't." Newt ran his hands through his already spiky hair. "Damn her. Damn her!"

I stared at him as the words sank in.

"I can't believe it," I said. "I mean I understand why she couldn't bring herself to defy the council. But I can't believe she'd lie like that. To me. Lie, about something that serious, about you. She said they'd grant me amnesty if I wanted to visit you in the hospital, that they wouldn't try to seize Carson if I came. She said you kept asking for me. That you needed me."

"Good thing you didn't trust them." A muscle in Newt's jaw moved, before he forced a grin. "That is, I assume you didn't trust them and not that you didn't want to come see me, me with mortal injuries, asking for you?"

My eyes filled, even though I knew he tried to lighten the moment, to defuse the pain of Eliza's betrayal. I lifted my arms and he knelt down for the hug, careful not to squish Carson, but holding me close for a long minute. He felt so warm—funny, that in the early fall heat with the threat of fire all around his body warmth would somehow be so soothing. Like curling up in front of a hearth. I rested my cheek against his shoulder, so grateful he was okay.

Carson moved a hand and I jolted back to awareness. Newt let go of me slowly. Tony stared at us, but I couldn't read the look on his face. Carson's eyes fluttered open, his gaze fixed on my face, and he opened his mouth and gave one of his most ear-piercing shrieks.

"Shh! Carson, sweetie, you're okay. I'm here." I babbled, trying to soothe him. My hands started to prickle where they touched him, and I adopted a sterner tone. "Carson Roger Hall, do *not* change. Don't you dare. You're okay. We're all okay. Mama's right here. Shhh…"

Carson subsided into quieter whining noises and I sighed in relief.

"Julie."

I turned around, adrenaline kicked into high gear by the warning in Tony's voice.

James Robinson approached us, flanked by Eliza and two of the Weres we met at the hotel yesterday. Three other people—presumably friendly Salamanders or other Weres, my human senses couldn't tell the difference—accompanied the group.

I tried to mask the effort I spent to stand up, though from the look on Tony's face, I wasn't sure I succeeded. Holding Carson tightly to me, I braced myself on the tree. My shoulder brushed Newt, who had immediately jumped to his feet, and I felt tension thrum through him. I couldn't even look at Eliza—just seeing her made me so furious I had a hard time focusing on anything else.

"What's the status of the fight?" asked Tony. He

moved to stand on my other side, so he and Newt flanked me.

James raised his brows. "You're welcome," he said. "I believe we arrived just in time to save your lives."

He looked pointedly at one of the other Weres and her name popped into my head as she spoke: Yuko.

She reported in a crisp voice. "The woman calling herself Ma'at is dead and so are eight other Eclipsers. Two captured, four escaped into the woods, but our people are in pursuit. One Were dead. Three Weres severely injured but healing, albeit slower than I'd like. Luckily, the moon is nearly full and we outnumbered them nearly two to one. Oh." She glanced at Newt, then at a young woman slightly to her rear. "Four Salamanders killed, several more injured, right?"

As if non-Weres were an afterthought. I reeled at the tally, clamped my hands more tightly around Carson to stop them from shaking.

"All because you wouldn't listen to us yesterday," said James.

I asked, "What about the hotel? Did anyone die?"

A look of surprise crossed James's otherwise impassive face and then vanished.

He said, "We left when Eliza got your call. Carson's our priority, not tourists."

"What?"

Tony stiffened next to me.

"Was the hotel on fire?"

"Yes, Julie, the hotel was on fire, but we were needed here. Did you want us to wait?"

Eliza stepped in hurriedly. "The hotel is right downtown. Human firefighters would arrive there any minute."

"Don't talk to me, you—you—" I looked her straight in the eyes for the first time and the emotion burst out of me. "How could you? Did you think it wasn't a big deal? Lying to me? Using Newt as a lure? How could you?" My voice shook with anger.

Eliza looked shocked at the level of my ferocity. "Julie, I had no choice."

"You *always* have a choice."

"Orders are orders, Julie. Your friend recognizes that," said James, his eyebrows quirked slightly as if amused by my upset.

"Dammit, Eliza! I thought you were my friend."

"Julie." She took a step closer to me and I shook my head in warning. Her voice shadowed with a note of uncertainty for the first time. "I *am* your friend. That's why I want what's best for you and Carson."

"You don't get to decide what's best for us. None of you do. Not you, not the Greybull pack, not the council."

"You're not making any sense, Julie. We never wanted to hurt Carson. The council wanted to protect him. And it's a good thing we were here to help; otherwise, you'd both be dead in the woods."

"Right. So you left a bunch of humans to burn to death in the hotel and came here to rescue your pet super-Were."

Eliza looked at me as if I spoke a foreign language.

"You just left. Left that hotel on fire." I spat the words.

"To rescue *you*, yes," Eliza said.

"What about those people? Do humans matter at all to you?"

"Julie? What are you talking about? *You're* human and I care about you. That's the whole reason I'm here."

"You lied to me. Eliza, you lied to me. About Newt. How could you?"

Someone cleared a throat.

"Actually, about the hotel, a team of 'Manders stayed behind to help. Against the wishes of some." The young blonde woman spoke, the one Yuko had glanced at, presumably the Salamander leader.

Newt said, quietly, "Jules, we took care of it. We wouldn't leave the hotel to burn."

I continued to stare at Eliza, wishing she would say something—anything—that could actually justify her betrayal. To make it all right again. As if anything could.

James gave a theatrical sigh and attracted my attention. He gestured through the trees toward the house where firefighters emerged from their trucks. "Most of the fires in the woods are out, but we may have humans scouting the area soon. Perhaps we can take this pointless discussion somewhere else?"

Anger coursed up my spine at his tone, but I recognized he was right; we needed to move before we were discovered.

Tony reached out an unobtrusive hand to my back, supporting me as we followed the group deeper into the woods. Newt walked right by my side. For once, I didn't mind the help. Eliza hovered slightly behind me, her face still a mass of hurt and confusion. I didn't care.

James Robinson surveyed the group and said, "The council organized a raid on Eclipser headquarters late yesterday, so the threat to your son should be over.

Whatever ragtag remainder we might have missed won't be enough to mount another attack. We'll round up your belongings and head to Greybull tomorrow—or maybe the next day," he adjusted, with a quick look at my injuries. "Carson will be much safer with the pack."

Eliza gave me a tentative smile, her dark eyes earnest.

"The council's very pleased they didn't need to contain Carson's powers after all. I suppose in some ways your recklessness paid off," concluded James.

So the council *had* considered stripping his powers. Not that the details mattered at this point. The chasm between what I wanted and what the council stood for seemed to widen by the second. I knew I was supposed to feel relieved on some level. We'd been saved from the Eclipsers after looking death straight in the face. Instead, I felt more and more trapped, my resentment of the high-handed Were leaders rising by the second.

"Um. I should call Lily Rose, so she can arrange housing for you and Carson," said Eliza.

"I'm not moving to Greybull."

James swiveled to face me. "Yes, you are."

"No. I'm not. Are you going to kidnap us? Abduct us and keep us prisoners in Wyoming? Because I'm not going voluntarily." I showed my teeth in a smile. "Fuck you, James. Fuck you and fuck your Special Ops and fuck the council, too."

"If you don't come with us, your son will be a rogue wolf. Do you know what the council will do to him? A Were as powerful as Carson, uncontrolled, untaught, unsupervised?"

Beside me, I felt Tony's Were energy rise in response to James's threat. Newt moved a fraction closer to me.

"Julie, be reasonable. Come to Greybull. We'll sit down together and discuss everything with Lily Rose. You can even meet with the inner council and they will reassure you. They can explain," Eliza said. She reached out to touch my shoulder, but dropped her hand before making contact as I roughly jerked away from her.

My mouth twisted. I couldn't even look her in the face.

"Um. Julie? I picked this up for you. This is yours, right?" Eliza held out my gun, as if a token of truce. I took it automatically, repositioning Carson up on my left hip, well out of reach of the gun. I moved my shoulders in a shrug, not even sure what I meant by the gesture.

"Julie," Eliza said, "I didn't have a choice. Why don't you understand?"

"Eliza—"

She took a step toward me, her hands open, body slim and graceful, her eyes fixed on me as if she could somehow will me into agreeing with her.

I closed my eyes for a moment. When I spoke, I knew my voice sounded flat with utter weariness.

"Eliza. You always have a choice. Always. You may not like the choices you have, but you can *always* choose. That's—" I paused and shook my head, my mouth twisting around the words. "That's what makes us human."

She stood mute.

The moment broke when Carson gave an impatient grunt and reached for the gun held loosely in my other hand. I moved him farther up on my hip. He thrashed, bending at the waist and trying to get at the shiny new thing. When I held him tighter to prevent him from grabbing at the gun, his frustration from the crazy events of the last few days finally peaked. He screamed in anger and flailed at me with his hands, kicked me in the side, right where my ribs shot pain into my every breath. Then he lunged. Fresh pain shot through my shoulder and I nearly flung him away, but at the last minute caught myself and merely set him roughly on the ground so he couldn't hurt me with his tantrum.

"No! No biting," I yelled, then immediately felt bad for raising my voice. But dammit, that *hurt* and biting wasn't…biting…

Sucking in a breath, I yanked down the collar of my shirt and saw two red tooth marks on the meat of my shoulder. One deep indentation slowly welled with blood.

Blood.

The world tilted around me and my heart thumped frantically. I opened my mouth, but no sound came out. Eliza's head jerked up and she stared at me, then was suddenly by my side. James Robinson appeared next to her, scooped up Carson, and held him possessively. Tony yelled something. Newt's warm arms were around me.

I couldn't breathe.

The world went white.

I was going to pass out.

Or change?

Or die.

****

Lights. Voices. Something pulled me into a roaring vortex of noise, a whirlwind of pressure and pain and swirling colors that lasted forever. I screamed and fought for the surface, over and over again. The world drowned in gray, stinging agony until nothing else existed. I couldn't think. My body was a mass of stabbing pain. My throat felt torn and bloody from screaming. My head would explode. I begged for it to stop. I begged and begged and begged.

Finally, quiet.

I sank down.

Epilogue

Sunlight. Warm and bright. I felt sunlight on my face and dimly realized the sun reminded me of someone. I opened my eyes and blinked into the light, slowly brought the world into focus.

"Julie?"

She moved into my field of vision, smelling of worry and stress. When she bent closer, the sharp scent of lavender spilled from her fawn-colored ponytail. I stared up at Eliza for a minute before I placed her.

There were other scents. Carson had been in this room recently—his healthy baby smell soothed me on a deep level, gave me the strength to draw another breath.

Tony. I knew exactly where he stood, though I hadn't looked yet. I didn't need to. I sensed him, the particular mix of musk and sweat of Tony. Even now, he pulled on me and I suddenly wondered if his scent, rather than the sunlight, had called me up from wherever I'd been.

Other people had been in the room, but not now. If I focused hard enough, I'd know just who.

Something was missing and I frowned.

Oh, right. Ash. Blood. That's what I expected. Pain. Where was the pain?

Eliza's eyes looked dark as the shadows.

"What happened?" I asked. Though I knew. God, I knew.

"You made it." Eliza's face beamed and I sensed her pure joy, radiating out in a dizzying wave of scent that flooded me. "Oh, Julie, it's all going to be okay. You're one of us. You're a Were. You're one of us, now."

She was wrong.

She was a stranger.

I turned my head. My gaze unerringly found Tony's and read shared truth in the amber depths of his eyes.

I'd never be one of them.

A word about the author...

Sarah's love of reading, writing, and all things fantasy started with her explorations of Narnia, Middle Earth, and Pern. She is a huge enthusiast of all fantasy, paranormal, and science fiction. Flying her geek flag early, she started D&D with the good old boxed sets (and still plays today). Her stories focus on strong women, strong friendships, magic, and love.

She lives with her husband Gary, their three kids, and three cats. She's also an artist and a boardgame geek.

http://sarahestevens.com